Forgive No More

SEB KIRBY
FORGIVE NO MORE

CANELO

First published in the United Kingdom in 2014 by Seb Kirby

This edition published in the United Kingdom in 2020 by

Canelo Digital Publishing Limited
Third Floor, 20 Mortimer Street
London W1T 3JW
United Kingdom

A CIP catalogue record for this book is available from the British Library.

Print ISBN 978 1 78863 935 4
Ebook ISBN 978 1 78863 655 1

Look for more great books at www.canelo.co

Printed and bound in Great Britain by Clays Ltd, Elcograf S.p.A.

The sun went down in wrath at such deceit.

J.M.W. Turner, *The Fallacies of Hope*

Prologue

Everyone knew him here as one of the most devout, one of the few who had risen to the rank of *Ajahn*. Devout because of the time he spent in meditation and prayer. He was honoured they would think of him in this way within the monastery, given he was not Tibetan.

It was the centre of his universe, the place he went back to in order to replenish his life, to regenerate his energy and regain what was lost when he went out there, into the wider world.

The last time he'd been out into that world he'd killed fifty men and not a few women without a thought. Because he served a higher goal. And because, when looked at from here, from the centre of the universe, the deaths were not important. In the great flow of energy passing through this place and through him as he meditated and chanted, the lives of these people were as nothing. Could be nothing.

Still, a slew of naked thoughts ran through his mind and threatened to disrupt the state of truth to which he was all the time aiming in these two hours alone in the monastery cell – why had he been concerned that the little girl would have to die? Why did he have to meet her? Why did she have to speak to him before the killings at Town Lake? He'd checked the lists of those who'd died. The little girl had been spared. But that was not the point. It was the simple fact that her innocence had touched him and he'd been made to care what would happen to her. It would not leave his thoughts. Try as he might to let these ideas go, they hung on, confronting him.

I

With time and mental effort, his mind focused once more on the flow of energy through him, the flow that gave him the glimpse of the divine.

He turned to face the door as a novice *samanera* came for instruction.

Strange, he thought, that he was so far away now from the world where they knew him by a different name.

Wolfgang Heller.

Day 1

September 2nd

Chapter 1

Leaving Julia and heading for London was one of the hardest decisions of my life.

As the train gained speed out of Oxenholme, leaving the vivid green hillsides of the English Lake District behind, my thoughts turned to what had led me to leave.

It would have been easy to stay in Ambleside with Julia.

No one knew we were there.

We'd both made sure we weren't followed when we headed north. Julia had given birth to our son, Simon, the child for whom we'd waited so long. She needed me at her side and I should have been there to share with her the wonder of the new life we'd brought into the world.

But however much I wished it could have been different, I knew I couldn't stay.

The secret life we'd been living was over. There could no longer be anonymity here. Nothing had been the same since Detective Inspector Reid came to our door and told us Agent Jack Franks had died so soon after tracking us down. That was the signal to run for our lives.

The two Italians who killed Martin Craig would have killed Julia if she hadn't escaped. Those attackers were sent by the Landos. We were loose ends as far as they were concerned. With the two million reward placed on our heads by Matteo Lando still in place, there would be many seeking us out.

I knew it wasn't viable waiting there in the hope we could remain hidden. A chance sighting by someone who knew either

4

of us from our earlier lives would be enough. However difficult it was going to be, I had to be out here.

The shock waves of the killing of Agent Franks posed dangers just as strong as those posed by the Landos. We knew Agent Nate Craven ordered the Franks killing. Craven was running black ops within the Bureau and making millions by guaranteeing the safety of the cartel shipping drugs into the US from Tijuana. Agent Franks had been clean. He would have taken what he knew to his superiors when he discovered what Craven was doing. For Craven there had been no choice but to act.

We knew this but lacked proof. Without evidence our accusations would be brushed aside.

Craven wanted me killed because of what I knew.

What made our problems worse were not just these dual threats – the Landos and Craven – but that these threats were connected and fed off each other.

Alessa Lando was the source of the attack on the politician that brought Agent Franks into play. Her assassin, Wolfgang Heller, planted the bombs at Town Lake that killed the politician and most of his family. And the Landos were involved with the drugs cartel in Tijuana that claimed its protection from Craven.

These competing and overlapping rivalries were sure to lead to further deaths and Julia and myself, not to mention my brother Miles, were caught up in them. I wouldn't have escaped the US without help from Miles but I had to leave him there and he was now out of contact.

I had to find the evidence to bring this to an end.

I was dragged back from my thoughts as I saw the guard coming through the carriage. When I showed him my ticket, he paused as if he were about to question my right to be on the train. I began to think the police had briefed railway staff to look out for me. In the event, he was trying to be helpful.

He clipped the ticket. "Should be arriving into Euston at 14.50."

I thanked him and told myself I should stop believing I was the only wanted man in the country.

As the countryside sped by, my thoughts returned to my last conversation with Julia before I'd set out for London.

"I'm going back there in the morning."

She was close to tears. "You know it's too great a risk."

"I won't need more than a few days. You'll be safe while I'm away."

"You'll be in danger."

"We can't wait here until someone finds us. You know that would be worse."

"Why London? You know how difficult it's been for us there."

"That's where the evidence is."

I could tell she knew there was more to come. I'd never been able to keep anything hidden from her. She knew just by looking into my eyes. "Jim, you have another reason for going to London, don't you?"

I couldn't avoid telling her. "I don't plan being there for long. Just long enough to check out what Miles was investigating. Then I need to head for Florence."

Julia drew back, terror written on her face. "Jim. You can't go back. Not after everything we've been through in that place. It's the centre of everything harmful to us."

I held her hand. "And that's just why I have to go back. Don't you see, it's only by discovering the truth that we'll ever be free. Something dark was driving Alfieri Lando to do what he did to you and to who knows how many others."

A tear ran down Julia's face, followed by another. I could see I'd taken her back to those days three years before when she'd gone to Florence in her work as an art conservator and in all innocence begun studying the Lando art collection. And, in what she'd found the most difficult thing to confide in me, the memory of the ritualistic way in which Alfieri Lando, dressed in a red cape and mask, had defiled her.

"Jim, you know how hard I've worked to put all this behind me. Behind us. Alfieri is dead. His son is in prison for his murder. Can't you see I can't bring myself to allow you to bring that all back again?"

"But it's not us, Julia. Not us bringing this back again. The Landos are not going to stop until they find us. The harm they represent will never go away."

She wiped her eyes. "And if you were to go back to Florence, where would you start?"

"I've thought of little else. I've lived through everything that took place when I struggled to find you, when I thought I'd never see you again. And I now know I need to start with Zella DeFrancesco."

Julia didn't sound convinced. "But we know she went into witness protection after the Lando trials, just like us. How are you going to find her?"

"Florence is her only known address."

"You'll be going back into the heart of the Lando power base."

I shook my head. "That's not the most important thing right now. We need our family to have a safe future."

She closed her eyes. She knew I'd made up my mind.

I kissed her. "I won't be away long, I promise."

The train sped on.

We were approaching Stafford, the last stop before London.

Chapter 2

Agent Michael Bedford had been with the London Bureau for two years. As overseas postings went, this was good – civilised compared with the black spots of the Middle East where half the men he'd trained with were now based.

What took away the shine was his line manager, Bill Maynard, who demanded hourly updates. So here Bedford was, taking it like a man.

Nothing Maynard did was understated. He was full on and proud of it. "Bedford, I need progress. Not anytime soon. Now!"

Bedford found it difficult to tolerate Maynard's lack of manners. Where he'd grown up in Boston, you didn't talk to people like that. "We're getting there, sir. Adam Weston is all but tied in. We're about to locate him."

Maynard glowered at him. "Well, getting there isn't good enough. We're on high priority here. We need a result. PDQ."

Bedford had sought the backroom life, one of the better options the FBI had to offer. He'd majored in computing science, so it was a natural for him to aim for counter intelligence, taking on the hackers.

"I hope you understand, sir, we have to get this right. Weston has been taking information from our system. But he hasn't penetrated our deep encryption. Make it too easy and Weston is going to be suspicious. Make it too difficult and he's going to stay away for good. He's aware of not spending too much time in our database, worried we'll be on to him. He's cautious but still curious. That's the way we want it."

Maynard interrupted. "OK. All very creditable and subtle, but where's the meat?"

"It's coming. He could bite anytime now. He's intelligent and experienced. It's like a stealth fight between two people who are not sure the other is there."

Maynard banged his fist hard on the table. "Get it done. Draw him in. Locate him. It's not that difficult, Bedford. Just do it."

Bedford nodded in agreement. He knew why it was important to find Adam Weston. Miles Blake was a threat to national security. Not just because as an investigative journalist he was probing the corners of American life that the power elite wanted to remain hidden but because he was using a contact within the State Department and the organisation needed to clean that up. It was why Maynard was so exercised, so much on Bedford's back.

Weston was hiding behind a series of proxy servers that hid his location. But Bedford had an answer. He'd embedded a Java script into the code. The moment Weston took the bait, the script would seek out the man's IP address. From there, with a little pressure on the local authorities, it wouldn't take long to locate him.

"I understand, sir. I'll get onto it right away."

Maynard walked away. "Damn right you will."

Bedford knew he couldn't blame it all on Maynard. He was doing his duty as he saw fit, after all. No, the difficulties here were greater than that. Bedford wished now he hadn't taken money from Craven. It was all so straightforward then. A little on the side for providing information Craven wanted to access without others in the organisation knowing. Bedford didn't suspect the Craven money came from kickbacks in smuggling drugs out of Mexico.

It was a shock to Bedford when he found out. His own brother had died of a drugs overdose. One of the reasons Bedford had joined the organisation was to make a difference, to right some of the wrongs that led to his brother's death. And now here he was trapped in a black ops set-up with a man like Craven with no way back to the light. If he didn't go along with what Craven wanted, his career in the organisation would be finished.

This was what led to Bedford's part in the cover up of the killing of Jack Franks. Bedford had doctored the record. He'd removed the initial reports suggesting murder and replaced them with others to show that Franks' death was a tragic accident, the result of the Agent cleaning his Glock with the safety off.

Bedford was guilty about deceiving Maynard and his colleagues, feelings made worse by the knowledge that Jack Franks had an exemplary record. But there had been no choice. Craven had demanded it.

Now he was making more demands.

Bedford was backroom and wanted it to stay this way. But Craven wouldn't listen. He told him he was stretched after the Town Lake bombing, fully occupied in the States, meaning that Bedford was the only one who could fill in.

When Bedford complained, Craven told him it would be simple for the origin of the drugs money he'd received to be made known to the organisation. If he didn't want to do time for that, he'd be wise to get behind what was needed.

So, at the same time as he had Maynard on his back, Craven was insisting Bedford should work for him. He wanted all available local information about James and Miles Blake.

Craven called the shots with Bedford just as much as Maynard. He had to go along with it but hated himself for giving up on his ideals.

Back came boss man Maynard. He looked as angry as ever.

"Have you seen this, Bedford?" He slapped a print out of a database search onto the desk. "We know Weston is working for Miles Blake, a known target of interest. This report shows that Agent Franks died when contacting Miles' brother, James.

That's a big unexplained connection and one I do not like. I want to know what we have on James Blake and how he figures in the Franks case. You get me?"

"Jack Franks' death was an accident, sir."

Maynard ignored him. "And what's the connection between Franks and Miles Blake?"

Bedford held his head in his hands. "I'll get onto it, sir."

Something latent in Maynard was drawing him to look further into the Franks case. It could only spell trouble.

It was untenable. For different reasons, both men who had power over his life wanted him to take action on James and Miles Blake.

Chapter 3

As the London train sped on towards Euston station, I thought through the plans I'd made to ensure Julia would be safe while I was away.

Before leaving I'd bought two pay-as-you-go phones. Since they had no previous history, any calls made on them would be difficult to trace. Provided we were careful and used them as little as possible, there was no reason why they would come to the attention of those trying to find us.

This was how I would keep in contact with Julia.

I weighed the phone in my hand.

Should I call her?

I wanted to call, to reassure myself that Julia had come to terms with my leaving, but I decided against it. The phones were for emergencies. This was not that time. I returned the phone to my jacket pocket.

Obtaining the phones had been simple. Making the other arrangements was not as straightforward. Faith Webster was understanding in allowing us to stay with her in the 16th century farmhouse at the top of Rook Lane, high over the Ambleside Valley. Everything had been done to make the farmhouse secure before I'd left. There was no question of hiring protection while I was away – such men would be difficult to find in Ambleside even if we could have afforded them. Faith Webster had an old double-barrelled shotgun she kept for scaring rabbits but could not claim to be a practiced shot.

Faith accepted without question that we were in real danger. I think Julia must have confided in her enough about the degradation she'd experienced in Florence for Faith to understand.

Her nearest neighbour was Mark Stone, a local huntsman who kept a pack of beagles in kennels at the rear of his cottage just down the hill from the farmhouse. He was good with a rifle. I didn't think I'd ever get on well with a man like him but in our annual visits to the farmhouse, we'd become friends. He saw the funny side of my determination never to hunt with him and teased me with good-natured banter about how town-dwellers had no idea of the realities of life in the countryside. When I told him I had to leave on a matter of urgency and I was concerned at leaving Julia and baby Simon here, he was quick to want to know the details. I told him that in a weak moment we'd taken out a pay day loan at an interest rate that made it unrepayable and I'd received threatening letters from them. Two suspicious men had been seen looking over Faith's property and it was a near certainty they were sent by the loan company. The police were of no help since what the loan company had done was within the law and no offence had yet been committed. These lies would come back to haunt me.

Stone, who was incensed by the idea of the loan sharks sending heavies to intimidate a decent family, was keen to help. He knew amongst the local men he hunted with there were a number he could depend on. He agreed to keep a close watch on the farmhouse. I had confidence that he would make a professional job of this.

It had been one of the most difficult decisions. How to weigh the odds of my chances of success in discovering the truth about what was driving the Landos – and to find a way of outwitting Craven – against the risk of leaving Julia and our child at the farmhouse. Mark Stone and his men were skilled shots while I had no such training. Julia and baby Simon would be safe with their protection. I could defend them best by cutting off the threats against them before they materialised. No one knew they were there. If I made it known I was in London, it would draw attention away and make Julia and the baby safer where they were.

That's what I told myself, over and over.

That's how I made one of the worst mistakes of my life.

As the train thundered through the outer London suburbs, I turned my thoughts towards what I wanted to achieve there.

I had no intention of meeting Inspector Hendricks yet there was information I wanted him to know. The plan was to phone him on arrival at Euston from a pay phone and not overstay time on the line.

The priority was to find Adam Weston and enlist his help and gain assistance in discovering Craven's plans.

Then, I planned to make the cross-channel journey to Florence.

As the train drew into Euston, I gathered myself for the confrontation with Hendricks.

I found a pay phone on the main concourse and dialled.

It was the police station sergeant who replied. "You say you have information for Inspector Hendricks. You know he's a very busy man."

"He'll want to speak to me."

"And you are?"

"Mr. Blake. James Blake."

He asked me to hold the line.

In less than a minute, Hendricks came on. "Mr. Blake. I've been expecting to hear from you. I thought you might pay me the respect of a visit in person."

I could tell that nothing had changed his readiness to assume the worst of everyone he came in contact with, including me. "There's no need for me to take up too much of your time, Inspector. This is much more convenient."

"As you wish, Mr. Blake."

I realised his men would be seeking to trace the call. I knew I'd have to make this quick. "I have information about the killing of Martin Craig in the Allegro Hotel. A case I know you're investigating."

He took a deep breath. "You're going to surprise me by telling me it was no coincidence that we met at the hotel the day after the killing. When you told me you were there to look for a replacement room. When all along you had an altogether more compelling reason to be there."

I was unsurprised he'd lost none of his flair for understatement. "If you say so, Inspector."

"And your wife had also been there."

I could picture him sitting there at his desk relishing the opportunity to keep me on the line a little longer. When I didn't reply he continued.

"We're not as naive as you might think, Mr. Blake. Of course, we checked the CCTV record from the hotel in the days before the killing. We identified you and your wife when you registered. In fact, the identification was made by myself. The hotel staff recognised you as John and Elizabeth Meredith. So, why the assumed names, Mr. Blake?"

"You don't need me to tell you that."

He laughed. "Oh, of course. The Weymouth police records show you were visited by a DI Reid concerning the death of an FBI man. What was his name? Agent Franks? And you told Reid a lie and headed for London. Did you know that DI Reid is now missing, whereabouts unknown, and we're beginning to treat his disappearance as suspicious? You wouldn't know anything about it, Mr. Blake?"

I didn't like the inference. "I had no idea Reid was missing. We only saw him one time back in Weymouth."

"And that was enough to make you leave?"

"We were running for a different reason."

"And what was that?"

"We ran because of unfinished business."

"Unfinished because of what?"

"Because of what happened in Florence three years ago."

He didn't sound impressed. "The case is closed. I put Clinton Ridley away for the London killing. I put good time and resource into setting you up in witness protection with new identities and you say the case is ongoing?"

"That's what I have to tell you. There's unfinished business from that case. Craig's death in the Allegro is part of it. If you want to find his killers, look back into that case and at what the Lando family is doing now."

"And that explains why the hotel manager told me the murdered man was your wife's brother when it's clear he was no such thing?"

"He was protecting her."

"From what?"

"From the Landos."

He wasn't about to believe me. "Mr. Blake, let me give you some advice. The best thing you can do is to come into the station and make a clean breast of everything. You must know we need to interview you and your wife. Don't make this any more difficult for yourselves."

I realised time was up but I had one more thing to say, something Julia was convinced was in need of investigation. "By the way, Inspector, check into the death of Peggy Westland. It wasn't an accident."

Hendricks had been skilful in keeping me on the line and I had overstayed my welcome. I didn't know how much I'd told him that was new to him. It was clear from what he'd told me that he'd made the connection between Craig and Julia before I spoke to him. But I'd made sure the connection to Florence was now in his mind.

Hendricks had left me puzzled about the significance of the disappearance of DI Reid.

I replaced the receiver without saying farewell and walked away, mingling with the crowds of passengers on the concourse, waiting for departing trains.

As I looked back from within the safety of the crowd, I saw a squad of six uniformed officers surround the pay phone I'd been using.

I'd avoided being picked up by Hendricks by just a few seconds.

Chapter 4

Miles Blake sat at one of the tables outside *The Green Flash* and looked at the rolling waves of the Pacific Ocean. He'd come this far to honour a promise to a dying man.

He'd made it all the way to San Diego without being apprehended by Agent Craven but it didn't feel good.

The way the Town Lake bombing had played out in the press and on TV left no doubt that Craven was in control of a misinformation campaign and it was succeeding. The atrocity had been attributed to a newly-identified jihadist group operating out of the Horn of Africa who it was claimed had admitted responsibility. All of which meant the public was getting the kind of truth that Craven wanted. The cover-up appeared to be complete.

When he'd left his brother, James, at Dallas Fort Worth airport, Miles had avoided the security blanket mobilised in response to the bombing. He'd retraced his steps, taking a taxi back to the rail stop at Fort Worth and checking into a small hotel near the station. Next morning he'd taken the *Texas Eagle* to San Antonio. It was a seven hour trip but he didn't need ID traveling by train.

It took time to realise he was not a wanted man in the accepted sense. There was no manhunt, no request for information from the public. It was Craven and his operation within the FBI who wanted him and by definition Craven needed to keep that dark. But that wasn't to say Craven wouldn't be using every back door request for information and assistance he could muster. If Craven was out to fit him up it would be nothing to do with the Town Lake atrocity. More likely it would be concerned with Miles' attempts to get information from the State Department on the drugs trade out of Mexico. Yet it was just as probable Craven would go straight for a quick kill and dispense with such formalities. Outwitting Craven was the life and death priority.

In San Antonio, Miles had made contact with a freelancer he could trust. Annabel Kelly was one of the best photographers he'd worked with. They had faced danger together. She was unquestioning when he told her he needed her help with money. It took two days to raise the cash he needed. When she handed it over she would not hear of anything about when Miles would pay her back. Their trust for each other was enough. Annabel also asked no questions when he told her that no matter who might ask, and on whatever pretext, she had not seen him.

Miles had travelled west from San Antonio aboard the *Sunset Limited*. It took him to Los Angeles. From there it had been simple to get a bus to San Diego.

The journey across the border to Tijuana would be short with no need to show documentation on crossing into Mexico.

He took in again the Pacific waves crashing ashore. They were certain and sure. As sure as he was that he would respect the last wish of Luiz Reyas as he lay dying in Miles' arms in the abandoned railway station in East Texas. He would find Luiz Reyas' son and tell him what he knew about his father's mission.

Chapter 5

Inspector John Hendricks was annoyed he hadn't kept James Blake on the phone the minute longer it would have taken to apprehend him at Euston station. There was much more he wanted to ask him about the killing at the Allegro Hotel. Yet Hendricks was more disturbed by what had passed between them regarding Peggy Westland. What Blake told him appealed to the old copper in the Inspector, the part of his make-up that couldn't let an idea go without teasing it to death once it had taken up residence beneath his balding skull.

He called in DI Franklin, his second-in-command, and made it clear what he wanted. "Get me the autopsy report on Peggy Westland."

The report was on his desk in twenty minutes. It made inconclusive reading. The woman had died in her own bed by suffocation, but the coroner was not able to rule out self-suffocation. Hendricks knew this was rare. Yet it was possible. It was also possible that a killer who knew what he was doing could have suffocated her and made it look like self-suffocation. If that were the case there would need to be a motive. Hendricks could not find one. There was no sign of forced entry at the apartment near Sloane Square. Nor was there indication that anything had been stolen.

Was it material that Peggy Westland had been married to Richard Westland, the well-known artist, and he'd been killed in a car accident just three weeks before his wife's death? Not that Hendricks recognised what Westland produced as art. For him, it was a denial of art not to picture the world as it is.

There was nothing to indicate that Richard Westland's death had been anything other than an accident. Perhaps, Hendricks thought for a moment, he should be looking at the art world but he could deduce no motive there either. A shiver passed down his spine as he recalled that Julia Blake was a known friend of Peggy Westland and that the Blake woman was at the centre of his investigations into the Allegro killing. Julia Blake was involved in art and, as the events in Florence three years earlier had shown, there was deception and corruption in that world. James Blake had made a point of mentioning the Landos but, again, without more to go on, Hendricks could make little of these connections.

The breakthrough came from an unexpected source. There was a phone call from the front desk. Sergeant Billy Smith, duty officer at Charing Cross police station, wanted to see Hendricks.

When Sergeant Smith came in it was plain to see he had a lot on his mind. Hendricks knew the man as outgoing and confident. Today, he was withdrawn and hesitant.

"I don't know where to start with this, John. There's stuff here you're going to find out about me that you're not going to like. Stuff I wouldn't want to go outside of this room. You know what I mean?"

Hendricks could guess. Sergeant Smith had been on the take again and something had gone wrong with the arrangement. "It's all right, Billy. You can trust me. It will go no farther."

Smith started to look more relaxed. More like his old self. "That's a relief, John. You see, there's events concerning your Allegro investigation you need to know. Martin Reid asked me for a favour. I knew I shouldn't have helped him but he insisted."

"How much did he offer you?"

"Eight hundred."

"So, something important then."

"He told me he was here in London doing this for a friend who had a wife who was playing around. Reid thought she'd booked into one of the hotels around here with her fancy man but he didn't know which hotel. All he wanted was a list of any couples who checked with no ID, looking suspicious."

"You got the information for him?"

Smith nodded. "I didn't believe it was the real reason he wanted the information, but I got it for him anyway. One of the contacts I gave him was for a couple who'd checked into the Allegro. Thought I'd need to let you know, now it's become a murder scene."

"Do you remember the names?"

"John and Elizabeth Meredith."

Hendricks smiled. These were the names used by the Blakes when they'd checked in. "When was this, Billy? In relation to the killing at the hotel?"

"When I gave Reid the list it must have been a couple of days before the killing."

Hendricks thanked him. "OK, Billy. You've done the right thing to tell me. I appreciate it. As far as I'm concerned, I didn't hear anything about any eight hundred changing hands. You're all right with that."

He called Franklin once more and instructed him to search again the surveillance footage from the CCTV camera at the reception desk at the Allegro Hotel.

"What are we looking for, Inspector? We found the Blakes checking in."

Hendricks shook his head. "Not the Blakes this time. Go back forty-eight hours and check on DI Reid. You can get his mug shot from the material we're putting out to try to find him."

"I don't get the point, Inspector."

"Just do it."

Franklin returned with images from the tape running on a laptop and showed Hendricks the vital link. "Here it is, Inspector." He pointed to the screen. "Reid was at the Allegro. Here he is entering the hotel and being taken to the back-office by the hotel manager."

Hendricks knew this was important. "And what time was this, Franklin?"

"Thirty-seven hours before the murder."

Hendricks thanked him and returned to his thoughts. Reid had been based in Weymouth. That's where the Blakes had been relocated in the witness protection program. Now Reid and the Blakes turn up at the same time in the Allegro where a murder takes place. The conclusion was clear. Reid had followed Julia and James Blake from Weymouth to London. What could have been his motive for that?

And now Reid had disappeared and was a listed missing person. Whatever Reid was involved in, it didn't look good.

When Hendricks called at the Allegro Hotel he asked to see the hotel manager. He showed the man a photograph of Martin Reid.

The hotel manager had no doubt. "I recognise this man, Inspector. He's Detective Inspector Billingham."

Hendricks was puzzled. "You're sure?"

"I'm confident. He showed me his police ID card. That was the name. DI Billingham. He told me he needed to search our CCTV footage, that he was on a missing person case."

"You didn't mention this when we interviewed you."

"No one asked."

What was Reid doing using a false name? Hendricks knew his chances of saving Reid's reputation and the reputation of the Force were fast fading.

It got worse when Hendricks established a link between Reid and Peggy Westland.

Reid's vehicle was found abandoned in a street close by an old warehouse complex near Canary Wharf. In the glove compartment of the car they found a notebook. He'd been using this to record names and addresses. One of the names and addresses was that of Peggy Westland.

Hendricks didn't like where this tugging away at the truth was leading. Reid must be involved in something that any policeman in his position should run a mile from. This required further investigation, starting with why Reid's vehicle had been abandoned so close to those derelict warehouses.

It proved to be difficult to get permission for a forensic team to be established. Everything these days came down to a question of money. Cutbacks in the police budget were biting deep. He had to be insistent. A police officer, one of their own, had disappeared. There was a possible connection to multiple murder. He told his superintendent the cost of sending out the team would be insignificant against the need to find the officer and clear his name. To achieve that, a ten-man case team would be required to search the derelict warehouses near where DI Reid's vehicle had been abandoned. Hendricks won the argument and the team was sent out.

The search of the warehouse complex soon found a site that aroused suspicion. They found blood on the floor near a dividing wall in a warehouse that had been used for timber storage years ago. There had been no attempt to clear up the blood. Either they were amateurs or they were so confident they wouldn't be caught they had no interest in covering their tracks.

The forensic team discovered the blood to be human. It also contained a high level of salt, suggesting a man had been tortured there, his tears diluting the blood.

Officer Franklin summed up for Hendricks. "This is consistent with someone having been interrogated here, sir. Could have been strung up by the feet and mutilated."

The team took swabs from Reid's vehicle to identify his DNA. Analysis of the blood found in the warehouse showed a match. Hendricks knew it was Reid who'd been strung up and tortured. The amount of blood at the site further suggested that Reid had been killed. Hendricks announced a murder investigation in respect of DI Reid and was able to report to his superiors that the cost of the investigation so far had been justified.

The chance of saving Reid's reputation was ended when his DNA was discovered in the Peggy Westland apartment and on her body. Hendricks knew he should announce a murder investigation in respect of Peggy Westland but he decided to wait. He still had hopes of rescuing the reputation of the Force but had no idea how he might achieve this.

Hendricks didn't like it. He didn't like any of it. He now had three deaths and, if you included Reid, as he felt he must even though the body had not been recovered, that made four. All taking place on his patch. The only common thread Hendricks could find between them was James and Julia Blake.

He summoned the search team and told them they were now a criminal case enquiry team investigating the probable death of a fellow police officer and three others.

Franklin set up a large cork board on which they pinned photographs of persons of interest – James and Julia Blake together with those of DI Reid, Peggy Westland, Richard Westland and Martin Craig.

Hendricks spelt out the instructions. "The priority is to find James and Julia Blake. We know James Blake is in London. It's imperative we locate him."

Chapter 6

You don't get a Congressional medal of honour if you're an undercover FBI man. The award is secret but it means the same.

Agent Nate Craven preened as the Secretary of State pinned the Intelligence Star to his chest. How strange, he thought, to be here in uniform. How seldom he wore it in the work he did now.

The commendation read:

For exceptional bravery in the line of duty.

Craven saluted and took a pace back.

Beside him Agent Debbie Miller stepped forward to receive her medal. She looked good in uniform.

Things had moved on. Craven had been successful in placing enough evidence in the right place to implicate the jihadist group for the Town Lake bombing. Though he said so himself, he'd constructed a detailed and believable case that action should be taken in the Horn of Africa to eliminate this threat before it could grow. And the more attention focused on Africa, the more he felt sure his role in the events that led to the atrocity would never come to light.

He would need to keep a close watch on Debbie Miller. She knew nothing of the drugs shipments out of Tijuana and, as far as he was aware, that's the way this had stayed. What she'd seen and experienced was consistent with the fact that the jihadist group had help to launch the attack from men recruited within the United States. The evidence collected by Craven on the operative the Landos had sent to carry out the assassination of Elmore Ravitz pointed to a shadowy figure by the name of Wolfgang Heller who was familiar with the Far East and had most likely disappeared back there.

Miller was not told what little Craven had discovered so far about Heller. All she knew was that the trap they'd set for the assassin sent by the Landos at the Warren Stephenson hotel in Austin had succeeded in drawing out Heller but they hadn't been able to capitalise on this because of the attack on the Town Lake compound. It was logical, given the evidence Craven had produced, that she would associate the attack with Middle East terror and assume that the events in the hotel were unconnected with the jihadist outrage. At least this was the way Craven wanted Miller to see it. Everything she did and said suggested this was the case. Craven had her on watch to ensure this stayed that way.

All but one of the remainder of Craven's team, including all those who'd known about the drugs business, had died in the blast. His immediate future was secure. At least this was what he convinced himself of now the medal was pinned to his chest.

There would be inconsistencies. It was true of every attempt at disinformation he'd ever been involved with. Debbie Miller was intelligent. If anyone was to discover those wrinkles in the fabric of the truth it would be her. He would watch and observe if she began making moves in that direction. But for now at least he was pleased she was content to bask with him in the recognition they were receiving.

As they stood down to join their FBI colleagues in the hall and receive their congratulations, Craven took time to acknowledge her. "Well done, Debbie."

She whispered a reply. "I just wish it could have been without such loss of life."

Craven embraced her. "I know. I feel the same."

The celebrations lasted into the night.

So this was what it was like to be a hero.

Walking back to his vehicle alone as the party broke up, Craven found darker thoughts coming into play. The whole thing was like a stack of cards. Pull away one card and the house would fall down. There were those out there who had the knowledge to do it. Matteo Lando and his mother Alessa. James Blake and his brother Miles. El Romero and the Soto cartel in Tijuana. They all knew enough to take this all away. To ruin him.

Good, then, that he now had a new team and would be able to take care of this.

Chapter 7

I took a room at *The Rhondda*, a no-questions-asked hotel off Great Russell Street, close to the British Museum. The accommodation was basic, the room so small that even in this busy part of London you'd call it mean. It was uncomfortable but there were no questions raised at the reception desk when I paid cash in advance and there was no request for identification. The young woman at reception offered a knowing smile when I told her my name was Henry Mitchell, confirming my suspicion that it was not unusual for guests to be here under false names for one reason or another.

There wasn't time to rest in the hotel room. I'd delayed too long in tracking down Adam Weston.

I made my way over to Pimlico. Weston would not know that Miles had given me the address before I'd left the States. I knew I'd have to handle Weston with care since Miles had left me in no doubt just how scared of detention by the police or the FBI the young hacker was.

I knocked on the door of his small second floor apartment. There was no reply. I knocked again the way Miles had told me.

The door opened. Weston looked angry. "I told you not to come here." Then he paused, realising that I wasn't my brother. "You're not Miles. You look enough like him. Where the hell is Miles?"

I placed my foot against the door to stop it being closed. "I'm his brother. We need to talk."

"OK, you're not Miles and even if you were you wouldn't be welcome. Please go away. I won't be as polite next time."

"I need your help."

"So what's it to me?"

"I'm not asking for much. Just some information. You'll have nothing to worry about from me after that."

"And why should I care?"

I didn't want to do this but it was clear he wasn't going to respond unless I applied pressure. I decided that for him a good lie would have more impact than the truth. "I've just been talking with someone you don't know yet. Inspector Hendricks at Euston police station. He's very interested in the whereabouts of Miles Blake. He tells me the FBI has asked for help and want to speak with Miles and anyone who's been associating with him."

Weston's resolve crumpled. "You'd better come in."

He showed me into an apartment that was filled with computer hardware with the barest space remaining for life's essentials. Now I was beneath the veneer of the bravado he'd presented, he looked as frightened as Miles had said he would be.

His voice had a pleading note. "Let's keep the police and the FBI out of this, shall we? You're Miles' brother. I should have trusted you. I'm sorry I came on ugly like that. Tell me what you want?"

"I need to know how much further you've got in the work you're doing for Miles."

His hands were shaking. "They're this close to being on to me. The situation is changing fast. Every time I hack their database it's at a greater risk. And right now everything is nailed down tight."

"But you have been back in?"

He nodded. "Call it an addiction. Call it the kind of challenge that gets right under the skin. Or just call it what someone like me does because he needs the money. Yes I've been back in there and I've been careful."

I was sure I knew much of what he could tell me but I wanted to hear it from him so I could discover if he had any new evidence.

"So, you can update me."

"If you insist. But first you need to tell me why I'm not saying this to Miles himself. And why I should trust you."

I told him Miles was still in the States. "He made a great sacrifice for me. He let me travel here on his passport. He's still there, on the run."

"You've lost contact?"

I nodded. "Before we parted he said I should contact you and gave me this address."

"Still doesn't tell me why I should trust you."

"I was hoping you'd see that by helping me you'd be helping Miles. And if that doesn't make sense, there's always the matter of Inspector Hendricks."

He raised a hand. "OK, you've made your point. I can show you what I archived before I decided enough was enough and this was the last time I would go back into their database." He became furtive, as if reliving the tension and apprehension he experienced while hacking the most protected database in the world. Yet there was also a sense of relief that he could unburden himself of secrets he knew.

He started to pull up internal FBI reports onto his screen. "The key is to understand that the Town Lake bombing was not down to East Africa terrorists. It was about something much nearer to home. I've found the real reason for the atrocity was known within the organisation but that's being covered up with the terrorist claims. Someone has been working hard to erase the real record. They're good but they've left telltale signs."

"Such as?"

"Such as the details of how the FBI first got involved with protecting Elmore Ravitz and his family. Ravitz's political career was riding high and he was on track to become the next great white hope, so secretiveness and disinformation could be expected. But this goes beyond that. Ravitz overreached himself. He had a problem and I think he offended the wrong people. He thought he could use his influence with the FBI to get even and he was wrong. That's why he and most of his family died at Town Lake."

"And the reason for someone to be working so hard to change the record?"

"Is what it always is – greed and corruption. What else? You see, Ravitz made the mistake of contacting the wrong people in the FBI. It was a mistake that led to an agent called Jack Franks being assigned to the investigation to defend Ravitz. You look as if this isn't news to you?"

My thoughts were back in Weymouth on the night when Franks had first called. I decided to keep them from Weston. "I know something of Franks but not what you're saying about his connection to Ravitz."

He continued. "Once you grasp the fact that Franks was not meant to be involved, the rest falls into place. Someone was running a black op from within the organisation and they needed to cover it up. Franks was on the wrong side and they got rid of him. The official reports state that Franks' death was an accident and that's the accepted view. But reading between the lines, the idea it was an accident is part of the same cover up."

"You have evidence?"

He shook his head. "Nothing you could point to and say, that's it and shows what I'm saying is the case. It's more what you can deduce from the way the official record has been doctored to conceal the key aspects of Franks' activity, the snippets of information remaining as loose ends when someone's house cleaning has been good but not quite good enough. It's a kind of truth that emerges by omission and association."

He was losing me. "What do you mean?"

"Look, when you piece together the way the record has been modified, the story emerging is that Franks was in possession of information deadly to others within the organisation. Part of that was good fortune. The rest was solid deduction. The combination was enough for someone to want to eliminate him."

"Can you tell who's behind the cover up?"

He shook his head. "Whoever's been cleaning up has been skilled enough to stay concealed."

I knew who I wanted Weston to name. "Any mention of Craven? Agent Nate Craven?"

"Nothing I've seen. Why do you ask?"

I smiled. "Just someone I have an interest in."

He began closing down the computer systems, his signal he wanted me to leave. "Is that everything?"

"There's one more thing. I want you to help me rob a bank."

I expected him to be shocked but instead he showed a detached, professional interest. "Give me details."

"I want you to steal from my own account."

I explained to him how the money I had in my account in Weymouth was locked because it was certain it was being watched. If I used the online banking facility to transfer money to another account it would be tracked.

He listened and, unlike in our earlier discussion, he remained calm and collected. He was comfortable in this, the low risk end of his business. Then he had questions. "Tell me why you need the money?"

"Better you don't know."

"Tell me why you're on the run? It's not Town Lake, is it?"

I shook my head. "I just need the money."

He paused and looked as if he was on the point of saying he didn't believe me when he changed his mind. "It could be done. Ten per cent."

"Of what?"

"Call it a finder's fee. I take ten per cent of whatever I arrange for you to withdraw as cash."

The account held over fifty thousand, made up of the severance pay I'd received on leaving the radio station three years ago and what small amounts Julia and I had been able to save from our Weymouth jobs. Weston was heading for a good payday.

I agreed. "OK. How do you propose to do it?"

As he explained it to me, it was simple. He'd set up a barrier to shield the initial transfer from the account so it would be difficult, if not impossible to trace. The transfer would be into an international money transfer account. Requests to the transfer account for payment for various services would be made from a legitimate computer software business. The business was a front controlled by Weston. In order not to shock the system and create unwanted attention, the overall transaction would be divided into ten parts, each with a value of five thousand.

I shook his hand. "OK, we have a deal. You keep ten per cent. I get the rest in cash."

"It's going to take at least twenty-four hours."

"That's OK."

I had another reason to stay in London – the forger Miles had used to secure the passport for Julia in the name of Elizabeth Meredith. I had his contact details, courtesy of Miles. I needed a passport in a new identity if I was to make the trip to Florence without being stopped. The time it took for the cash to appear would give enough time for the passport to be made.

Weston worked at his main screen for the next hour. Code flowed across the screen as he set up the protocols to hide the money as it left my Weymouth account. He stopped periodically to ask me details of log-ins and passwords for my account.

I wanted to be sure. "Won't whoever's watching the account see that the money has been withdrawn?"

He wasn't fazed. "Yes, but they won't know where it's going."

"Won't they put a stop on the account?"

"That's why we take the money out of the account right away. By the time they call to stop it, the fifty thou will be gone.

They'll have left it open as a trap to try to get you to give away your current identity and location. Once the money's gone, it's gone. They'll be reduced to trying to find out where you've sent it and we'll have covered our tracks too well to let them get far with that."

After an hour, he sat back in his chair. "We're done. It's all in place."

I wanted to know how I was going to collect the money.

He became defensive. "Not here. We don't meet here again, you understand. It's too risky."

"Then where?"

He handed me a Post-It note on which he'd written an email address and a password. "This is secure. Access when you think is right but use a cafe with free WiFi. When the money is all here, I'll send a mail to let you know the time and place we can meet."

"And that's all I get to know right now?"

"It'll be somewhere public. I give you the cash in two deliveries. We meet twice and that's it."

I had to trust him if I wanted the money and the chance to get to Florence. "OK. I'll wait to hear."

He looked long and hard at me as I thanked him and prepared to leave. "And we've forgotten about saying anything to Hendricks."

I smiled. "Let's say he's someone I'd go a long way to avoid right now. You can be sure of that."

When I reached the door, he called me back. "What do you want me to do about the work for Miles?"

"Nothing's changed. Miles will find a way back from the States. So, carry on. See what else you can find."

Chapter 8

Agent Bedford thanked his stars. The stakeout of the Adam Weston apartment was failing to yield results but, just when he should have been calling it a day and heading back to the safety of the Bureau, here came a tall man approaching Weston's place and going inside.

Finding Weston had been straightforward. Once he'd taken the bait, the Java script that Bedford had inserted in the database had done its work, delivering the IP address used by the hacker. A little pressure on the Internet service provider had delivered Weston's address.

Bedford adjusted the laser microphone to focus on the window-pane of the second floor room where he'd seen Weston moving around. He tuned the settings on the compact control box that sat on the vacant front seat of his vehicle and listened to what he could pick up through the earpiece that came with the equipment. Yes, the sound quality was good.

Few people knew that these days you didn't need to do anything as crude as breaking into the target's apartment and planting bugs in the light fittings or electrical sockets. Just shine the laser on their window-pane, use the ever-so-versatile ray of light to pick up the vibrations in the glass as the people inside talk and let the box of tricks turn those vibrations back into sound. Why, the clever little box even recorded what was being said and beamed it straight into the FBI main database to be accessed whenever needed in the future. It was just one of the smart surveillance techniques he could call upon.

Still, he needed to concentrate. They were talking.

"I told you not to come here."

A pause. Then the same voice.

"You're not Miles. You look enough like him. Where the hell is Miles?"

The second voice.

"I'm his brother. We need to talk."

Yes, this was James Blake, the brother of Miles, the principal target of the investigation. The same James Blake that both Craven and Maynard wanted a fix on. Bedford smiled. He could use what he was hearing to keep both men satisfied. Not that he'd be telling them both the same thing.

He listened as Blake and Weston discussed their plans. Weston was being guarded, not because he was concerned at being overheard but because he didn't know if he could trust the man. That was good. It meant they weren't close and divisions between the two could be exploited.

Weston was admitting he'd removed documents from the database. The recording of this conversation was enough to put the hacker away for twenty years. That would make him pliable. Make him susceptible to doing what the Bureau wanted.

And Blake needed money. He must be planning a trip.

Now Blake was leaving. That was a problem. There was no way he could follow, even if Bedford had the appetite for such a thing. He had to concentrate on Weston. The hacker would deliver Blake and more.

It was time to take the initiative. Time to show Maynard he could return with the goods.

He left his vehicle, made his way to the second floor of the building and knocked on Weston's door. He could hear the man moving about inside but the door did not open.

Bedford shouted. "It's James Blake. Let me in."

Weston's muffled voice came back from the other side of the door. "Why are you back?"

He lied and picked a significant name he'd just heard in the bugged conversation between Blake and Weston. "There's something important I forgot to tell you about Ravitz."

37

Bedford drew his Glock-23 as the door opened. At the sight of the weapon, Weston froze and fell back.

Bedford pushed his way in. "Get inside and sit down."

He looked around as he followed Weston inside, all the time keeping the pistol aimed at his man. So this was what a hacker's place looked like. Not much different from his own set up back at base.

Weston had his hands raised. "Don't fire. I don't know who you are but just put the weapon down. We can talk this through, whatever it is."

Bedford was surprised how straightforward this was.

The target.

The weapon.

The fear.

The response.

He wasn't used to this feeling of undiluted power. It wasn't the kind of thing you experienced in backroom work. He decided he liked it.

He spoke the magic words. "FBI."

Weston, hands still raised, went white. "I knew you'd find me."

"Yes, Adam. You've been known to us for a while. You're good. But not good enough. I want you to listen to this."

Bedford placed the clever little box he'd brought with him from the vehicle and pressed play. It was the conversation between Weston and Blake recorded just minutes before.

"OK, you've made your point. I can show you what I archived before I decided enough was enough and I'd never go back into their database again."

Weston's mouth sagged open.

Bedford smiled. "So, Adam, what do you say to twenty years in Walls Unit Correctional Facility? It's a federal offence. Stealing classified information. And, in case you're thinking there's some way out of this, the little box I have here is WiFi connected. What you're hearing now is safe and secure and filed in our database under something like: *dangerous subversive, prepare for imminent arrest.*"

Weston's words came one by one. "You have me. Why tell me this?"

"Because there's a way you might avoid that trip to Huntsville. What you've done is bad. And you have no future if things stay as they are. But I'm here to help. I'm here to give you the chance to make amends."

Weston was not the type to resist. "What do you want me to do?"

"That's better, Adam. You can put your hands down now. We want you to tell us everything you know about Miles and James Blake. Then we want you to do what we say as you relate to them in the future. That's simple, isn't it?"

"You mean you want me to inform on them?"

"Yes, if you want to call it that. Let's just say you'd be given the chance to redeem yourself by at last living up to your duty as a responsible citizen who's turned his back on wrongdoing. We're saying we'll take it into account."

Weston had all the look of a defeated man. "OK." Then, after a long break, he pleaded. "What happens next?"

Bedford could see the man was so frightened he would do as was asked. The agent put the Glock away. "Adam, you stay as you are. We'll stay in close touch and tell you what we expect you to do. Someone will come here to give you the chance to tell us what you know. And don't think you can get away with anything stupid. One slip and the deal's off. You know what that means?"

Weston nodded in agreement and said no more. He didn't notice as, during the interrogation, Bedford sprinkled RFID, radiofrequency identification, dust on the floor beneath the computer where Weston spent most of his time.

Bedford took time to pack away the clever little box and let himself out. It had been a successful day after all. He'd accomplished more than enough to keep Maynard off his back.

Bedford made his way back to his vehicle. He didn't see the two Italians sitting in the parked car on the other side of the street who turned their faces away as he left the building.

Back inside, Adam Weston could not stop the shaking that had taken control of his whole body. The paranoia he'd been feeling had been made so real he knew he could no longer call it that.

Chapter 9

Retired Chief Superintendent Giles Cleary was worried about John Hendricks. The man was unreformed, so much a throwback to the old school of London policing that he was a danger to the whole enterprise.

The Italians had got carried away and this could mean serious problems if Hendricks put the whole story together.

The killing in the Allegro Hotel had been botched. The Blake woman had escaped. Another man, most likely her protector, had been killed instead. It wouldn't take Hendricks long to make connections beyond Julia Blake. But what was worse was the Italians had killed DI Reid. At least that's what Cleary was forced to assume.

Cleary had never intended them to go that far when he'd sent Reid to the old warehouse down the river from Canary Wharf. He'd expected they would frighten the policeman off, convince him to return to Weymouth where he belonged and put behind him the dream he had of collecting on the two million the Landos had offered for James and Julia Blake. The Italians were under instruction to achieve that and no more. But they lacked discipline. Reid had not been heard of since. The conclusion that loomed large for Cleary was that the Italians had killed Reid and disposed of the body goodness knows where.

So far Reid was listed as missing. It would be enough to alert Hendricks. The unreformed copper would be bound to make the connection between Reid, the Blakes and the Allegro killing but the significance would remain in the world of speculation without hard evidence.

Cleary hated the idea of damage limitation. It was a sure sign that things were not as they should be. Yet damage limitation was needed now. If Reid's body was found Hendricks would have the evidence he needed and it would spell trouble indeed.

The retired Chief Superintendent picked up the phone. He called the special number. The number he knew should only be used with the greatest caution.

Alessa Lando picked up the call.

Cleary began. "Signora Lando, you must forgive me for calling like this but it's imperative we speak."

She sounded perplexed that he had called. "What can I help you with, Chief Superintendent?"

"We have a problem. Something we need to deal with sooner rather than later. It concerns two of your men. The ones who were sent to target the Blake woman."

"I thought it had been taken care of."

"There are complications. Unavoidable problems. It's likely that your men killed a policeman. Name of Reid. DI Reid. Then they disposed of the body no one knows where. If the body comes to light everything could be on the line. We need to find the body and make sure it doesn't become a problem."

Cleary had used all his influence to secure a safe existence in London for Alessa Lando. As the Kolakov business interests had continued to prosper in this city, so had the importance of ensuring that the oligarch's new wife, Alessa, could have confidence in her security. Dmitri Kolakov had paid well to ensure it was so. Cleary didn't want anything to interfere with that. It's what made the present conversation so difficult.

Alessa was not impressed. "I hear you, Chief Superintendent. I'll deal with it."

"That would be best."

Her annoyance was plain to hear. "More to the point, Mr. Cleary, what are you doing to find the Blakes? With your resources I would have thought you'd have tracked them down by now."

Cleary could feel his blood pressure rising. He couldn't say what he wanted to say. The Italians had botched the killing at the Allegro and left behind the kind of mess no one, least of all Cleary, should have to clean up. But he could say none of this. It would be madness to be out of favour with this woman. Instead, he tried to sound matter-of-fact. "The Blakes have disappeared from view. The Blake woman is untraceable, though I have hopes of finding her. The husband, James has been seen in London. He was close to being apprehended at Euston station."

"Close is not good enough. I want him disposed of, you understand? Surely, the two million is enough to loosen tongues. Surely, with all the resources you can count on, you can locate him?"

"We'll find Blake now he's in London. It's just a matter of time."

"OK, Chief Superintendent. We know we can depend on you."

"You'll let me know about Reid's body?"

"I'll let you know." She closed the line.

Cleary took a deep breath.

It was good she had treated him with such contempt, as if he were her underling. That meant she did not know the truth about the power he had, a power bequeathed to him by Alfieri Lando.

Chapter 10

Luigi Bandini thumped the iron bar into his cupped right hand. It was an unfashionable instrument, but one he liked, at least in the early stages of breaking down the resistance of an opponent. That's the way he'd opened up the policeman Reid before he was dispatched. Bandini smiled at the thought of using it again on whoever was inside the apartment.

The British police were fools.

They were no match for him.

Not for once had Bandini felt he was on the run since the killing in the Allegro Hotel.

Yet he knew he could not call the current state of play a success either. Sure, they'd killed the bodyguard, the one the police had named as Martin Craig, but they'd lost the Blake woman, the one they were supposed to kill. Matteo Lando was not impressed. If they returned home to Florence without addressing this problem their own lives would be short indeed.

Getting on to the FBI man had not been difficult. The Lando man inside the FBI organisation was still active, though the recent events involving the German Heller had strained matters almost to breaking point. So, here they were watching Agent Bedford leave the apartment where he'd spent the last thirty minutes involved in something they needed to know about.

It had been difficult to know if they should have followed the tall man who'd left the apartment earlier. Bandini had not recognised him as anyone of importance and had chosen to stay to observe Bedford. He had a photograph of the unknown man and would seek to identify him later.

Bedford was no professional, that much was clear. He was unaware how simple it was to follow him as he left the office in the Haymarket, now identified as the front for the FBI in London. If it went on like this, it was going to be as simple as ever could have been wished for to keep following Bedford and discover each and every one of the suspects he was investigating.

Asputi, the man seated beside him in the vehicle, was not bright. "So, we take down the American."

"No, Asputi. He's our meal ticket. Now, we discover what he's been doing up there in the apartment."

Bandini opened the car door and motioned Asputi to climb out. He got out himself and pressed the key fob to lock the vehicle.

The two men headed towards Adam Weston's apartment.

When there was no reply, Bandini used the iron bar to smash a hole in the door so he could reach through and open the lock from inside.

They were too late. The apartment was empty.

–

Minutes earlier, Adam Weston had packed everything important to him into a small hold all. This comprised a dozen terabyte pocket drives onto which he had backup of the entire contents of his elaborate hacking system and all the information files that went with it. Then he'd wiped the hard drives of each of his computers before taking a hammer to them. Giving one last look back he'd commiserated with himself at leaving such valuable equipment behind before pulling up the sash window and making his way down the fire escape at the rear of the building before he had any more unwelcome visitors.

Chapter 11

The bus from San Diego Old Town to Tijuana was peopled largely by those ill-informed tourists who believed there were cheap pickings to be had across the border. Miles Blake climbed aboard, paid the fare, and hoped for an uneventful trip.

Leaving the US was straightforward as the whole busload was waved through an exit channel that looked more like a highway tollbooth than a border control post. Miles expected the same easy entry into Mexico but he was mistaken.

The alarm must have been raised. The Mexico police were looking for someone. A moustachioed and uniformed official boarded the bus when it was stopped at the Mexico border and began checking papers. The person they were searching for was James Blake. That was the name in the passport Miles now carried after the swap of passports with James at Dallas Fort Worth. When Miles showed the passport he was told to stand and leave the bus. He was shown straight to a waiting police car, handcuffed and forced into the rear passenger seat.

"Why are you doing this? Where are you taking me?"

The arresting officer had taken up position in the front passenger seat. A uniformed colleague was driving. They both ignored Miles' questions.

Miles' Spanish was poor to nonexistent yet he suspected that even if he had been fluent in the language they would have shown him the same response. The Mexico authorities now believed they had apprehended James Blake. Miles had to decide if it might be best if it stayed this way.

They drove for thirty minutes on a highway that cut through the desert before they arrived at central Tijuana. He was taken straight to a police station in the Zona Norte.

There were no charges, yet he was placed still handcuffed in a cell. His protests were answered with a silent smile. After four hours he was walked upstairs to the top floor of the building and into an office marked: Pedro Martinez – Chief of Police.

Martinez looked up as Miles was brought in and seated on a chair facing the chief's desk. He nodded to one of the officers. "Remove the handcuffs. I think we can trust Senor Blake to remain seated while we talk."

Miles whispered. "Thank you."

Martinez was welcoming. "Senor Blake, can I call you James?"

Miles nodded.

"So, James, I'm pleased you chose to visit us here in Tijuana. I'm pleased we have this chance to talk. Do you mind telling me why you are here?"

"I thought you might be telling me why you've arrested me."

Martinez smiled. "I think you already know that, James. Still, if you wish, I will be formal with you. We have concerns about whether it is appropriate to you to be in Mexico when you have so many unresolved matters with the authorities of our good neighbour, the United States."

"You mean the FBI put out a wanted call for me."

"You should not be surprised. You should understand that those who think that Mexico is, as you say, a soft touch, when it comes to evading authority are mistaken. The days when Tijuana was a byword for lawlessness are coming to a close. I am here to see that those days are in the past once and for all. I think you understand?"

Miles knew of Pedro Martinez. He was aware of the personal risk the man was taking in seeking to overcome the cartels running this town. There were constant threats to himself and his family and corruption inside and outside his own force. He was a brave man who had achieved much in the short time he'd been there. Yet it was clear he was overstating the case.

The time had come to tell Martinez who he was. "James is my brother. I'm Miles Blake."

Martinez was surprised but not fazed. "I have bad news, Senor Miles Blake. There is also a notice from the FBI regarding you." He paused. "Tell me, why do you travel with your brother's passport?"

"It's a long story."

"Try me."

"We swapped passports."

"So he could leave the US as you?"

Miles nodded. "That's a crime here in Mexico?"

"It is not regular. So, tell me Senor Blake, why are you here in Tijuana?"

"I'm seeking a man. Luiz Reyas. I'm hoping you can help me find him."

Martinez frowned. "A man of that name died in a shooting in East Texas. His body is due to return here this week."

Miles was lost for a moment. He was back in the abandoned train station in East Austin cradling Luiz Reyas in his arms as the Mexican died. He turned his mind back to the matter in hand. "No, not him. His son. He is also called Luiz Reyas. I need to speak to him."

"About what?"

"About his father."

"And why would you expect me to want to help you contact him?"

"Chief Martinez, I know about your stance against drugs. How you are the best chance this town has had in years. If we work together I may be able, in some small way, to help you beat the cartels."

"This is the investigative reporter talking?"

"You know about that?"

Martinez smiled. "It's on your record." And then he continued. "How is Luiz Reyas a part of that?"

Miles told Martinez about the investigation he was carrying out on the Lando operation smuggling drugs out of Tijuana for the European market. "They're not working alone. The people they're working with are the same people you're trying to root out here. We can help each other."

Miles knew this was a risk. Martinez was not the first police chief in this town to have been appointed on a wave of optimism that he was going to make a difference. The corrupting power of the cartels was everywhere. Miles did not know if Martinez would be just another amongst the many who'd tried and failed.

Martinez had not rejected Miles' offer out of hand. "And why would Luiz Reyas make a difference?"

"He has a reason, a motivation that means he could succeed if we decide to help him."

"We know more than enough in this town about revenge, if that is what you mean. It is the biggest part of where we are today."

"This is about more than revenge. It's about a man's right to control his destiny."

"And your motivation, Mr. Blake? What do you get out of it?"

"A story. Just a story."

Martinez was silent for a while, leaving Miles in doubt about the outcome. When the man spoke it was clear he'd made up his mind. "Well, Miles Blake, tell me what I can do to help."

Chapter 12

To travel to Florence I needed a passport that wasn't being tracked.

I phoned Alex Bishop using the number Miles had given me and he agreed to meet me at the *Miller and Ploughman*, a pub overlooking the Thames at Wapping. It was one of the oldest in London with parts of the building dating back to the 1500s and Henry VIII. It was known for a chequered history involving all manner of skulduggery as it served as a meeting place for sailors, smugglers and just about every kind of criminal lowlife in the city of London.

Knowing this did nothing to calm my fears as I approached the building.

It was evening, already dark, by the time I made my way there via Shadwell Underground station. As I walked in, no heads turned. They were used to ignoring strangers here. The cramped bar area was peopled with the expected array of drinkers absorbed in their own conversations. The building had been rebuilt after a fire in the eighteenth century. Dark mahogany wood from a salvaged ship had been used. This explained the gloomy, nautical feel of the place.

There was no surprise either when I asked at the bar for Alex Bishop. "His table's out the back."

Bishop made me as soon as I set foot on the terrace. He called me over with a wave of the hand.

He'd taken control of a prime position, looking out across the Thames towards the bankers' towers of Canary Wharf with their lights shining out across the river as if there was no tomorrow. There was no need for sailors or smugglers in Bishop's entourage nor amongst the boys on the opposite bank of the Thames – their skulduggery was all of the digital kind.

Bishop looked me over, eyeing another payday, calculating how much he thought he could take me for.

I tried to sound matter-of-fact. "I need a passport."

He smiled. "You've come to the right place, then. When do you need it?"

"As soon as."

"Affects the price."

"One day."

He exhaled. "Makes it different. That's five thou, that is."

"Make it four."

He looked at me long and hard. "Cash up front."

The cash I had left was running low. There was nothing yet from Adam Weston. This was going to be a problem. "I can give you five hundred up front."

He leaned back and looked away, across the Thames. "Then it's no deal. It has to be cash up front. What if you don't come back?"

"What if you run away with my money?"

He feigned being offended. "And damage my reputation? I don't think so."

"You know I'll come back with the money. I need the passport." He was gazing at my Rolex, the gift they'd given me when I'd left the radio station. "Must be worth a couple of thou."

I removed the watch and handed it to him. "I want it back."

His hand was still outstretched, palm open. "And the five hundred."

I handed him the notes. "Adrian Gillespie. Use it as the name on the passport."

He smiled again. "OK. I expect the other two thou on delivery. Four thou if you want the watch back. Be here same time tomorrow."

He paused and nodded to two of his men. "Oh, and you'll need to go with Mr. Spinks and the other gentleman to get a head and shoulders, won't you?"

They walked me away from the pub along deserted and dark East End streets. I didn't know where they were taking me. The further we walked the less I was any longer sure that the whole thing wasn't a setup to relieve me of my money and my Rolex. I cursed myself for being this foolish, leaving myself in such a defenceless position, trusting those who I had no instinct to trust.

When we reached the all-night pharmacy on Wapping Lane, they walked me inside and sat me down in the photo booth. One of them, the ugliest, Spinks, was in control. "Now, make sure the seat is the right height so your face fits the frame. And let's make sure the curtain is out of the way so there's a nice white background. You wouldn't want people to think this wasn't a proper passport photo now, would you?"

They fed the machine money. I sat still as the four shots were taken. When the photos popped out, Spinks dismissed me. "You can go now."

I walked away, heading back towards Shadwell Underground and the light.

Back at the hotel, I couldn't resist any longer the impulse to call Julia on the mobile phone. She picked up.

"Just to check you're all right."

It was good to hear her voice again. "Everything's fine. Mark Stone is serious about protecting us and Faith's property. He's got a couple of local men with him. It's helping me feel secure. Faith took me to the postnatal clinic. That's all fine, too."

"Baby Simon is progressing well?"

"He's doing fine."

"That's what I wanted to hear."

"Jim, you're not taking risks?"

"I'm OK. No need to worry. I'm going to get off the line now. Love you."

"Love you."

I closed the line.

I hadn't told Julia what I still needed to do to get the passport to allow me to travel to Florence. There was no need to worry her with the details.

Chapter 13

Agent Michael Bedford congratulated himself that he'd found a way to get his life back again. He'd gained enough information from Adam Weston to keep Maynard off his back. And he'd found a way of dealing with Craven.

The first step back to control was to make sure the recording of the conversation between Weston and James Blake was placed in an encrypted location on the FBI database where Bedford alone would have access. Bill Maynard knew only that Blake was in London and was under surveillance. Bedford wanted to keep it this way. This was his insurance policy. The information that would be key to his future. Hiding the recording was a simple enough task for someone with his computing knowledge.

The second step was to contact Nate Craven and let him know the game had changed.

Craven picked up as soon as Bedford accessed the secure line. He was in no mood to talk. "What is it, Bedford?"

Bedford took his time. "I have something you should hear."

He placed the phone close to the speaker of the computer so Craven could hear the recording Bedford had brought back from Adam Weston's apartment.

It was Adam Weston's voice.

"The key is to understand that the Town Lake bombing was not down to East Africa terrorists. It was about something much nearer to home. I've found the real reason for the atrocity was known within the organisation but that's being covered up with the terrorist claims. Someone has been working hard to erase the real record. They're good but they've left telltale signs."

And now James Blake.

"Such as?"

Back to Weston.

"Such as the details of how the FBI first got involved with protecting Elmore Ravitz and his family."

Craven's voice sounded tense as he interrupted. "Just what are we listening to, Bedford?"

Bedford stopped the playback. "Can't you tell, Nate? That's Adam Weston talking with James Blake. About what happened at Town Lake."

"The hacker?"

"The very same."

"How did you get it?"

"By doing my job, Nate. It's from my surveillance of Weston."

"And James Blake was there?"

"Like I said. OK, so listen to this."

Bedford resumed the playback.

Weston was speaking.

"Franks was in possession of information that was deadly to others within the organisation. Part of that was fortune. The rest was good solid deduction. The combination was enough for someone to want to eliminate him."

Now Blake.

"Can you tell who's behind the cover up?"

Weston's reply.

"Whoever's been cleaning up has been good enough to stay concealed."

And more from Blake.

"Any mention of Craven? Agent Nate Craven?"

Craven called a halt once more. "OK, Bedford. What's this got to do with anything?"

"It's got to do with the fact that I want out. You understand. If you don't want to hear about this again, you count me out of Mexico and you stop treating me as if you own me."

"On the basis of hearsay from two English targets under our active surveillance? I don't think that's any kind of threat."

"So you're prepared to take a chance?"

"On what?"

"On what happens if I give this to Bill Maynard. I can't think he'll do anything but draw conclusions from this, not if he hears the whole conversation."

"What else is on it?"

"That's what you're going to have to pay to hear, Nate."

Craven hesitated, making it clear that the mention of Maynard's name had affected him. "Where's the recording now, Bedford?"

"I have it secured. For my sole use."

"You have a way of not revealing it to Maynard?"

Bedford was relishing the feeling of getting the upper hand, just like he felt when he'd pulled the Glock on Weston. "Maynard doesn't know any more than I was tailing the target. He doesn't know there is a recording. Not yet. It can stay like that if you want. I have a one-to-one meeting with him just about now."

"OK. OK. Let's say we keep this between us. Tell me what you want."

"That's better, Nate. I want what I asked you for, nothing more. I want out. I want you off my back."

Bedford closed the line. There was no need for anything further. Craven had got the message. He had no way of knowing what else was on the recording. It had real power over him. He would have to agree to Bedford's terms.

Bedford sat back and congratulated himself once more. It felt good to have stood up to Craven. The second step along the way to getting his life back had gone well.

The third step was Maynard. The one-on-one meeting was sure to be a trial. But this time it would be different. Tracking down Weston was a success. Maynard needed to know about that. But Bedford would not reveal the recording. He wanted to tell Maynard enough to build the pressure on Craven, nothing more.

Maynard was his usual blustering self when the one-on-one started and Bedford was not surprised when the man piled straight in. "OK, you had a brief to do something about the Adam Weston target and to make progress on Miles Blake. So, Bedford, what progress have you made?"

Bedford would not cower this time. In fact, he felt a confidence in dealing with Maynard he hadn't felt before. "I have a success to report, sir. I traced the target Weston to an apartment in Pimlico and put it under surveillance. A farther key target was identified arriving at the premises."

He tabled a print out of a photograph of the target.

Maynard gave it a sceptical glance. "The target is Miles Blake?"

"No, sir. In fact it's the brother, James."

"You're sure?"

"The facial recognition software is clear on this, sir. This is James Blake."

"How long did he stay?"

"Under half an hour."

"You had them bugged?"

Bedford lied. "No, sir. I wasn't set up for that. I wasn't expecting they would both be there."

"So what use is this?"

"When Blake left, I paid Weston a visit. He became cooperative when I showed him a little extra attention."

Maynard smiled. "I was beginning to think you didn't have it in you, boy."

"As we thought, he's scared stiff we're going to take him in. He's prepared to co-operate. It should be no problem to get him to wear a wire when he next meets Blake."

"You know where and when that is?"

"No, sir."

"So if he makes a run for it, you've lost him?"

"That's not the case. I took the precaution of sprinkling RFID dust on the floor where he'd walk. Those little transponders will be stuck to the soles of his shoes. Whenever he goes near enough to a strong enough magnetic field and electricity can be scavenged, we'll get back a radio signal that gives us his location."

"If it works so well, tell me where he is now."

Bedford pulled out the tablet he was carrying and called up the custom locator app. He had to hope that the tagging system on Weston was active. Much to Bedford's relief, the screen showed a blinking blue dot indicating the target. "He's on the move, sir. He's in the West End."

Maynard looked impressed but didn't show it. "Anything else, Bedford?"

Bedford wanted to get this right, to make it sound like he was reluctant to say what was coming next. "I don't know if I should mention this, sir. There's almost certain to be nothing in it but I think it's something you should know."

"Get to the point."

"Weston told me the Blakes are making claims about corruption in one of our own."

"Who might that be?"

"Agent Nate Craven."

"And you think that might be credible?"

"Of course not, sir. But there was something about the way Weston told me this that made me think others might come to believe him if we were to let this ride."

"But there's no hard evidence for that?"

"No, sir."

Bedford was growing ever more confident. "I ran some checks on James Blake. He's a target on our system but there's something about the audit trail on him that doesn't add up. There are gaps in the data and it's possible someone has been messing with it, covering their tracks. But one thing stands out. He was in Austin at the time of the Town Lake bombing. Maybe it's just a coincidence."

Maynard's eyes sparkled. "Bedford, there's no such thing as coincidence. That's what I've learned in all the years I've been in this game. Whenever there's an appeal to coincidence there's something someone, somewhere wants to hide. So, you're saying this is somehow connected with Craven?"

"I don't know, sir. It's the way the data looks."

Maynard grunted and said no more. It was clear he was taking in the possible consequences of what Bedford had told him. When he next spoke, he was constructive. "So, tell me what you need."

"Sir?"

"To close in on Blake. To make sure we bring the mother's son to book."

Bedford knew he had to be careful not to reveal information that would lead Maynard to suspect he had the recording of the conversation between Weston and Blake at the Pimlico apartment. There was a way round that. "There is one thing, sir. When I questioned Weston, he told me Blake needed to have a passport made. That's going to be by someone here in London. If we knew who it was, we'd have a second fix on Blake if anything was to go wrong."

"What do you propose?"

"Put the word out to our contacts that there's money for anyone who tells us who the passport maker is."

"How much?"

"Five thousand would do it."

Money was not one of the Bureau's problems and Maynard obliged. "OK. Have ten. Make sure you get the intel."

The second request was more difficult. They were under-manned. If that wasn't the case Bedford wouldn't be out in the field himself. Yet he made the request anyway. "I need another man. With one more and the right back up when the time comes, I'm sure we can get a result."

"You can call in backup. But only when you have Blake ready for capture. Another man on the case isn't going to be possible, Bedford. Give me one good reason."

"It would be for just two days, maybe three. It could make the difference."

Maynard's snarl made it clear this was against his better judgment, but he agreed. "OK. I'll assign McGraw. But he'll work with you for three days max, you got that?"

When the meeting finished and Bedford walked back to his office, he could not help thinking that the third part of the plan to get his life back had been another success.

Chapter 14

Alessa Lando waited for the message from her son, Matteo. She knew it was difficult to get calls out of Sollicciano even if you were as powerful amongst the inmates as her son. There were bribes to be paid. There were officials who wanted more. It was the routine of life within the Florence prison. Yet it didn't stop such delays from being an annoyance.

She rued the day she'd let the Blakes into her life, the chain of events that had left her husband Alfieri dead and her dearest Matteo imprisoned for life for his murder. She should have stopped the tragedy from unfolding. All along she'd tried to shield Matteo from that corrupting hand. All along she'd tried to prevent Alfieri from perverting the good she knew Matteo must have in him.

Just what had Alfieri wanted of their son? It was something that remained a mystery to her to this day.

How could something that Alfieri had been so involved with have been kept secret from her? What had he been doing with those women? She was shocked on his death to realise the secret life her husband had been leading. When they were together in the early years, when it had appeared to all the world they belonged together, she realised now, he must have been all the time living a secret life and that it had continued and intensified after their split and the tussle over the future of their son, Matteo.

These realisations had cast a shadow on the past and caused Alessa to reflect on all that had gone before. How the whole of their life together had been a sham. And with this had come the concern over just what Alfieri had in mind for Matteo. How he kept insisting their son achieved his real potential while all the time seeming to drive the boy down, to destroy his confidence. How he had hardened the boy and made him into a merciless man. Just what had Alfieri been preparing their son for? It was more than the expectation that one day Matteo would head the family. The more she thought about it, the more she realised it was connected with the secret life Alfieri had kept from her.

Perhaps the Blakes had been no more than a symptom of the disease that had been their lives. Perhaps Matteo was destined all along to kill his father. But this did not change the hatred she felt towards James and Julia Blake and the brother, Miles.

Somehow, she knew nothing had been changed by Alfieri's death. The secret life, the way he used the women, spoke of something else. Something more enveloping. Something more confining. Something that might yet threaten to engulf Matteo.

It was her sincerest wish to understand this and make sure Matteo did not become like his father. In life, she had not been strong enough in curbing her husband's excesses. In death, Alfieri must not get his wish.

The phone rang. It was Matteo. "You want to talk, Mother?"

"I need to know you are well."

"As well as anyone could be confined in a place like this. But it's not the reason for your call."

"It is, Matteo. A mother's wish to see her son released from the pain these people have placed him in."

"So you have the Blakes?"

"No, Matteo. We don't yet have them. And we have problems. You know we have to talk about Wolfgang Heller."

"Wolfgang does what he sees fit, you know that. And he gets results."

"At what cost? What he did at Town Lake threatens to bring the whole of the American security service down on our heads."

"It's not like that, Mother. Heller made a calculation."

"That more would have to die."

"You have lost your stomach for the fight?"

"But we have never strayed so far from the path that has served us so well. We have never taken such risks with our future."

Matteo paused before continuing. "Mother, you want to remove the loose ends threatening us?"

"Of course."

"Then, step aside. Leave it to those who have the stomach to do what is needed to keep the family safe."

"Not at any cost. Not if that risks everything as at Town Lake."

"Mother, you need to understand. We knew Agent Craven was involved in protecting the Ravitz family. Our FBI insider told us. We knew he would be forced to compromise himself. That's how it has worked out. So as far as the world is concerned, Heller was never at Town Lake. African terrorists did it."

"You knew about such a calculation?"

"Yes."

"Then you were taking too great a risk, indulging Heller in such a plan, You must understand why I am concerned. You had no certainty that Craven would be able to deliver and that placed us all at risk. Still places us all in danger."

"Success is about risk, Mother. Heller is safe for now in the monastery in Lhasa. He can't lead them to us. But you must know we need Heller. He's the difference for us. Isn't he delivering?"

"Yes. But at what cost?"

"Everything is under control. You need to trust me to lead the family now."

"I do trust you, my dearest. But I cannot face the thought of losing all we have worked for down the years."

"Then leave to me the remaining loose ends."

Alessa Lando was beginning to feel relieved that her son was in control but she had a confession to make. "Bandini and Asputi are failing."

"I know. I can have them dealt with."

"No. Not yet. We need them to take care of the body of the policeman they killed in London. Before it comes to light. You understand?"

She paused. "I agree you now lead the family. How can it be otherwise? Close off the loose ends. That includes the Blakes."

"Yes, Mother."

"Prosper in all you do, Matteo. It is a long race we run."

She closed the line. She cursed Alfieri all the way to his grave for making their son as heartless as he himself had been.

Alessa Lando was aware of the fatal flaws in Matteo's logic and the plain facts he would not face up to. The *calculation* he had been party to led to the atrocity at Town Lake and was heartless. Too many had died. Too many of those had been on the side of the authorities. The Landos had never carried out their business in this way. It could mean the ruination of the family.

Chapter 15

The euphoria of the award of the Intelligence Star didn't last long for Agent Debbie Miller. The growing feeling of unease was not helped by an unexpected call from Bill Maynard.

Before his dispatch to London, the two had worked together for three years in the Chicago office. During this time Debbie had learned to value their relationship despite Maynard's irascibility, putting this down to his dedication to success in the work.

"I wanted to catch up with you, Debbie."

This was unlike Maynard. He didn't often have time for small talk. He must have something on his mind.

"You heard I got the Star?"

"Yes. Made me feel proud. Your time with me wasn't wasted, then?"

"Chicago was great. I learned a lot. You heard that Nate got the Star along with me?"

He paused. "I heard that too. It's part of the reason for my call. I know I can trust you with this. I'm hearing doubts about Craven. I need to let you know since you're in his team."

Debbie's feeling of unease went up a notch. "What kind of doubts, Bill?"

"I don't think it's right to say just now. Not since he's just been given the Star. But there's intelligence coming my way that might paint the man in a different light."

"But you're not about to tell me what it is?"

"No, Debbie. It may not be reliable. Then I'd have wronged a decorated hero. I'm not about to do that until I'm sure the information we have here in London is sound. I'll check it and check it again until I'm sure. All I can say is the intelligence concerns Town Lake."

"I can't convince you."

"Take care around Craven. Watch your back. That's why I called. And to let you know I've emailed you a report about the Blake target."

Maynard said his farewells and was gone.

Debbie Miller had been given no time to discuss the report on Blake with Maynard. She checked it now. Something unexpected. Something she would have to report to the team meeting scheduled in ten minutes time. And she'd been given no time to let Maynard know she had her own doubts about Nate Craven.

As she thought more about it again now, for some time she'd been on the edge of admitting to herself something was wrong. It had begun with the feeling that Craven was watching her, using others to report on her. Why would he do that?

Then she couldn't stop her thoughts returning to the events of Town Lake and Craven's role that day. There was something not right about the way he'd appeared out of the smoke and rubble as she'd been leading the Ravitz girl to safety. Something too casual about the way he'd spoken, something that told her he hadn't been through the trauma of witnessing the mutilated and twisted bodies, as he claimed.

As she visualised the scene that day, it was a single perception that weighed most on her mind. Something about the way the grime on Craven's clothes, face and hands made it look as if he'd applied the dust and dirt himself to make it look as if he'd been toiling in the rubble amongst the dead and injured. If this were true it sickened her that he was now considered a hero. It cheapened any recognition she had received herself. It made the muscles in her abdomen clench tight with hard-to-conceal rage.

And these feelings led to further unease. She had not been able to follow through on what had happened to James Blake in the Warren Richardson hotel bar. Craven had been right that the Englishman would draw out the assassin sent to attack Elmore Ravitz. She'd seen the tall German draw the pistol and aim at Blake and herself as they sat at the bar. But that had come at the same time as the whole team had been scrambled to the Ravitz compound at Town Lake to deal with the destruction created there. Blake had escaped after a life-and-death chase. There were bodies found in the abandoned railway station in East Austin to prove it.

She'd developed a soft spot for the quiet-spoken Englishman, she knew, but that didn't affect her judgment. There were questions that wouldn't go away.

Could she believe it was a coincidence that the bombing at Town Lake took place at the same time as the stakeout at the Warren Richardson? It was possible. The evidence linking the atrocity to threats made against Ravitz by East Africa jihadists looked genuine and compelling. So, why did the fact of the coincidence stick in her throat?

She found herself asking the same question over and over. If Craven had implicated the jihadists in the Town Lake atrocity for some reason of his own, what was he trying to hide?

These doubts had been building. The call from Bill Maynard had shifted these doubts up a gear.

It was time for the meeting with Craven. It was time to face the man again.

As soon as the team assembled around the meeting room table Craven began. "OK, let's bring the latest intelligence together. Miller. You want to start?"

Debbie Miller could have done with more time to compose her thoughts but that didn't matter now. She had to get this right if she wasn't to compromise her position within the group. They were a new team, hand-picked by Craven. Early impressions counted. "I've been following intelligence on the London connection. We have an anomaly. The flight records and 1-91 show that Miles Blake left the US on 23rd August. There is no record of his brother James leaving the US, but maybe it's not too surprising given the way we brought him here."

Craven interrupted. "Debbie, we agreed not to question the means by which we brought the Englishman here. That's water under the bridge. We don't have time to go there again, I thought you understood."

"Nate. This *is* relevant." She smiled. "Just bear with me. I have a report from Agent Maynard from the London office. James Blake, not Miles Blake, is in London. They have him under surveillance."

"James Blake. How did he get there?"

Debbie could not help thinking Craven was being careful to act surprised but she let it pass. "Maynard believes he swapped passports with his brother. They look enough alike to pass as one another."

"Then Miles Blake is still on the loose in the US and it's even more urgent that we find him. The charge that he's obtaining secret information out of the State Department still stands. I want him located and brought in."

Debbie Miller did not air her doubts about Craven. He was a cool customer. The way he handled the meeting was efficient in assigning tasks to the ten-man team. Find Miles Blake. Check for financial transactions. Check for seat reservations. Check for police reports. Check hotel registrations. Check on what was known on James Blake's activities in London.

Craven addressed them all but his gaze remained on Miller. "We lost them. It's an embarrassment. Find them and bring them in."

As she left the room at the end of the meeting, Craven called her to one side. "You are comfortable with the investigation, aren't you Debbie?"

She nodded. "Of course, Nate. You know I'd be the first to let you know."

Craven appeared to be assuring her everything was fine. "What we went through at Town Lake has had effects on us all. Don't let it get to you. I've always got time for you if you need to talk."

She was beginning to know why she was finding it so hard to believe him.

Day 2

September 3rd

Chapter 16

The meeting with Adam Weston couldn't come soon enough.
I needed to pay Bishop for the passport and time was running
out before my next meeting with the man.

I found an Internet cafe in one of the back streets across the
road from the British Museum. It was run by a surly Egyptian
whose every word and gesture told me he would rather have
been anywhere else but here.

Every hour, I checked for a message on the email address
that Weston had given me. Each time the Egyptian made a
great show of explaining that he was not allowed to give access
without checking a passport and logging the name of the user.
Each time I had to offer a bribe and each time he demanded
double the amount of the previous bribe. I was soon getting
close to giving him the last of my money. If Weston's message
didn't arrive soon, I wouldn't be able to buy a coffee let alone
pay him again.

On the fifth visit, he asked for more than I had in my wallet.

I lied and told him the reason I needed to check for a message
was that my wife was in hospital expecting a baby.

He wasn't convinced. "Then why are you here? Why are
you not with her?"

"She's in Scotland. I have to be here to earn money to pay
the bills."

He looked long and hard at me. "How much do you have?"

I told him.

"So, give me half."

I didn't know if he'd believed me or if he'd worked out that this was the most he was going to get out of me but he took what I offered and logged me on to one of the battered machines.

Here was Weston's message.

HiTec Store. Covent Garden. Today. 3.30.

I deleted the message and prepared to leave. The Egyptian was standing behind me and had been looking at the screen. I had no way of knowing if he'd been able to read the message.

Chapter 17

Madeleine Jamieson, visiting London from Seattle, jumped at the chance to become a mudlarker. She'd always been interested in history and when she heard about the London walk that took in the chance to beach comb on the banks of the Thames it was too good to miss.

At low tide, the Thames retreated along the river bank between Somerset House and St Paul's to reveal a distinct beach made up of shingle and the detritus of earlier centuries. Back in the 1600s, clay pipes filled with tobacco had been smoked and discarded into the river. These were abundant and formed the main treasure to be found at low tide now, though in the mind's eye of any self-respecting mudlarker there was always the chance of real treasure in the shape of a Roman coin or something more valuable such as mediaeval jewellery. In Victorian times, to be a mudlarker was a recognised profession, given the wealth discarded into the Thames each day when the Port of London was the gateway to the world. These days, mudlarking was, at best, archaeology for everyman.

When the tour guide in the bright yellow T-shirt finished telling the small group these things she wished them well and sent them out on their search for the remains of London's past. "Good hunting to you all. Come back with plenty of treasure."

Madeline Jamieson turned to her husband. "Phil, let's separate. We'll have more chance of making good finds."

Phil Jamieson was less interested in any of this but was keen to please her. "OK, Maddie. See you back here in twenty minutes."

Madeleine made her way along the shore, searching as she went, and before long she'd found the first of the half-dozen clay pipe fragments she was to collect. She couldn't help thinking, *now, if only I could find an intact clay pipe, that would be something to show Phil.*

She'd walked further than intended and was by now some distance away from the main group. In fact, she was approaching the buttress supports of Vauxhall Bridge.

When she saw the body she gave out a long and piercing scream heard a quarter of a mile away.

The body was bloated and in the late stages of decomposition. It had been dumped in the Thames some days before and the weights used to keep it beneath the water had now slipped. Brought in on the morning tide it had been washed against the supports of the bridge where it was now lodged.

The tour guide was the first to reach her and tried to calm her. "Just take deep breaths. Did I see you were with your husband? He'll soon be here."

When Phil Jamieson arrived, the guide was quick to attempt to reassure him. "It's one of those unfortunate events we can't guard against. I'm sure your wife will be able to get over this with your help."

He wrapped his arms around his wife and walked her away from the scene. He tried to cheer her. "We didn't expect to find anything as Charles Dickens as that, eh?"

She attempted a smile. "And this town is supposed to be so peaceful."

Chapter 18

When Bedford returned to the apartment in Pimlico he was disappointed. Colin McGraw was with him in the expectation that Adam Weston would be willing and able to take detailed instructions on how to assist the Bureau.

They knew something was wrong when they arrived at Weston's smashed front door. When they looked inside it was clear the apartment was unoccupied. The computing equipment that all but filled the small space was smashed. Weston had run.

Bedford tried to remain analytical. "Maybe he wasn't as scared of us as we thought."

McGraw rolled his eyes. "No way you can second-guess these computing types. They've got to be on the spectrum in the first place to be into serious hacking. No one knows which way they might jump."

"It's not going to please Maynard."

"Nothing's going to please Maynard, you should know that by now."

Bedford held his arm across the doorway as McGraw was about to walk through. "Hold on, Colin. You need shoe covers and gloves."

They pulled on the protective gear and went in. Bedford was first, walking toward the smashed computer equipment, reaching down, pressing his gloved palm to the floor and showing it to McGraw. "RFID dust. We don't want to end up following each other."

McGraw smiled. "That would be a waste. So where's Weston?"

Bedford opened the cover on his tablet computer and selected the locator app. "Let's see."

The locator gave a time-averaged summary of the places where Weston had triggered the transponders attached to his shoes. "He's moving around. Unsettled. He's too clever or too paranoid to give us a new address where he's holed up or just plain lucky that if he has a new base there's no EM source near enough to trigger the tags."

"But we can follow him, right?"

"Yes we can, though it's not perfect. But there's a problem." Bedford showed McGraw the screen. "Even if he is that paranoid, there's no way he should be in two places at the same time." The map showed two blinking blue pinpoints in real time.

McGraw looked puzzled. "What does it mean?"

"More than one target has picked up the tags."

"Someone else has been here and picked up the dust?"

Bedford nodded. "There's no other explanation."

"So what do we tell Maynard? We can't tail Weston?"

"No. We split. You take one trace. I take the other. That way we'll catch up with Weston and we'll find out who else is spoiling our game."

Chapter 19

Inspector John Hendricks surveyed the body of DI Martin Reid, fished out of the Thames, now in the morgue.

So, this was where all those dreams of serving the public had ended. Thrown up by the tide as scum on the back of humanity.

Hendricks was more concerned than ever. He now had to admit to four deaths on his patch. He turned to Franklin. "Just what makes an honest copper like Reid go off the rails and end up like this?"

Franklin looked shaken but trying not to show it. He hadn't seen many corpses in his short career in the Force. "It's a fair question, boss."

"I don't like the idea of one of our own being on the take. I don't like the idea of Reid being involved in the Peggy Westland killing. I don't like the way he attached himself to the Blakes, following them from Weymouth, checking them out at the hotel where another murder took place. And you know what I like even less, Franklin? I don't like the idea that there are people running free in this town who can do these things and think they can get away with it."

"I know that, sir."

"So why do we think Reid wanted to follow the Blakes? And what led him to the Peggy Westland apartment?"

"Could have been something in it for him, sir."

"What do you mean?"

"Just the rumours going round the Force. There's money to be made, big money, if you can deliver the Blakes."

"Deliver to whom?"

"Don't know that, sir. As far as I've heard you need to ask Andrew McKenzie. He's drugs squad. He's the man."

Hendricks smiled. "Not much point in my asking anything of him, is it? But you might get a result."

"What do you mean, sir?"

"I mean, if Martin Reid was on the make, McKenzie could be the one who put him up to it. But there's no way McKenzie is going to believe that a tired old copper like me would have anything to do with anything as shady."

"Your reputation precedes you, sir."

Hendricks nodded. "You're right. But if you were to go talk to McKenzie, he might think you were trying to drink from the trough. Enough to let on."

None of the men in the drugs squad deserved much respect as far as Hendricks was concerned. They sought credit for the risks they took and the lives they led when all along those undercover identities so often led them to be too close to those they were seeking to police. Hendricks was scornful of their whole approach.

Franklin tracked down Andrew McKenzie in the *Anzil Bar* at London Bridge. It was early afternoon and the drugs squad man had been drinking.

He sat beside McKenzie at the bar. "All right if we have a word?" McKenzie didn't hide his displeasure at being approached by a rookie who, though out of uniform, still looked for all the world like a copper. "No problem. If anyone says anything, I'll tell them you're feeling my collar."

Franklin was uncertain how to play this and decided to jump straight in. "I hear there's a reward being offered on the Blakes?"

McKenzie exhaled. "What makes you think I know anything about that?"

"Look, I have a lead to where they are and I need to make some serious money fast."

"You got personal problems?"

"The mortgage. I can't pay it back with what I'm getting from the Force. The house is in negative equity, so even if I sell it, I'm still stuffed. The wife is saying we should post the keys with the building society and scarper. It means we lose everything."

"You got real info on the Blakes?"

Franklin nodded.

The drugs squad man looked for a moment as if he might take the bait. But he was playing with the rookie. "Tell Hendricks I don't know why he would send you to talk to me. I don't have any idea why you think I could help you."

McKenzie waited a few minutes after Franklin left before phoning Cleary. "Giles. I've just had one of Hendricks' men sniffing around."

"You didn't tell him anything?"

"Course not."

Chapter 20

Police chief Pedro Martinez got the result he wanted with a speed that surprised Miles.

"Senor Blake. It is all in the name. Reyas is not usual, not here in Tijuana. The name is common as Reyes or Reyez but not as Reyas. We have Luiz Reyas here."

Miles was shown into the interrogation room where the young man was seated.

Martinez shrugged his shoulders. "He has not spoken since his arrest. I will leave you with him, Senor. But I don't think he will be any more responsive with you."

Miles sat opposite the young man and said nothing for a long time. He was observing how much the young Luiz was like Luiz senior would have looked when he was nineteen.

When Miles spoke, he chose his first words with care. "Tell me, Luiz, just how many men are you going to have to kill to keep your place in the cartel long enough to avenge your family?"

Luiz remained silent.

"You don't think I understand. Is that it?"

More silence.

"I was there when your father died."

The young man jumped, not sure what he'd just heard. Unsure enough to need to break silence. "You are playing with words, Senor. You do not know how we live."

Miles leaned closer. "No, Luiz, I mean just what I say. I knew your father. I was there. He died in my arms. And I made him a promise."

Luiz sneered. "You will not convince me this is not some kind of trick."

"Show me your right arm. I'll prove it to you."

The young man shrugged his shoulders as if to say he had nothing to lose. He rolled back the shirtsleeve on his right arm.

"Three stars. You've killed three men. Your father had over a hundred stars."

"So?"

"He told me what it meant."

"He had killed a hundred men. So what? Anyone could know that about him."

"No. He'd killed so many and wasn't proud of it. He'd killed so many to keep close to those who knew enough for him to complete his mission, handed down to him by his father, just as that mission is now handed down to you."

Luiz looked shocked. It took time for him to reply. "If you know this, you knew my father. Is that why you are here?"

Miles nodded. "It's a promise I made to him as he died."

Luiz Reyas continued talking but his gestures made it clear his words were not important. They were meant for whoever might be listening. Instead he pointed to Miles' notebook and pen, inviting him to pass them over. He wrote at speed in good English and passed the pad back.

> *We cannot talk here. There are as many from the cartels inside a place like this as there are outside. The more we talk here, the more it is certain we will both be killed. Tell Martinez that I would not say a word to you. Let him think I am not the one you search for. When they release me, I will find you. We will talk then. Do this and we may both have a chance to survive.*

Miles read the message and gave back a knowing look. They talked about matters of no consequence for a few minutes more, all the time aware that Miles was going to act as requested.

When the meeting was over, Miles told Martinez this was not the Luiz Reyas he was seeking. The police chief accepted this with a shrug. "I wish you well, Senor. I will help where I can in finding the one you seek. You understand this cannot be a high priority. But you are free to go."

"I understand. I'm grateful." Miles was careful to not overdo the sense of disappointment. He had done enough, he hoped, to guard against any informer from within the police station. Yet he could not be sure that, once released, he would see Luiz Reyas again.

His fears were unfounded as later that evening the young man came to Miles' hotel room.

"Senor, we can now talk."

Miles welcomed him in and they sat on the hotel room balcony, concealed from the city square below. "Thank you for coming. We have a lot to talk about."

Luiz appeared defensive. "I hear you are a journalist. You are here for a story. When you have your story you will be gone. Me and my kind will still be here as we were. Nothing will have changed. You will have used us just as everyone else seeks to use us."

"I'll be straight with you, Luiz. It was like that at first with your father. You're right. I needed a story. He offered information. I paid for information. But we found we had a common cause, your father and I. Something we didn't expect when we first began to work together. It's the greater reason why I'm here. I promised your father I would find you."

Miles told the Mexican about the events in East Texas, about how Luiz Reyas senior had been following the German, Wolfgang Heller. How they had been pursued by Heller and cornered in the abandoned railway station in Austin where Luiz Reyas senior had been killed. When Miles told the young Mexican about the role of El Romero in helping the German target those he was employed to assassinate, Luiz could not hide that he was shaken.

83

"I did not know he was involved. You should know, Senor, that in El Romero you are talking about a very violent man, even by the ways of Tijuana."

"And I need to tell you even by the ways of El Romero, Wolfgang Heller is a very violent man. He was responsible for the death of your father."

"Then I will find him and kill him."

Miles leaned forward and looked deep into the young man's eyes. "I know there is more to it. I know about your father's mission – your mission to avenge the harm done to your family long ago. And I know who was behind the shame brought upon them."

"How could you know that, Senor?"

"It's what your father and I discovered. The family that commissioned Wolfgang Heller to carry out those killings is the same family that shamed your family all those years ago."

"They have a name?"

"Lando. The family name is Lando."

"Then, if it is true, Senor, and you can prove this to me, I'm in your debt."

"I can show you proof enough. There is something more you should know. This same Lando family is a threat to me and my family, to those who are near and dear to me."

"So, just as with my father, Senor, we have common cause."

Miles nodded. "Yes, common cause."

"You're asking me to trust you with my life, Senor. That's how it is here."

"We'll find a way to right the wrongs. Just as with your father."

"It got him killed."

"I understand. I'll also be trusting you with my life."

They shook hands. The young man's grip was as sure as his determination to fulfil the mission handed down to him.

He had more to say. "Since we now trust each other with our lives, I must show you this."

84

He pulled out a wallet. It opened to reveal a gold badge. "Something I do not often carry, Senor."

It was the gold badge of an officer of the Policia Federal Ministerial, the PFM, the Federales, the Mexico equivalent of the FBI.

Reyas smiled. "You see, Senor, there is more than one way to complete my mission."

Miles was still trying to come to terms with what was being said. "Back there in Zona Nolte, that was all for my benefit?"

"Yes, Senor. There are agents of the cartels everywhere, even inside the PFM. Many are forced to work for them out of fear for their families. Others do it for money. Whoever was listening needed to hear the right things about me."

"And which side are you on?"

"That is something you will have to trust me with. In any case we have common cause, I think you agree."

"The three stars?"

"Are men I killed. But I killed in the line of duty, nothing more."

"What about Martinez?"

"Is he straight? Yes, he is. He arranged our meeting. He is one of the few in this town you should trust."

"The FBI?"

"They want you. It was me who requested that Martinez should not turn you in. I wanted to know what a man like you had to say about my father. Now I know, I have no interest in turning you in." He was a changed man, confident, with an authority that belied his years. Miles realised then that the role of inexperienced young cartel member was a cloak he wore well.

Chapter 21

They were aware of being followed as soon as they caught sight of the tall American.

Luigi Bandini was quick to alert Asputi. "Gianni. The one behind us, crossing the street. Looking like he is shopping."

Asputi was about to turn and look. "Which one, Luigi?"

"Don't look. We want to lead him to where we want him."

They were on Oxford Street, shopping for presents to take back home once the issue of the Blakes had been sorted out. It would not be easy to trap the man following them here in such a busy part of London. Yet it was a universal truth that had served Bandini and so many others over the years. If you are going to act, do it immediately and with sudden, unexpected violence.

Bandini called in Carlucci who was circling in the SUV. "Come pick us up."

Before the vehicle arrived, Bandini was careful to give their tracker every chance of keeping in touch with them while avoiding the impression they knew they were being tailed. He wandered into a side street with shops that you could walk through and exit on an adjacent street running parallel to it. Leaving Asputi in place to draw the tracker's attention, Bandini entered a shop halfway along the street, walked back along the parallel street and remerged in the first street unseen and behind the tracker.

As the SUV drew up, Bandini acted. He drew out the Uzi from beneath his coat, ran towards the tracker and held the weapon to the man's head, motioning him towards the SUV.

As the side door of the vehicle opened, Asputi joined in as the tracker was pushed into the back seat with Bandini following, all the time holding the weapon to the tracker's head.

A woman shopper screamed. Other passers-by sought to care for her, assuming she'd been hurt in some way. In that time, Asputi had clambered in, the doors of the SUV had been closed and Bandini and his captive were on their way.

The captive was quick to protest. "My name is Agent McGraw, Federal Bureau of Investigation. What you're doing is a crime under US International law. I advise you that my government is pledged to address every transgression of this law."

Bandini was unconcerned. He removed the iron bar from the rear document pouch of the vehicle and struck McGraw hard across the face, breaking his teeth. "This is the one law."

Bandini smiled. As he'd supposed, capturing the man in broad daylight in one of the busiest locations in London had presented no special problems. It was no more difficult to lift a man off the street here than it was at home in Florence. All the rewards were for those with the courage to act. The rules were the same here.

They searched McGraw, took away his Glock, found his phone and disabled it.

They took him to a deserted factory unit on an industrial estate in Harlow.

McGraw soon learned about the power of raw, unannounced violence. Ten minutes with the iron bar, much enjoyed by Bandini, was enough. His man was talking as if he was not going to stop.

Bandini stood back to admire his work in bloodying the man. "Tell me, Signor McGraw, why it is you were following us?"

McGraw replied through broken teeth. "Because it's my job."

Bandini unleashed another blow with the iron bar, breaking the fingers on McGraw's right hand. "When I say *why*, I mean *why*, not *because*. You understand me?"

When McGraw stopped screaming, his reply was more precise. "You are a target."

"Target, how?"

"Dust on your shoes. From the hacker's apartment."

Bandini smiled. "So, someone knows we are here?"

"No, I'm following to know who you are."

Bandini raised the iron bar again, as if to strike.

McGraw flinched.

No need to hurt the man any further. He was his now.

"So, Signor McGraw, tell me the real point of your mission?"

"To find Blake."

Bandini was intrigued. "So, tell me, how do we find Signor Blake?"

McGraw was pleading for his life. "I'll tell you if you let me go."

Bandini smiled. "You tell us. We let you go."

"We have intelligence where Blake will be. Tonight. That's how to find him."

"So, where?"

"In the East End. The *Miller and Ploughman*. He'll be there to collect a parcel."

"And you know this from where?"

"From one of Bishop's men."

"Bishop?"

"The one Blake will be meeting."

"And tell me, Signor McGraw, why would you know this?"

"We paid good money."

"Ah, money. That is something everyone can understand." He paused. Maybe it was time to end the misery of this man. But then a further thought. "Who has been assigned to Blake for the visit?"

"Just me."

"No one but you?"

"No one."

The iron bar was raised once more.

McGraw winced. "It's the truth. It's all I know."

Bandini turned his back and addressed Asputi. "Finish him."

The Glock was placed to McGraw's temple. Asputi fired. McGraw was gone.

Bandini was pleased with the day's work, even though shopping for presents now had to wait for another day. He had a fix on Blake. Bandini couldn't wait to get to work on him. Blake would capitulate in the same way they all did and give up the location of his wife. Bandini would kill them both and be back in credit with Matteo. And the presents would then be needed for when they went home.

He looked back at the agent's body. It was necessary to be more careful this time. It had been a mistake to allow Asputi to deal with the body of Reid. It had been foolish to dump it in the Thames. No wonder Alessa Lando was alarmed.

They dragged the body into the back yard of the deserted factory. There was no one to see them as they raised the hatch on the empty fuel storage tank and pushed the corpse in.

Chapter 22

Agent Bedford caught sight of Adam Weston for the first time as he walked across the cobbled street on the East side of Covent Garden.

He needed good news. McGraw had been out of contact for too long. Bedford could not begin to think how he could explain to Maynard how he had lost touch with him. Having Weston in full view was the first break of the day.

It was a rewarding moment. The RFID dust had done its job. Following the blinking blue pin on the locator app for the past hours without knowing how much latency there was on the tracking system had been stressful. But there must have been enough EM sites in this crowded part of London to activate the transponders on the soles of the target's feet to produce a continuous trace. And now real time contact had been made.

Bedford followed and watched as Weston entered the HiTec Store. The agent knew at once this was the meeting place with Blake. Where else would a geek like Weston choose but a computer store?

It was time to take a chance. If he got this wrong, Maynard would be loath to send backup next time.

Bedford called his boss. "I have the location of the meeting, sir." He gave the coordinates. "I'm requesting backup."

Maynard made no attempt at encouragement. "OK, you have it, Bedford. But make sure you get it right this time. You hear me?"

"Loud and clear, sir."

It would take fifteen to twenty minutes to get here from The Haymarket. Bedford hoped it would be quick enough. The likelihood was that Weston had arrived early. His mind worked like that. He would need to be clear everything was as he wanted before Blake arrived.

Bedford waited and watched.

Still no sign of Blake.

Here came backup. Three agents and no sign of McGraw. He must have his reasons. The sting on Weston and Blake still needed to go ahead.

So, four men counting himself. That should be enough.

He wanted to get his hands on Weston. Running like that had been an embarrassment Bedford could not afford. The threat of Walls Unit was still real. Weston must not be allowed to run this time and then with a little work he would become compliant. He was the type.

Bedford checked the Glock in the shoulder holster beneath his jacket and felt the rush of satisfaction that came with knowing he was in control.

He deployed the agents as would-be customers inside the store.

When Blake arrived they'd be ready.

Chapter 23

Recent events worried Nate Craven.

True, he now knew where James Blake was. But beyond this almost everything else pointed downhill.

Debbie Miller didn't know that Craven had taken the precaution of bugging her phone. Her conversation that morning with Maynard in London had made interesting listening. The tie-up between Debbie Miller and Maynard was a matter of real concern. They'd worked together in Chicago and were still close. Just what was the intelligence Maynard was sitting on? Was it the same material Bedford had?

Overall, Craven knew he'd been right to be wary of the inconsistencies. More of the loose ends from Town Lake were beginning to show.

And the bigger picture was now also worrying him.

He'd lost touch with the Landos and had no idea where he stood with them.

He called Agent Marvin Bryce into his office and seated him in a chair facing the desk.

Bryce was the remaining member of the team apart from Debbie Miller and Craven himself who'd survived Town Lake. He was the only one left standing who knew the full detail of the arrangements Craven had in Mexico. And he was the only black man on the team. He was Craven's one true ally. There was no doubt their friendship was the kind that would survive even if there was an end to the easy money coming out of the drugs business in Tijuana.

After playing Bryce the recording of Debbie Miller's phone call, Craven began. "Marvin, I hope you can see that Debbie Miller is becoming a problem we need to find a way past."

Bryce wasn't fazed. "It's not good. Just what's coming out of London?"

"I thought we could depend on Bedford but now I'm not so sure. I don't think he can do a job for us after all. He's too controlled by Maynard."

"And Maynard is talking with Debbie Miller."

"Bedford tells me he has a recording in which James Blake is saying stuff that's best not spread around."

"Where's the recording now?"

"In a secure location Bedford knows but he's backing out of helping us. We could maybe still get to it. Before it gets out within the Agency. We need to find a way."

"Sure, Nate. Just give the word. Whatever you need. You know I'm here for you."

"Maynard's the bigger problem. You understand?"

Bryce nodded. "As you say, we'll find a way. We've done it before."

Craven was encouraged enough to go on. "It's not the only reason I called you in, Marvin. I want you to give some time to working on where we've got to with Matteo Lando. You know Town Lake wasn't terrorism, don't you?"

Bryce showed no surprise. "I didn't have to work too hard to see through that. And it hurts."

Craven looked serious. "I know how you're feeling. We lost too many of our own."

Bryce was becoming angry as he visualised again what he'd seen that day. "Men and women I would have laid down my life for. Men and women who saved my life more than once."

"I feel your anger, Marvin. You know Ravitz was targeted by Matteo Lando."

Bryce nodded. "What do you want me to do? There's no way it can be business as usual with the Landos. Not now."

"It has to be that way for a while. Until we can find a sure fire way of moving against them. And anyway, the money from Mexico is good. You have to think of getting your kids through college."

"What do you want me to do first, Nate?"

"Go to London. Clean up the problem with Maynard. Make it look good. Get us some closure. Then we can have a clear run at the Landos. Give it back for what they did to our own."

Chapter 24

It was afternoon and the street performers around Covent Garden were out in force to make the most of the opportunities presented by the crowds of tourists and local shoppers thronging the place. The old market had reverted to the mixture of shops, cafes and street theatre it had been in the days before it had been pressed into service as a wholesale vegetable market. With the vegetable market now relocated, it was free to do what it had done best in the previous two hundred years – offer itself as a melting pot for those seeking the unusual and the remarkable.

I wanted to mix with the crowds. I needed to forget my solitary existence since leaving Ambleside. The smiles of pleasure of the watching couples and families as they took in the street entertainers made me feel alive again.

You couldn't help being engaged by the street performers. Here was one who somehow presented himself as a crouching dog that could have come straight from *The Wizard of Oz* lying flat on the pavement, long furry ears hanging down the sides of his face, the main part of his body somehow concealed to reveal just that dog's face looking out through a kennel entrance. When he spoke, unsuspecting passers-by shot back in surprise. What he said was dry, philosophical. "I don't mind if the world is about to come to an end just don't include me in it."

Further round the square on the area of cobblestones at the far end of the market another entertainer held a large audience spellbound. He was perched on top of fifteen-feet-high stilts and made much of how difficult it was to stay balanced there. In his hand he held a tennis racket with the strings removed.

To the amazement of the crowd, and while still perched on the stilts, he succeeded in passing his whole body through the head of the racket, first his head, then his arms and shoulders, then his chest and pelvis and then down his legs and under his feet, all the time fifteen foot aloft on the stilts, teetering and about to fall off. And all the time maintaining the most brilliant banter, cajoling the crowd into placing money in the upturned hat left on the cobbles beneath him.

Just being here, in the sunlight, surrounded by so many smiling people, brought me back to the realisation that life was never meant to be as difficult as it was for Julia and myself. People knew ordinary lives with ordinary pleasures and I envied them every bit of that. But I knew I couldn't remain here. I had to tear myself away. It was time for the meeting with Adam Weston.

I made my way into the HiTec Store that faced onto the square. Inside was the expected hubbub of activity as, campus-like, young and old tried out the products. I'd been there just a moment when a twenty-year-old girl in jeans and sweatshirt came up to me and whispered. "Don't look around. Adam sent me. Just follow me. Make it look like we're not together."

I followed her to the rear of the ground floor where amongst the throng of shoppers Weston was waiting. He looked different. More determined than when I'd met him at his apart-ment. "They tried to put the bum on me, to get me to inform on you but you need to know I'm better than that."

I whispered back. "You mean the police?"

"FBI. Look, we don't have time. They're over there."

He gestured towards two men seated at the bank of consoles on the far side of the room. "They followed me here. The tall one on the right is the one who visited me just after you left my apartment and threatened that if I didn't play ball and spy on you they'd put me away. I told him I'd go along with it. But I was never going to make it easy for them. And I'm sure they have more men here, trying to make themselves look inconspicuous."

He handed me an envelope containing the first half of the money. "Take the money and get out of here."

"What about you?"

There was a determination and resilience about him I had not expected. "I know a way out of here and they won't be able to follow. We'll both be OK."

The girl in the T-shirt who'd first approached me typed numbers into the keypad next to the door nearby marked *Staff Only* and it opened for her. We went inside and closed door behind us.

"She works here?"

Weston nodded. "Out the back, downstairs and into the street. There will be enough people milling around for us both to get away. The Feds don't have the door access code."

I was impressed by his courage, surprised that he'd overcome his fears.

We made it out to the rear of the building and mingled with the crowds heading towards Covent Garden station.

I was concerned again as we parted. "Thanks for taking the risk. It means a lot to me. You have somewhere you can be safe?"

"I'm with good people. You don't have to worry on my behalf."

With that he was lost in the crowd. I had half the money I'd arranged Weston to acquire for me. Given what he'd just told me, it would have to be enough.

Chapter 25

When the message came through to Debbie Miller she knew as soon as she saw it she wouldn't pass it on to Craven.

Miles Blake had been traced to Tijuana. Instinct told her to say nothing and get down there to find out what the Englishman knew. The problem was finding a way of doing this without alerting Craven.

She called in to Craven's office and sat down opposite him. "Nate, I've been thinking about what you said about the aftermath of Town Lake getting to me and making it difficult to see things straight."

He smiled. "I hear you, Debbie. We're both in the same place. We're both still in shock. It's good you've taken care to understand what I was saying to you."

She worked hard not to register her disbelief at Craven's attempt at sincerity. "I'm trying to make sure it doesn't get to cloud my judgment."

"So, how can I help?"

"Maybe I need a break, Nate. Some place to unwind. Come back refreshed."

He was smiling. "Take ten days. We can manage while you're away."

She was playing him well. Appealing to his desire to sideline her. "It might be for the best, Nate. I've always wanted to spend time in Hawaii."

She thanked him.

When she went to the travel agent to book the tickets the only destination under consideration was Tijuana.

Chapter 26

Weston thought he was clever disappearing from the back entrance of the HiTec Store with Blake like that. Blake was gone but Weston was still there to be caught. It was the least Agent Bedford could do to appease Maynard.

The beauty of the RFID dust was that Weston had no idea it was there. Bedford noted that the movement of the flashing blue pin on the locator app had stopped. Weston must have decided it was safe to lie low until those searching for him gave up. He was about to find that was an unwise assumption. More puzzling was the fact that the second trace was no longer there. Perhaps McGraw could provide an answer but he still hadn't made contact.

Bedford briefed the backup crew and gave them Weston's position. "Move in on him as a group. Make out he's a friend."

The location was the crypt of St Martins-in-the-Fields just off Trafalgar Square. It served as a vast underground coffee place. If you weren't being tracked as Weston was, it was a good place to hide.

They found him seated alone at one of the wooden-benched tables on the far side, nursing a coffee and pretending to read one of the brochures about the work of the church. He flinched as Bedford and the three in the backup crew moved in and took seats beside and opposite him and began acting as if they'd just met up with a long lost friend.

"How did you find me?"

Bedford smiled. "You don't get to know that, Adam. It was foolish to run."

Weston was trying to remain strong. "I'm a British citizen. You can't just trample on my rights. I'm out of your jurisdiction."

Bedford leaned forward. "Then we'll have to ask you to place yourself in our jurisdiction." He reached under the table and stabbed the syringe deep into Weston's thigh and pressed the plunger. Before Weston could protest, Bedford whispered, "It's a lethal dose of digitalis. Causes death in thirty minutes. Twenty in some cases. We have the antidote back at base. If you shout out or make any other move to alert anyone, we walk and leave you to die. What's it to be? Do you want to place yourself in our jurisdiction?"

Weston struggled not to shout out at the pain as the syringe was withdrawn. "You mean you're giving me the choice?"

"Isn't that what it's all about? The kind of freedom to choose you and the hacker crowd vent about so often?"

Weston stood and disguised the pain in his leg as he walked out with Bedford and his men.

Bedford was pleased. He had a captive to show Maynard.

Back at base in the Haymarket, Weston was agitated. His shirt was soaked with sweat and he was pleading for the antidote. "It's been too long. I need it now. Do you want me to die?"

Bedford was enjoying this. This was better than pulling the Glock on him. This was real power. And there was satisfaction in delivering the punch line. "Didn't I tell you, Adam. The syringe was filled with distilled water. Pure and simple. You won't need an antidote for that."

Weston lowered his head. "What is it you want?"

"Just what we asked. Take the chance we're offering you."

"To lie and deceive like you?"

"No, Adam, to do the right thing for once in your life. Or do you prefer Huntsville? It's your freedom to choose."

Chapter 27

There was no point in denying it. Alessa Lando was aware she would have to take matters into her own hands, no matter how much she wanted Matteo to take control of the affairs of the family. Perhaps it was Sollicciano that had blunted his understanding of the dangers out here in the real world. She hated to think that, after all, Alfieri was right and their son was destined never to amount to anything. No matter what, she knew it was time to act.

She placed the call to Tijuana and waited. When El Romero picked up he sounded as if he'd been expecting a call. "Senora Lando. It is always a pleasure."

Alessa showed her customary caution. "The line is secure?"

"As always, Senora. How else can we do business?"

It was El Romero who had first alerted her to the consequences of the events at Town Lake. She was ready to take his advice once again. "Then tell me what can be done to reduce the risk to our business."

He did not need to pause to find the answer to her question. "I have thought of little else since we last spoke, Senora. The threats are real. Our resources are not as great as those ranged against us. But we have certain things on our side, like the power and influence of the Lando family."

Alessa determined to not be distracted by the obvious flattery. "So I can help?"

"Senora, indeed. Since we last spoke, Town Lake has stabilised to an extent. The greatest risk now is not from outside but from within. The protectors we have always depended on may no longer be at our side."

"You mean the FBI?"

"Without them our couriers cannot make it. And if we can no longer deliver, others will move in. The rival cartels here in Tijuana will be on our backs."

"I understand but I still don't see how I can help."

"Make peace. A woman of your standing could succeed."

"With who?"

"With Agent Craven."

Chapter 28

There was no sign I was being followed from Covent Garden.
The more I checked, the more I was certain Adam Weston had
planned my escape well and I'd lost them in the crowds leaving
the area. I knew now it was the FBI who'd sent the squad after
us. That could mean Craven was on to what I was doing here
and I knew it was now ever more unsafe to be in London.

I took the train to Guildford.

Julia had spoken little about her adoptive parents in all the
time we'd been together. They were prosperous, middle-class.
Her father, William Morley, was a dental practitioner. He'd
made good money drilling teeth and retired at fifty-five. Julia's
mother, Constance, was a fashion model in her early years and
settled into life with William in prosperous Guildford with ease.

There had been nothing but secrecy regarding the adoption.
People were less enlightened then, it's true, but Julia's parents
had been even less forthcoming than most. They concealed her
origins from Julia until she was sixteen. While this would have
thrown many youngsters, Julia adjusted well to the knowledge
that William and Constance were not her biological parents.
Yet it must have been painful for her to know she hadn't been
trusted with the knowledge of her origins until so late in life.
It led her to be defensive, to downplay consideration of everything to do with her relationship with her adoptive parents.
Their relationship was civilised and polite more than warm and
understanding.

I'd always had the feeling there was more behind why Julia's adoptive parents weren't forthcoming with her. And the only way to test this was to talk to them.

They'd never liked me. Whatever future they'd imagined for their daughter hadn't included me. To say the least, this was not going to be an enjoyable meeting.

I took a taxi from Guildford station and asked the driver to set me down at the end of the street where the Morley house stood. It was tree-lined and elegant with large well-kept shrubs in well-kept gardens that led up to large well-kept properties that signalled wealth and status in the reserved manner regarded as so essential by the English upper middle-class.

When I rang the doorbell to the Morley house, it was Constance who answered.

I spoke first. "It's Jim. Can I come in?"

She stared and I thought for a while she was going to blank me. When she replied, she didn't hide her reluctance to recognise me. "James. Why are you here? It's not Julia, is it? She's not in any kind of trouble?"

I lied. "No, she's fine. I was in the area. I thought I'd call in."

She was suspicious. "It's just that we see so little of you."

"I know. It should be more often, but here I am."

She remained cold but opened the door further. "All right. Come in."

William was in the large rear garden seated at a table and chairs under a mock China gazebo. Constance walked me out to meet him. The introduction was formal, as if otherwise he might have had a problem remembering who I was. "Bill, dear, it's Jim. Julia's husband."

He looked up but showed no enthusiasm at meeting me. "James, to what do we owe this pleasure?"

The conversation turned straight to Julia. Why weren't she and the baby with me? William's medical training was well to the fore. "The pregnancy, everything went all right?"

"Of course. They're both doing well. Everything's fine." I lied again. "You must come to visit us in Weymouth. Your first grandson."

His eyes narrowed. "You know we aren't grandparents in the biological sense, don't you?"

This gave me my chance. "That's why I want to talk to you. I've never felt Julia has been able to share with me enough about her background. It's like a barrier between us."

"You're not having problems?"

"No. It's just that the more I know, the more I'll be able to understand her. Help her. Tell me about the adoption."

William was defensive. "What is there to tell you that you might want to know?"

"Tell me about her birth parents."

"They're unknown. She was delivered into the hands of the Catholic Church when she was just a few days old. Left in the crypt of the church in Waterville, in Ireland."

"And her sister? She was abandoned at the same time?"

Constance jumped with shock. Both looked as though the moment they'd feared for half their lives had just arrived. She spoke first. "You know about her sister?"

I tried to make this as easy for them as possible. "Yes, I know she had an identical twin sister. It's one of the issues that Julia has been trying to work her way through. She found out by accident she was a twin. No one had prepared her for that. She told me she'd always felt incomplete. When she met her sister, she realised what the feeling of absence was that she'd been carrying with her all these years."

"You mean they met?"

I nodded. "She felt if she'd known about her sister earlier, things might have been different."

Constance was close to tears. "We couldn't tell her. It was part of the agreement. That we didn't tell her. That we couldn't tell her about her sister. And we stuck to the agreement. You're not here to criticise us for that, are you?"

I tried to reassure her. "I just want to understand so I can help Julia."

William was still unmoved. "Why would she need help?"

"I hoped you knew. I hoped Julia had told you. She found her sister, Emelia, after all those years. Within days, Emelia was killed. It's left a scar on Julia's life. She's worked so hard to overcome this but there are times when it overwhelms her. It's why I need your help. I want you to be as open and frank with me as you are able, given all this means to Julia."

"When did the sister die?"

"Three years ago. The wounds still haven't healed."

"Why is this the first we've heard?"

"It would have been better to have told you. It was Julia's wish that we didn't."

They both seemed offended by the suggestion that Julia had been unable to confide in them. "You know, we've done everything for Julia."

"So help me understand."

Constance moved closer to her husband and took his hand. "Bill, I think we should tell him as much as we can about the adoption."

He placed his other hand on hers. "Perhaps it's better this way." He cleared his throat and began. "James, I want you to realise that adoption was not as well-organised back then as it is now. Childless couples like us could not get a child. It was heartbreaking to see families around us. We were as good as them. We had as much or more to offer a child but try as we might we couldn't produce one. Then along came the Sisters."

"Sisters?"

"The Sisters of the Carpasian Order. We received a message from our parish priest who knew we were seeking a child. There was a baby in Ireland and we could be considered for adoption. There were special conditions. We had to meet the requirements laid down by the Order. There was to be absolute secrecy about where the baby came from and the fact that she was a twin, and she had a sister."

"You weren't considered for the adoption of both? You must have thought it was unusual to separate them?"

"We were told not to question anything. If we asked too many questions or broke their rules we'd lose the baby. You can't imagine what pain that would have brought when we'd come so close to fulfilling our dearest wish. We were told the first of the twins had been sent to Italy to be adopted there. This had been decided at the highest level by the Board of Deputies that had oversight of the Order, by the President of the Board himself."

Constance joined in. "We had to be interviewed by him to see if we were fit to have the child. He was thorough in questioning us to see if we were suitable parents. And if we were prepared to sign the agreement to promise that the arrangements made for the adoption would be kept secret."

Her husband agreed. "He left us in no doubt that if we ever broke the agreement once we'd accepted the child there would be consequences."

I knew I had to get this clear. "You mean he threatened you?"

"Not in so many words. On the surface it was all about the agreement with the Order and how it would be enforced, through the courts if necessary. But the implication was that if we broke the agreement there might be something much more immediate."

"Why couldn't you just walk away?"

"We wanted a child. You can't imagine how that feels. When Constance saw the baby, so beautiful, so small and fragile, there was never any doubt we would agree, no matter how threatened by that man we felt."

"The one you made the agreement with, the President of the Board, do you have a name?"

"It was a long time ago now but it was a name neither of us could ever forget. His name was Lando. Signor Alfieri Lando."

The train journey back to London was filled with thoughts of what I'd discovered from Julia's parents.

The remainder of our meeting was inconsequential, over-shadowed by the single revelation that Alfieri Lando had a determining hand in the destination of the twins. Julia to a middle-class family in Guildford. Emelia, as Julia and I knew, to the Rossellini family in Bari in Italy.

I had to try to make sense of this. I knew from the events in Florence three years before that Emelia had been enticed to Florence by Matteo Lando under his father's orders. It had appeared to be chance that Julia and Emelia were both in Florence at the same time. But now I wasn't so sure. If Alfieri Lando had so much power over their lives when they were born maybe he was behind their being in Florence at the same time all those years later.

And that raised the possibility that Alfieri Lando had somehow been behind the decision of Julia to go to Florence to survey the Lando art collection.

Yet both Julia and myself had always known it was Miles who'd suggested she went there. It was Miles who'd made the arrangements for her to go. And it was Miles who'd suffered the shame and guilt of what had happened to Julia there.

I needed to talk to Julia. I needed to ask her what she recalled about Miles' role in the invitation for her to go to Florence.

When the train pulled into Charing Cross, I left the station, crossed The Strand and walked up Bedford Street. As I walked, I used the pay-as-you-go phone to call Julia.

It was not an emergency but I needed to talk again.

Julia must have been waiting for my call. Her reply came back straight away.

"Jim, are you OK?"

"I'm safe, love. I'm well. How are things there?"

We knew we needed to stay on the line for as short a time as possible to minimise the chance of being detected and Julia was keeping her end of the bargain. "No change. We're being well protected."

But this couldn't wait. "There's something I need to ask. Where did Miles get the idea to recommend you go to Florence to survey the Lando paintings?"

"Why do you want to know?"

"Just trust me. It's important."

"I'm trying to recall. It seems so long ago now. He knew I was looking for a suitable collection of works that might have been overpainted and perhaps conceal a masterpiece. Miles heard about the Lando collection through an intermediary. I'm struggling to remember which one but I think it was called the Arpeggio Foundation."

"OK. I'll check it out." I changed the subject. "By the way, I met your parents. They're well. They send their love."

"Now I know there's a lot you're not telling me."

We wished each other love and closed the connection.

I'd reached Covent Garden and entered the HiTec store once more. I reasoned this would be one place they were no longer looking for me. I found a vacant machine and searched the Internet for information on the Arpeggio Foundation.

There it was. *Arpeggio Foundation*. An obituary posted three years ago about their founder and patron: Signor Alfieri Lando.

I didn't want to call back to tell Julia what I'd just discovered until I had a clear idea of what it meant. But I couldn't help thinking Lando had found a means of priming Miles with the idea that Julia should go to Florence and all along the Italian's motive had been to ensure that Julia and Emelia were in Florence at the same time.

If this proved to be the case I knew I'd need to take great care in breaking this to Julia.

It was time to head for the East End and my appointment with Alex Bishop.

Chapter 29

The action was becoming stretched. Nate Craven had personnel he could trust out in the field. It was what the new team was for. But who could he trust with the black ops part of the business?

Debbie Miller wouldn't go to Hawaii. He knew that. He was sure he hadn't telegraphed it when he'd agreed to her taking leave. She must be on her way to Tijuana by now to work out whatever agenda she had with Miles Blake. None of that would be favourable to Craven. But the merit of letting her go was that Miller would lead him to Miles Blake and, if he played his cards right, to what the Blake target was trying to achieve by being there. Yet, the problem was who to send after her.

He'd thought about going himself. Marvin Bryce would cover the situation in London, deal with what Maynard was developing with Bedford and narrow the search for James Blake. Leaving Craven free to concentrate on Tijuana. But this wasn't the best way forward long term. Craven was needed here at base and, if he were to go to Tijuana and was spotted there, it would make it too easy for Debbie Miller to see through the game plan. And he'd make no progress in rebuilding the black ops side of the business.

It all came back to the same question. Who amongst the new recruits could be trusted to join him in the dark side of the business?

He'd chosen the new team well. Still in the afterglow of the Intelligence Star, the Bureau had been keen to let him choose from the best it had to offer. While there hadn't been as much time as he would have liked, he'd spent considerable effort looking through the career records of those available. Looking for those who were both effective and corruptible.

Why did he dislike the sound of that last word?

Perhaps because he'd hate to hear anyone apply it to himself.

He looked over the list of possibles once more. One name stood out. Dillon Ashley. Ex-military, spotless record and expensive tastes.

Craven arranged to meet Ashley in a favourite bar in downtown Washington. After two rounds of drinks and the expected pleasantries, Craven popped the question.

Ashley didn't have to think about a reply. "Why, Nate, I thought you'd never get round to asking."

Chapter 30

I knew I'd made a mistake as soon as I saw them coming up on me from behind at speed as I walked through the East End.

I could have taken a taxi to the *Miller and Ploughman* and the meeting with Bishop to collect my passport but I'd reasoned it would attract less attention if I came in from Shadwell Underground station and walked along Wapping Wall, the long, narrow street running behind the warehouses that faced onto the Thames.

The first thought – don't look round. Don't give whoever was approaching at speed in the SUV the opportunity to see you're scared. After all, they might just pass by. The second thought – run. If I was quick enough I might be able to reach one of the nearby shops and seek help.

Too late.

They were on me.

Two men. Italian. Heavy. Dark clothes. Determined faces.

The first took me by the shoulders and forced me against the high brick wall flanking the street at this point. The second, the leader, hit me hard in the small of my back with an iron bar, the kind of sickening blow that made me think he'd ruptured my kidney.

The leader knew my name. "Signor Blake. We have you. Don't resist. Take this like the man you are."

My face was pressed so close to the wall I had to struggle to make myself heard. "If you're from Matteo Lando, tell him I won't stop. I won't stop until I pay him back for what his family has done to my wife."

They were laughing. "Matteo would want to know how you intend to do that."

A second, harder blow landed in the small of my back. I struggled not to retch.

There was a third with them, driving the SUV. It drew up and stopped beside me. I braced myself for the moment they would force me into the rear of the vehicle. My only thought was to make as much noise as possible in the hope that someone nearby would hear. A third blow was aimed at my kidneys. A large hand came across my mouth, preventing my shouting.

It was inevitable I'd be forced into the SUV and it would be then a matter of time before I'd have to face whatever fate Matteo Lando had planned for me.

Another vehicle, a white van, approached at speed. It pulled up alongside the SUV, close enough to prevent it from taking off. Four large Londoners piled out. One brandished a machete. Another carried a baseball bat. The third carried a compact machine gun I recognised as an Uzi. A burst of shots was released, aimed at a point on the brick wall ten feet or so from where I was being held, bringing down shattered fragments onto the pavement.

The three Italians were overpowered with surprising speed. Seeing the Uzi, my attackers appealed for calm, raising their hands above their heads as if this might prevent the onslaught that was to come. This did nothing to deter the Londoners. The driver of the SUV was pulled out and dumped onto the street. Under threat from the Uzi and the machete, the Italians were helpless as repeated blows with the baseball bat piled into their heads and limbs. The more the Italians protested, the more the blows rained in.

Now released, I recognised the ugly Londoner who led the rescue. It was Spinks, one of the Bishop men who'd taken me to the pharmacy to have my head and shoulders photograph taken.

"Mr. Blake, I hope you don't mind us helping you out like this. Mr. Bishop takes a dim view of anyone who tries to get in the way of him and his customers."

Julia had described the men who'd come close to killing her in the Allegro Hotel. Two Italians, one tall and in charge, the other smaller and subservient. This, and the failed abduction, told me that two of the three men lying prone on the street were the same men who'd killed Craig at the hotel.

I replied to Spinks. "What are you going to do with them?"

He smiled. "Well, we'll tie them up tight and leave them here." He signalled to one of his colleagues who used snap-on plastic cuffs to bind the legs and arms of the Italians. "It's the punishment of the streets. You see, it's a rough neighbourhood round here. These gentleman look smart enough to me to suggest they could have more than a few prized possessions on them. So I'd say it's more than possible they might attract the attention of some of the less than dependable types that lurk around here."

He pulled open Bandini's coat and pulled out the Uzi that the Italian had been unable to use because of the speed and ferocity of the Londoners' attack. He placed the weapon across the Italian's chest. "Very juicy. Just what the less dependable types round here might want for Christmas."

I had a better idea.

When we arrived at the *Miller and Ploughman*, I made the excuse that I needed to clean up after the attention I'd received out on the street. Out of sight, I used the mobile phone to call Euston police station to leave a message for Inspector Hendricks. "If you want to arrest those responsible for the killing at the Allegro Hotel, send your men to Wapping Wall right now."

I was still shaken when I made my way to the pub terrace where Bishop was waiting at his usual table overlooking the Thames.

He greeted me like a friend. "Mr. Blake. Good to see you!"

I tried to thank him. "I owe you."

He would have none of it. "Just business, Mr. Blake. You see, we do things proper round here. If we make a deal, we see it through. We promised you a passport. You have to be here to collect it, don't you?"

He handed me the passport. I flicked through the pages. Name – Adrian Gillespie. My head and shoulders. It looked genuine.

He read my mind. "It's genuine, all right. As genuine as anything you can get from the Passport Office because it *is* from the Passport Office, if you know what I mean." He tapped the side of his nose. "You didn't hear me say that."

I pocketed the passport, handed him two thou and prepared to leave.

He called me back. "Haven't we forgotten something?"

I hadn't paid the full amount. "Keep the watch."

He smiled. "I was hoping you'd say that." He pulled back the shirt cuff from his wrist to reveal my Rolex. "Looks good on, don't you think?"

Spinks and two other Bishop men escorted me back to Shadwell station in the white van. As we travelled along Wapping Wall, I could see my call to Hendricks had been a success. Four armed police were in the process of loading the three Italians we'd left on the street into a waiting police truck.

Spinks smiled as we passed. "Told you there were some less than dependable types on the loose in this part of town."

When they dropped me I decided to head for the hotel to get some rest ahead of catching the 5.25 AM *Eurostar* out of St Pancras. Armed with the new passport, I would be in Paris in three hours and in Florence by mid-afternoon.

Chapter 31

Now that today's *samanera* had gone, Wolfgang Heller knew it was time to return to matters more of the world outside the monastery.

It was still a wonder worth remarking on that with the slim tablet computer, small enough to conceal beneath his clothing, he was connected to the world through the WiFi waves coursing through Lhasa and right here into the monastery. Yes, the world had been transformed. So much more of what he was destined to achieve had been made ever more possible.

He turned on the music player and inserted the ear buds. Richard Wagner's *The Valkyrie*, Act I, the source he needed to return to again and again to set his mind at peace with the perils that awaited in the world outside.

He let the power of this part of the opera wash over him. He tried to underplay his anticipation at the climax of the Act when Siegmund and Sieglinde, twin brother and sister, separated at birth and now reunited, approached the point of realisation. Sieglinde telling Siegmund she is his twin sister. Siegmund replying she is his bride *and* sister. Siegmund drawing the sword that no man has been able to remove from the oak tree.

Heller did not stop the tear that ran down his cheek. This was Wagner's finest moment. Heller had every right to feel this way.

He looked up at the wall above him where he'd positioned the images of Siegmund and Sieglinde. Here were the children of Wotan, one of the keys to the divine. The sure pulse of the energy running through his body in this centre of the universe.

Strange, he thought, that so many had experienced this music, had this moment placed before them, yet failed to understand its significance.

To think he was one of the few who had true knowledge, one of the few who understood that this was the path to immortality. To his own immortality. And that day was fast approaching.

He turned off the music and selected the phone. Time to engage with the wider world. He knew he must return there again if he was to seize the moment.

He dialled. He waited as the digital signal bounced from satellite to satellite around the world. Yes, we *are* gods now.

Matteo Lando picked up. "You called at a good time."

"Why good?"

"Because we need your help again."

Day 3

September 4th

Chapter 32

I spent most of the time on the way to Florence trying not to think of all that had happened in the three years since I'd last made this journey. I knew I should not dwell on the past. The only way to be free for good from the threats to my family was to be clear about what I should do next and not let the memory of those tragic events deter me.

As soon as I stepped off the train into the heat at Florence station I made the decision to present myself at the Questura and demand to be seen by Inspector Manieri. It was not a decision arrived at with ease. If Hendricks or Craven had put out calls for my detention, there was every chance these would have reached Manieri.

I took a taxi to the Questura on Via Zara and walked up the grey stone steps and into the entrance hall where the uniformed sergeant made me wait while he shuffled paperwork on the desk before him. When I asked for Inspector Manieri, he looked at me long and hard before giving a knowing smile and gesturing that I should follow him up the stairs.

Manieri looked up as I was brought in. "Signor Blake. It is always a pleasure but I am sure you will forgive me when I ask, what are you doing here?"

I decided to come straight to the point. "Inspector, I need your help."

"I see you are wanted for questioning in London."

"Hendricks?"

He smiled. "Yes, he has been in touch. He wants to talk to you about a murder in a West End hotel. The Allegro, I believe."

"I need you to trust me."

"He was insistent that I send you back if, as he suspected, you were found to be in Florence."

"You trusted me before. Look where that led."

"Yes, of course, James, we are grateful for your help in apprehending Matteo Lando and for the information you provided to allow the prosecution of the Lando family."

"So trust me again. Finish the job."

"Do I detect criticism?"

"No, Inspector, I'm not suggesting that. But the Landos have regrouped. Matteo Lando is as powerful as his father ever was, even though you have him locked up in Sollicciano. They're behind the cocaine trade out of Mexico now flooding Europe and it's being channelled through your town."

He held up his hand. "Wait, James. How can you be sure?"

I told Manieri what Miles had discovered in Albuquerque. The Landos were still in direct contact with the cartel that controlled the drugs traffic out of Tijuana. They had an assassin who was targeting their rivals. A black ops FBI mission was involved that had its sights set on myself and Miles. And Julia was back in danger because the Landos had not forgotten what had happened three years earlier in Florence and had offered a reward of two million for our murder.

He didn't appear to be shocked. "Those are powerful accusations, James. You will have to prove them. So, why did you not go to the British police? Why not confide in my colleague Inspector Hendricks?"

"Because the way I understand what's happening to Julia and me is that the British police are as compromised on this as the FBI. There's no other way of explaining what's happened to us since we left witness protection in Weymouth."

"You are not implicating Hendricks?"

"No. I don't doubt he's straight. Things aren't right elsewhere in the British police system. There are forces at work undermining everything."

"And you are sure the Landos are behind it?"

I nodded. "Sure enough to come here and place myself in your hands."

He looked interested but not yet convinced. "That still doesn't tell me why you are here in Florence."

"I need to talk to Zella DeFrancesco."

Manieri shook his head. "You should know that is not going to be possible. Like you, she is in witness protection. The highest priority is being given to keeping her location secret. After giving evidence against the Landos, she placed herself at great risk. That situation remains today."

"I understand. I know what she's going through. But there's a reason why she will want to talk to me. Her work in avenging the loss of her husband and children is not complete so long as the Landos are able to continue as they are. Put it to her that I want to talk with her. Let her decide. That's all I ask."

Manieri seemed puzzled. "What makes you so sure she'll want to speak to you?"

"I'd like to tell her myself."

"Signor Blake. If you are to have a chance of my agreeing with your requests, you need to tell me. Take it or leave it."

Even if I felt I could trust him, it was likely the Landos still had informers inside the Questura. But he'd left me with no choice. "Inspector, you know the reason Zella DeFrancesco spent ten years of her life infiltrating the Lando operation?"

"Of course. To avenge the deaths of her husband and children at the hands of the Landos and the Rossellinis."

"Well, Zella may have thought that justice had been done when Alfieri Lando was killed and Matteo was imprisoned for the murder. I'm here to tell her that the evil Alfieri embodied is still with us. And she's the only one who has the knowledge to bring this to an end. Trust me. Give me three days before reporting I'm here."

"You're asking that my office, on behalf of the Italian State, should choose not to respond to a request for assistance from a fellow Interpol member? You're asking that the same office ignores a request from the FBI, one we're treaty bound to reply to?"

"If that's what it takes."

He stood and looked out the window for a long time before replying. "You have seventy-two hours. Up until then I can claim there has been an administrative delay in replying. But not an hour more."

Chapter 33

Miles Blake was an expert at hiding in plain sight. His work had taken him to more trouble spots than he cared to remember and what he'd learned in each and every one of them was that to be safe was to be with people, as many people as possible.

Here in Tijuana that meant being in and around La Revo, where, night and day, life passed in an unending confusion of comings and goings allowing no explanation. Tourists, mainly young, came looking for cheap alcohol, drugs and the edgy excitement that came from being close, but not too close, to real danger. Just about every other inhabitant of the city was out and about hustling the tourist dollar, from the men on the cheap roadside food stalls, to the legal prostitutes with their improbable shoes and their nearby protecting pimps, to the callers-in trying to boost the trade of the bars and clubs lining the street. Nothing disturbed the steady flow of commerce, not even the appearance in the street every now and then of the dead body of one of the locals.

A good place to disappear.

He was surprised, then, to find he was being followed and his pursuer was an American woman. She'd made the attempt to dress down and appear to be just another tourist but there was something much too smart about the linen clothes she wore.

He walked past the next alleyway that led off La Revo and waited just long enough for the woman following to begin to cross it. Without warning, he turned, ran towards her and forced her into the alleyway. Not one of the throng around them bothered to depart from the much more urgent business consuming their lives.

She was strong and resisted. She reached for the weapon in the holster beneath her jacket but Miles was able to pin her arms to her side and turn her round to face him.

He recognised her.

He never forgot a face and this served him well as a journalist. He had the ability to visualise not just the person but also the location of the encounter. The image that came placed him back in the Warren Stevenson hotel in Austin. His brother James was seated at the hotel bar beside an attractive woman. As Miles came in with Luiz Reyas at his side, Wolfgang Heller was drawing a weapon and preparing to fire at James. The woman seated with James at the bar was the woman he now held.

He released her. "We've met before."

She was surprised and relieved to be free. She said nothing and reached for the weapon beneath her jacket.

Miles stood back. "No need for that. We need to talk. Beginning with why you were with James in Austin."

She let her arms drop to her sides again. "OK, you made me, Miles. Agent Miller, FBI."

"You know who I am?"

"You're the reason why I'm here."

"And why's that?"

"You said we need to talk. Let's talk."

They went to Miles' hotel, a short walk away on Avenida L'Ascencione, looking for all the world like one of the American tourist couples who stayed in this more respectable part of town. In plain sight, over drinks in the bar of the Anglia Hotels they talked.

Miles began. "Give me a good reason why I should be talking to the FBI after all you've done to myself and my brother."

"Call it, *that's what journalists do — talk to people.* Call it anything you like. You know there are questions that need answers."

"Like why did you render my brother James to the United States and set him up as a target for a hit man sent by one of Italy's most notorious crime families? And don't tell me it was all about national security."

She wasn't fazed. "It's not something I would have authorised."

"No, you have Craven to do that. Did he send you here after me?"

"Craven is my boss. He gives an order, I follow it. That's what was happening at the Warren Stevenson. But, no, he didn't send me down here. The questions I have are mine and mine alone."

"What makes you think I should believe you?"

"Give it a try. You might be surprised."

There was something about Debbie Miller that made Miles want to believe she was not here to trap him. But he knew he had to be careful. "OK. So, you're wired and you're going to relay back everything we say to the folks in Washington. Where's that going to get me?"

She opened her hands in exasperation. "And I might just as well say you have a hidden recorder and you're going to put anything I say into one of your articles. Where's that going to get us?"

He smiled. "We both spy on each other?"

"Trust me and I'll trust you. You have my word."

It wasn't enough. There was risk in this but without taking this chance, Miles would never know if he'd passed over the opportunity to get at the truth. He looked into her eyes for a long time. She did not blink or look away. "OK. So, start by telling me if the Agency has a fix on where James is now."

"I shouldn't be telling you this, but I'll level with you, as a sign of good faith. James has been seen in London. I can't tell you any more."

"OK, what I asked before. Why did you render my brother James to United States and set him up as a target for a hit man sent by one of Italy's most notorious crime families?"

"It was the best way to protect Elmore Ravitz. To draw out the assassin."

"Didn't work too well."

"What do you mean?"

"Ravitz died. Along with his wife and too many other poor souls."

"That was something else. Ravitz was campaigning on increasing the war on terror and winning the argument. The terrorists got to him at Town Lake. It was unconnected to what was happening with your brother."

"You don't believe that?"

She was trying to hide her anger now. "Careful what you say, Mr. Blake. I was there. I saw the destruction, first hand. When the second bomb went off, I thought I was going to die along with everyone else. I lost good colleagues that day. Don't you dare say anything that takes away the sacrifice they made."

"What if I know it was different? What if there was a way of proving it?"

"Then that would be a good reason why we're talking. Even if I'm going to find it hard to believe you."

"What if I told you it was Wolfgang Heller who planted the bombs at Town Lake?"

"I'd be even less inclined to believe you. What allows you to say that?"

"Because it makes sense and you'll know it makes sense the more you think about it. Heller knew all about the trap you'd set for him by setting up James as bait in the Warren Richardson. So he used that as a diversion while he planted the bombs. Then, when the bombs went off he was ready to take out James at the hotel. We escaped from him but only just. There are bodies to prove it."

She still seemed unconvinced. "At the abandoned railway station. I know about that. There's nothing to connect it to the Town Lake attack, even if it played out as you say it did. It's separate. Heller chasing you, trying to kill you. Craven has evidence implicating East Africa jihadists for Town Lake."

"So it's a coincidence that the Town Lake bombs go off just as you and the rest of Craven's team are protecting Ravitz from a threat not connected to East Africa, is it?"

"Ravitz campaigned on the war on terror."

"You know that's not enough."

"You don't think I haven't thought about that? No one likes coincidence but it's a fact of life. It happens. Get used to it."

"Such as?"

"Such as Fleming leaves one of his specimens and a mould infests it and he plays a hunch on finding out what effect the mould might have on one of his samples, discovers antibiotics and saves the lives of a few hundred million people. That kind of coincidence. Or, I don't know, Mark Twain was born the same day as Halley's comet appeared and he died seventy-five years later on the very same day as the comet next appeared. You tell me?"

Miles was not going to be diverted. "We're not talking that kind of coincidence and I think you know it. We're talking convenience. We're talking *cuo bene*. And that's something I've learned as a journalist. Whenever you see an incident that can't be explained, ask the question. Who benefits? There's always someone there to pick up an advantage. And in this case it's Craven."

"How so?"

Miles could see from her downcast expression that he'd hit a mark. "You're worried about Craven. I know it. I can tell."

"I'm not going to agree with you. Just how do you think Craven benefits if it's East Africa terrorists? You could say it was still his fault they got in and planted those bombs. And that includes me. I'm part of the same team."

"Except, there was never any real doubt that a terror attack would have to be accommodated within your system. Because it was unexpected. You should have seen it coming but with best efforts you didn't. You don't get sacked for that. You get to be called heroes."

She gave him a warning stare. "But?"

"But if there was another motive – to obscure Heller's role as the real perpetrator – the idea of a terror attack would be perfect cover."

"For what?"

"For the fact that the people who sent Heller after Elmore Ravitz know things about Craven that he'd do everything in his power to conceal."

"Such as?"

"Such as Craven is making it rich big time out of the drugs traffic out of here. Out of Tijuana. Such as the Lando family who sent Heller know all about it since they're involved in the same traffic themselves."

"And you have evidence for this."

He nodded. "I have it from someone inside the Soto cartel."

She was not convinced. "Show me him. Let me hear it from him." It was Miles' turn to look downcast. "I can't. A man, a man I trust, died at my side in East Texas. Before he died he told me. I believe what he said."

"You're not going to convince the world with the second hand testimony of a dead man."

"I know that. Doesn't mean what he said is any less true. It's why I'm here. To gather the evidence."

She was dismissive. "That's what you have to go on?"

"And the fact that I know where the explosive used at Town Lake came from."

"And you know that from where?"

"From the man who died in my arms in East Texas."

"How's it going to help?"

"You must have analysed the residue of the explosive used in the blast. It will have its own signature. If I can show it matches explosive from here in Mexico, would it convince you?"

"It would depend on how good the evidence was."

"But you could access the report on the Town Lake explosive?"

She nodded. "That wouldn't be difficult. Finding your proof is a whole different matter."

Miles was becoming more certain this was not a set up and he decided to try to show it. "I'm sensing there's more here than you're telling me. The fact that you've come down here on your own."

"I didn't say I was here alone."

"But it's right, isn't it? And why would you say the questions you're asking me are yours and yours alone? Doesn't it mean you have your own doubts about Craven's version of events?"

"I don't know how you can think that. As I said, I'm part of his team. I'm loyal to him."

"Yet you know I'm right. You don't think Craven is right. You're here to find out for yourself what happened at Town Lake."

She smiled. "You're not going to get me to agree to that. But I'll make you an offer. I'll do what I can to help you test your theory. I'll file no report on what you're doing here. In exchange, you agree to include me in everything."

Miles agreed. "OK. On condition that when I come back with the evidence you need, you help me deal with Craven."

She said nothing. Her silence was enough to say she agreed.

Chapter 34

Inspector John Hendricks was baffled when he received the message from DI Franklin. Someone had called the operation room the night before to say that persons of interest connected to the killing at the Allegro Hotel could be found in Wapping Wall in the East End. When the police squad was sent there, they found three Italians lying in the street, hands and feet secured by the plastic snap-on bands.

Franklin was not being precise enough for the inspector. "They were the worse for wear, sir."

"What does that mean, Franklin?"

"They've been beaten, sir. Looks like they'd been battered with something blunt like a baseball bat."

"Italians?"

"Yes sir. Two of them match images taken from the Allegro security cameras. They were there in the hotel the day Craig was killed."

Hendricks was beginning to think this was his lucky day. "Hold them. I want to question them about Craig's death. Take prints and DNA and run both against the evidence collected from room 301 in the Allegro."

"Of course, sir."

"And while you're at it, Franklin, run the prints and the DNA profile against the evidence from the murder scene in the warehouse."

"Where DI Reid was tortured, sir?"

"Exactly."

"Any good reason to do that, sir?"

"Call it a hunch, Franklin. Just one of my hunches."

Hendricks closed the line. He was looking forward to interrogating the suspects about the killings of both Craig and Reid. Something told him he was going to wipe more than one name off the list of unsolved murders on his patch. One thing that worried him was the nagging question of who knew enough about the Allegro killing to send that message linking the beaten-up Italians with the murder committed there.

Chapter 35

Zella DeFrancesco agreed to meet at the Peggy Guggenheim Gallery in Venice, the place we first met three years before when I'd been searching for Julia in order to release her from Alfieri Lando's grip. Perhaps the symmetry of events appealed to her. Perhaps this was where she felt more anonymous, most secure.

She would not speak at first. One by one, she introduced me again to each and every painting in Peggy Guggenheim's collection, standing with me before them, taking in their beauty in silence. She spent longer in front of one of the paintings – Max Ernst's *The Attirement of the Bride* – the painting that summed up her life, as she'd told me. She took me out into the sculpture garden and again we stood in silence before each piece.

When we'd finished, we sat on chairs overlooking the Grand Canal beneath the Mario Marini statue.

The three years had not been kind to her. I'd imagined that with the lifting of the stress and concern of being within the Lando family and doing their bidding, she would look younger but that was not the case.

She started with a question. "You know the worst thing?"

"No, tell me."

"Having survived. Having come out unscathed when so many around me have perished and will never sit like this again and look out at the beauty of such a place. Why should I have survived when they have not? There is guilt and shame in that."

I tried to reassure her. "It's because you had the courage to stare evil in the face and not look away as so many do."

"I think about the women I betrayed, using and exploiting them to serve the Lando name. To play the Lando game. To stifle whatever hope of happiness they had in their lives."

"You had to stay strong to overcome such evil. You had to win the Lando's trust so you could denounce them."

She smiled. "Try telling that to the women whose lives were ruined. Try telling that to the ones who did not make it."

My mind turned to thoughts of Julia's sister, Emelia, but I knew that remorse for her death would not help at this moment. "You can't blame yourself. It was beyond your control."

A deeper sense of sadness came upon her. "I have never had control. Not even to save my own family."

Nothing would take away the loss she'd suffered when her husband and children were killed when their vehicle had been caught in crossfire in the Lando-Rossellini turf war. Only she had survived.

"I feel shame and guilt also about that. It is why you should not be talking to me, Signor Blake. I can only demoralise you. You should look elsewhere for the answers you seek."

I looked away, at the fine buildings across the waterway. "I need your help, Zella. I need you to help me to save my family."

I told her how we'd been targeted once more by the Landos, about the loose ends Alessa and Matteo Lando were now seeking to clean up. And I told her Wolfgang Heller was their paid assassin.

She shot back in shock. "Heller! He's more than an assassin. I thought they'd finished with him."

"You know him?"

She nodded. "As much as anyone could know a man like that. He was close to Alfieri, almost like a son to him. Almost like the son Alfieri wished Matteo to be but couldn't be because of Alessa's opposition."

"He's killed many people. Many who will not again be with their families. If you know anything, please help me find a way through this threat to the existence of my family. I'm begging you to tell me."

She shivered. "James, there are things Alfieri was capable of that no one should know. Just knowing about these things can corrupt even the most determined. You're sure you want to hear this?"

"I need to know. Nothing else matters."

"Then, I have to begin at the point that is the most painful for you. If you are to understand the true depth of evil of the Landos and all they represent. I have to tell you what happened to your wife."

"To Julia?"

She nodded. "Something I've told no one to this day. Alfieri Lando used me as his handmaiden. He made me become Hypnos to his Zeus."

"I don't understand."

"It goes back to the painting, to *Leda and the Swan*. What it represents. Why the myth was so important for Michelangelo."

I was out of my depth but not afraid to admit it. "I don't see where this is going. What does this have to do with what happened to Julia?"

"Then I must tell you. In the moment Alfieri appeared to Julia, he believed he was all powerful, that he was Zeus, the most powerful of the gods and that he could have anything he wanted. As in the myth he could take on any form he wanted and take any woman he wanted. He wore a flowing red cape and a mask to conceal his identity, just as Zeus had concealed his identity to Leda. And just as in the myth Zeus was helped by Hypnos, the goddess of sleep who charmed Leda into submission with the sound of dripping water from the river Lethe, so Alfieri had me as his handmaiden, only the drugs I used were more powerful. Cocaine and heroin. Available from the Lando drugs trade."

"You were there when Julia was raped?"

She hung her head. "I did warn you there were things I would have to tell you that you would not want to hear. It was expected. It was a test of loyalty that I was there."

I tried to hide the distaste of what I was hearing. I tried to drown out the image forming in my mind of Julia being raped by Alfieri Lando while Zella DeFrancesco held her hand and wiped her brow. "You had no choice."

"You begin to understand now the evil of the Landos. How they taint all they touch. How I still struggle to come to terms with what I did to stay inside their world as long as was needed to gain revenge for my family. The fact is that in the end the revenge I won was not enough to compensate for what I put your wife and all those other women through."

"There were others?"

She nodded. "Too many to remember. I try to forget them all but there are some, like Emelia, I cannot shake from my mind."

"Julia's sister. He did the same to her?"

"In the same way. To my shame, I have to tell you I was there as his handmaiden as she was raped too."

I was holding back the tears. Tears at the thought of what Julia had been through. Tears at how inadequate were my own attempts to understand how Julia was able to overcome these horrors of the past and start a new life.

She could see the tears in my eyes. "If only I could cry. I gave up trying to cry long ago."

I was finding it difficult to hold onto the logic of what I needed to achieve here in Venice, talking with this woman. I found myself thinking about my conversation with Julia's adopted parents before leaving for Florence. "Zella, let me put this to you. It was no accident that Julia Blake and Emelia Rossellini were in Florence at the same time and that Alfieri targeted them both."

"Yes, Signor Blake. You are beginning to know the true nature of the evil of the man and what he represents. Yes, it was no coincidence that they were both here. And yes, before you ask, it has everything to do with the fact that they were twins."

She waved her arm across the scene to indicate its scale and beauty, the shimmer of the sun on the glinting waters of the Grand Canal and the Renaissance buildings lining its banks. "We have to hold onto beauty, Signor Blake. In the end, it is all there is between us and the ugliness, the death and destruction of a world made in our own image. It is what art insists upon, that we force beauty into the face of evil and demand that the ugliness of the world is overcome. No one gets to choose the world we inherit and struggle to make sense of. It is the tragedy of our lives. By the time we start to work out how it should all be, we are caught up in the corruption we inherit."

"That's why you brought me here?"

"Yes, I wanted to remind you of the beauty of this place. I wanted you to experience that beauty while I told you what you have to know. So you might be able to bear it and, perhaps, help myself to be blessed with some of that redemption."

"Then help me understand what lies behind the evil that took root in Alfieri Lando."

She upturned her hands in a gesture of resignation.

"I have been there, Signor Blake. Like you are now. Seeking to answer the same question. There was a time when I was strong enough to dare to ask, but those days are gone from me."

She reached into her bag and pulled out a business card. She handed it to me. "Back when I still had the strength to search, my path led me to this man. Go to see him. Ask your questions of him."

I took the card.

Professor Niccolo Ferrara, Professor of Comparative Religion, University of Padova.

I thanked her and said my farewells. She'd made it clear I should not try to contact her again.

As I walked back towards the vaporetto station, I couldn't help thinking I would indeed see her again.

Chapter 36

It didn't take long for Luiz Reyas to find the key fact that would make or break Miles' investigation of the Town Lake bombing.

They met in Miles' hotel room.

Luiz was keen to tell what he'd discovered. "Senor, I have found someone who overheard El Romero talking about Town Lake."

Miles was questioning. "Why wasn't he being more careful?"

"It was the maid. She was cleaning the room. He was on the phone."

"And?"

"She heard El Romero complaining that the explosive used for the bomb came from Mexico."

"From the Soto cartel?"

"No, Senior. From a rival. From Johnny Rivenza in Juarez."

"Why would Rivenza do that?"

"Because he has no sense, like so many here."

Miles was aware how Rivenza was seeking to move in on El Romero's patch. "Things are bad between the two men?"

"Yes, Senor. It's the biggest cause of death in this town. El Romero claims the drugs trade as his own, given to him by the council that oversees the cartels. Rivenza says he does not care about that. He is going to move in and take over. Too many men have died as a result."

"Except, the FBI doesn't think the bomb came from Mexico."

"From what you told me, Senor, you know that cannot be true."

Miles agreed. "So, the explosive came from Juarez. But the only way this could help is if we have solid proof."

"It's not so simple, Senor. Rivenza is as ruthless as El Romero. His operation is locked down tight."

"Before we go any further, Luiz, there is more you should know about the risk to both of us."

"Yes, Senor?"

Miles could see so much of the father in this young man. He didn't want to find such a young life lost in pursuit of the same goal. "What do you know about Craven, Nate Craven?"

"He is FBI. He is one of those involved in the fight against drugs from the US side."

"You don't collaborate?"

Luiz shook his head. "That stopped a long time ago when the Americans got to know how many here in the FDM are in the pay of the cartels."

"Then you won't know about what he does for El Romero?"

"It is suspected, Senor, that El Romero has protection from someone inside the FBI but he keeps that secret, even from those closest to him. You are saying Craven is the one?"

Miles nodded. "That's what your father discovered. It's what got him killed. Craven runs black ops. He protects the El Romero shipments to the US and the Lando shipments to Europe. And he makes himself rich."

"The man has much power."

"Yet he has a fatal weakness that we will exploit. If we succeed we will bring him down."

"And if Craven falls, the Landos fall with him?"

"And we achieve our common cause."

Miles paused. He knew if they were to succeed, Luiz Reyas would have to know about Debbie Miller. That multiplied the risk. Miles had to be sure his judgment of both of them was correct and both would accept the other. "Luiz, there's someone else I want you to meet."

"Now?"

"She's here in the hotel."

When Debbie Miller came in a few minutes after Miles' call, she eyed Luiz Reyas with caution before addressing Miles. "You didn't say there would be anyone else here."

He smiled. "This needed to be face to face."

She listened in silence as Miles told her about Luiz Reyas, the mission he had inherited from his father and his undercover role in the El Romero cartel. The sight of Luiz's FDM shield helped to convince her.

When Miles told Luiz that Debbie Miller was part of the Craven team at the FBI, Luiz was unable to hide his agitation.

When Debbie Miller offered to shake hands, Luiz did not offer his hand back.

Miles turned to face Luiz. "I understand. How do you know I haven't been taken in by the FBI?"

"You are sure, Senor?"

Miles looked at Debbie Miller, waiting for an answer. When she spoke her words carried conviction. She turned to look at Miles. "This man has put his trust in me." Then she turned to Luiz. "If you *trust* him, put your trust in me. It's the only way we will succeed."

Miles agreed. "You have my word, Luiz. What she says is true."

The Mexican showed nothing more than resigned acceptance. "If you say, Senor."

Debbie Miller offered her hand again and Luiz shook it. "To our common cause, Senora."

It was a moment of understanding that Miles wanted to build on. "We need to plan how we'll work together."

He explained what Luiz had discovered about the origin of the Town Lake explosive. "Debbie, we need to get a sample of the explosive from Johnny Rivenza, tie the signature of the plastic he supplied to the analysis of what was recovered at Town Lake."

She could see where this was leading. "You're not planning to go out there?"

Miles nodded. "I suggest we leave for Juarez first thing in the morning."

"That place makes Tijuana look safe."

"We'll take our chance." He paused. "You stay here."

"You're not trying to protect me?"

"It's just going to be better this way. But there is one thing we need to get clear and it does involve you."

"Which is?"

"When we get back you need to tell the Agency that the explosive came from El Romero."

"That would be a lie."

"A small lie to out a bigger lie."

Chapter 37

Before Inspector Manieri agreed to arrange the meeting with Zella DeFrancesco in Venice, he gave me a mobile phone.

"You must carry this with you."

I was in no position to refuse. "So you can track me?"

"For your safety. And to make sure you do nothing to disable the phone you must call my number every four hours. There will be someone here to check. If you do not phone in, I will issue the order to act on the request from England and from the FBI for your capture. Do you understand?"

I took the phone and agreed to the conditions.

Traveling by train from Venice to Padova to meet Niccolo Ferrara, I checked the time and saw that another call to the Questura in Florence was required. I was hoping Manieri picked up rather than one of his assistants.

I dialled the number.

It was Manieri. "Signor Blake, it is good you have checked in. I trust the meeting was satisfactory?"

"Thank you, Inspector. The arrangements worked well," I lied. "She sends her best wishes."

"She was of help to you?"

"She answered as best she could. But I have to say she is a disillusioned woman."

I wanted to move on with the conversation. There was an important question I needed to ask him now I'd spoken with Zella DeFrancesco. "Tell me, Inspector, how many twins have gone missing in Florence in the past ten years?"

He sounded surprised. "This came out of your meeting with DeFrancesco?"

I could see no reason not to let him know. "It was something we talked about. Do you have an answer?"

"The simple fact, Signor Blake, is we do not keep records of such cases. There are many disappearances. Most are quite understandable. Women leaving their husbands. Children escaping from abusing parents. Not all are suspicious."

"But you could find out?"

"Male and female twins?"

"No, just female."

"If it will help you, I will investigate and let you know when next you call."

I thanked him and ended the call.

When the train arrived in Padova, I called the number for Professor Niccolo Ferrara, as shown on the card given me by Zella DeFrancesco in Venice.

After a long wait, a secretary answered the phone. "Professor Ferrara is not available. He is lecturing."

"When does the lecture finish?"

"At five. But I can give you no guarantee he will see you then. His diary has been full all week."

Before she had time to deter me, I told her I'd take my chance in seeing him. I ended the call.

The train was due to arrive at 4.45. There was just time to taxi to the university and head off Professor Ferrara as he came out of the lecture theatre. In the event, the lecture overran. I waited outside until he finished and the students began to file out. I ventured inside. With steep, tiered seats sufficient to hold three hundred, the place reminded me of my own time as a student of physics back in the UK. Except here in Padova, the university had history on its side since the Physics Chair could claim descent from Galileo.

Ferrara had stayed behind to answer earnest questions from one of the students. When he saw me approaching, he used this as an excuse to bring the session with the student to a close.

143

As the student left, he addressed me. "Signor, what do you want with me?"

I introduced myself as James Blake. It felt good to use my real name. "I hope you can find time to give me some advice."

He took a step back. "It is out of the question. It is Friday. The end of a long week. I am leaving in fifteen minutes for the weekend. You may come back on Monday."

"I don't have time for that, Professor. What I need to talk to you about is urgent."

"What could it be that you could ask a professor of comparative religion that cannot wait, Signor Blake?"

I was unsure where to start. "Do you recall a Signora DeFrancesco who came to see you sometime ago?"

His manner changed. "Come this way."

He walked me along the corridor leading away from the lecture theatre and showed me into his office.

As his secretary saw me she tried to apologise for not protecting Ferrara from me. He reassured her. "It is OK, Gisselda. I am pleased to talk with Signor Blake."

He told me we did not have long. He was scheduled to drive to Puglia this evening and that could not be changed. He was expected there. If I was prepared to travel with him to Ostuni, he would answer my questions during the journey.

I had just one question. "When do we leave, Professor?"

"Right now. And please stop calling me Professor. My name is Nico."

Chapter 38

Finding Debbie Miller wasn't difficult. Agent Dillon Ashley knew who to bribe in Tijuana. The name of her hotel was with him in less than the time it took to shower and dress after the flight from Washington and the drive down from San Diego.

Ashley bided his time. He wanted to know if Miller had met the Blake target here, as Nate Craven supposed.

He saw them together for the first time in the lobby of the hotel. Miles Blake was with a young Mexican. Both were talking with Miller. They were saying farewell, saying they were going on a trip and they hoped to be back by the next day. She was wishing them well.

What to do? Ashley's first thought was to wait until the men had left, then follow Miller back to her hotel room and confront her with the fact that the Agency now knew she was here. But that wasn't what Craven wanted. He'd been clear. He wanted to know why Miller was in Tijuana, why she would risk her career to meet the Englishman.

The correct course of action was to report what he had seen back to Nate Craven. It was up to Craven what happened next.

Ashley called in on the secure line. "She's here, Nate. With Miles Blake and an unknown local. You want me to move in on her?"

Craven was quick to respond. "No, Dillon. Keep her under surveillance until I advise different. I'll get back to you with more later."

When Craven ended the call, Ashley went to the bar in his hotel and ordered a large whisky. Just what was he getting into with Craven? Carrying out surveillance on a fellow agent didn't feel right, even for all the money Craven was offering. But he could use the cash, there was no doubt about it.

The warm glow of the whisky began to take hold. Ashley steadied himself. Time enough to sit on the sidelines and see how this would play out.

Chapter 39

The bright red Alfa Romeo Giulietta was brand new. To his clear delight, Niccolo Ferrara had collected it from the dealer this very day.

I had to remind myself I was sitting beside the fifty-year-old academic with the flowing grey hair who was more noted for expounding a treatise on the history of religion than for being a boy racer.

He could not contain his delight. "It is the top of the range model. 1.7-liter turbocharged engine. 0–100 km in 6.8 seconds. Top speed 240 km/hr. That is 150 in your miles per hour. And I am sure we will able to coax a little more out of it with the Dynamic Driver setting."

The way he admired the vehicle was everything you would expect from a youngster opening presents on Christmas morning. The illuminated control panel with its multitude of features that were new to him was a treat to be enjoyed. He enthused at the built-in climate control, sound system and satellite navigation. The smell of newness was like an aphrodisiac to him. Above all, there was no question that the most enjoyable aspect of the Alfa Romeo for the professor was its power to turn heads. And, like all boy racers the world over, the overriding interest was the prospect of speed. It was going to be a breathtaking journey on the Autostrada to Ostuni.

We'd soon left Padova and were approaching the tollbooth at the start of the Autostrada A14. As we waited in the line of traffic to take the biglietto from the entry machine, Ferrara punched data into the satellite navigation system. "Padova to

Bari. It's 658 km. About 400 miles." He gave a boyish smile. "It's going to take about six hours if we obey the speed limit but we should be able to improve on that."

Once through the tollbooth area, Ferrara began to deliver on the short journey promise. He treated the outside lane as his own, tailgating any vehicles occupying it at the legal speed limit of 110 km/h, causing them to head for cover in the slower lanes.

I tried not to sound too much like a nervous passenger as the display showed we had just exceeded 130 km/h. "Professor Ferrara. You're not worried about the fines?"

He tapped the small electronic box hidden beneath the dashboard. "Not when I have this. It tells me where the speed cameras are. We will pass them at the legal speed." He paused. "And, James, did you not hear me? My name is Nico."

We fell silent for a while as the North Italy landscape scudded past at threatening speed.

When he next spoke, it was clear he'd been sorting through the pressing issues weighing on him and now, with the freeing hand of the journey before him, he'd found the space to take an interest in me. "So, James, what is it you came all this way to ask me? And what has this got to do with Signora DeFrancesco?"

"She said she'd been to see you. Some time ago. And she'd begun to get answers to her questions."

"You have the same questions?"

"Zella told me you would be able to help."

"You need tell me more than that, James."

I started with what had happened to Julia. I told him about her art conservation work and how she'd been drawn to Florence in search of missing masterpieces. She was a twin and she and her twin sister had been abused by Alfieri Lando. I said we were being threatened now and I needed to know what lay behind the chain of events now visited on us. I ended with a question. "Tell me, Nico, why would Zella DeFrancesco consider it so important I speak with you?"

He did not reply for some time. He was involved in a difficult lane-change after tailgating a vehicle that could not move to a slower lane occupied by three twelve-wheel delivery lorries. He was swearing in Italian and railing against those who abided by the speed limit.

When the road ahead began to clear, he made his reply. "I need you to understand, James, I have to be sure I can trust you. Here in Italy, it is not unknown for people to be other than they say they are. I hope you will not be offended."

He was testing me. I couldn't blame him. He knew about me only from what I'd said. I would have wanted more assurance if I were him. Yet I didn't want to complicate his view of me by letting on I was on the run from the British police and the FBI. I decided to be as open as I could without going too far. "I'm not offended. I understand your reservations. What can I do to prove to you I'm genuine in what I say?"

He paused as he pushed the Alfa Romeo to greater speed as a clear section of highway opened up and then he continued. "So you don't mind if I ask questions?"

"Of course not."

"We both know Signora DeFrancesco. You said you met her at the Peggy Guggenheim in Venice. There is a painting in the museum that has a special significance for her."

I interrupted him. "Ernst's *The Attirement of the Bride*. She told me it sums up her life."

He smiled. "Good! And what jewellery does she wear on her right hand?"

"Nothing. She wears no rings on either hand."

He smiled. "Good."

His questions continued until he had covered every detail of what I should have known if I had been truthful in what I'd said about my meeting with Zella. When he was finished he gave another smile. "So, James Blake, you are either who you say you are or you are one of the most well-briefed imposters I have had the misfortune to meet. However, I am pleased to say I believe the former."

I leaned back in the seat. "Glad I made it."

We talked about London and about Florence, now as two men who were beginning to trust each other, though I could not be sure he wasn't still testing me.

When we neared the halfway point of the journey, Ferrara pulled off at the Autogrill service stop at Torre Cerrano Ovest to refuel the Alfa Romeo and for coffee.

I welcomed the break. If I didn't call Manieri in the next half hour, he would have every reason to act on his threat of reporting me to Hendricks and the FBI. While Ferrara ordered panini and coffee, I made the excuse to go to the restroom from where I called Manieri.

"It's me. Reporting in as requested, Inspector."

He was business-like. "Signor Blake. A pleasure to hear from you. You left me with a question. I have an answer. There are eleven cases of twins who have disappeared in Florence in the last ten years under circumstances that warrant investigation."

"They were all women."

"That is correct."

"Tell me, Inspector, what was the outcome?"

"What do you mean?"

"There were investigations, were the missing women found?"

"Within the limits of our resources, the cases were investigated. I cannot tell you anything more."

"You mean they weren't found?"

"That is beginning to sound like criticism, Signor Blake. The investigations were not brought to a conclusion. Except in one case, the disappearance of your wife and her sister."

I swallowed hard. I knew I could not get drawn again into what had happened to Julia. "And tell me, Inspector, has the number of disappearances declined since Alfieri Lando died?"

"On the contrary, Signor Blake, they have remained at the same level. Why would you expect it to be otherwise?"

I chose not to answer. "Yet unresolved cases remain?"

"It is possible they have resolved themselves. It is what often happens. People go missing every day. They start new lives. There is nothing to suggest that the law has been broken. If you are asking if we found bodies or evidence of foul play, the answer is *no*."

"But you don't know what happened to them?"

"As I told you, they slip out of sight in our system. There is nothing untoward in that."

I decided I wouldn't get any more than this from him. I thanked him and ended the call.

I felt that Inspector Manieri was satisfied I was keeping my side of the bargain. Yet time was not on my side. I was already eating into the seventy-two hours he said was the absolute limit on how far he could delay before reporting my whereabouts. And here I was in the middle of nowhere with a speed crazy academic of comparative religion. But there was no going back. I had to hope Zella DeFrancesco was right and Ferrara's enthusiasm and knowledge held the key to understanding what lay behind what had happened to Julia.

Chapter 40

It was known all across the Baja that Johnny Riveriza wanted to move in on the territory controlled by the Soto cartel. El Romero claimed this was against the agreement made by the cartel owners down in Mexico City but that hadn't stopped Rivenza. The result was predictable as El Romero defended his territory – killings too many to count, beheadings, the wiping out of whole families.

Now Luiz Reyas and Miles were traveling to the Rivenza cartel base in Juarez to put their proposition to the man himself. Luiz was optimistic. "He will want to listen, I know."

They were driving through El Paso heading for State Highway 45, preparing to re-enter Mexico. It was not long before they were sighted as they passed through the desolate outskirts of Juarez. An agricultural wagon piled high with guava fruit stopped ahead of them while a brand-new SUV pulled up behind. Three men piled out carrying Uzis and threatened Luiz Reyas who was driving. They were searched for weapons and escorted to the hilltop ranch house where, in an air-conditioned room, Johnny Rivenza was waiting.

He looked them over with contempt. "You should know, Senors, you are not welcome here." He gave Luiz Reyas a penetrating look. "Why would someone from the Soto cartel presume to arrive here without an invitation?"

Luiz held his nerve. "I don't come here from El Romero. I come here for myself. There is no other way. What I have to tell you can only be told in person."

"Important enough to risk your life?"

"Yes, Senor."

Rivenza stared at Miles. "And to do this you bring the *gringo* with you?"

Miles spoke for the first time and decided there was no option but to be honest. "My name is Miles Blake, Senor Rivenza. I am a journalist." What came next was a risk. But then the whole idea of bringing the proposition to Juarez was a risk. "I know about the explosive."

Rivenza was trying not to show how startled he was. "What explosive?"

"The plastic explosive you sent to Austin. The material for the bombs that killed all those people at Town Lake."

Rivenza reached for his gun and signalled to the two guards standing behind Luiz and Miles. "Then you give us no choice but to kill you now." He levelled the gun. "Give me one reason not to pull the trigger?"

Miles fought to resist the fear engulfing him. "Kill us and you'll never know about the key to unlock everything you wish for."

He lowered the gun a little. "So, what is this *everything* you dangle before me?"

Miles pointed a thumb at the two guards behind him. "Not while they're here."

"You expect me to agree to that?"

"You have the gun."

Rivenza signalled the two men to leave. He raised the gun again. "So, tell me."

Luiz Reyas took over. "We have a proposition."

"To deliver to me *everything* I wish for?"

"You give us a small gift. We give you the key to finishing El Romero. It is a straight trade."

"What kind of gift?"

"A sample of the explosive you supplied for Town Lake. We return to Tijuana. You do not hear from us again."

Rivenza smiled. "And why would I do this?"

"Because we tell the Americans that the explosive came from El Romero. The Federales will have no choice but to act once they know the part he played in the outrage."

He was not convinced. "You must take me for a fool, Senor. You leave here. I don't see you again. You tell the Federales that I supplied the plastic and all along you have been working for El Romero."

"You have our word."

He laughed. "And you think that would ever be enough in a place like this where every truth is a lie. No, I do not need to take such a chance. I kill you now."

Luiz was not fazed. "We would not be here if we did not think we could convince you. Would any men come here as defenceless as we are if that was not the case? Give us the chance and we will tell you why we will keep our side of the bargain."

Rivenza agreed. He listened as Luiz told him the history of the Reyas family, how his mission since birth was to seek revenge for the wrongs that had been unresolved for so long. He told him about the killing of Luiz Reyas, his own father, in Austin. "Senor, you can see I have every reason to implicate El Romero. He is in partnership with the family that humiliated my forebears. He helped the Landos when they sent their man to Mexico, the man who killed my father. I will do everything in my power to bring El Romero down. And when he falls, the Landos will fall and I will have achieved my life's goal."

There was silence as Rivenza considered what he'd been told. "It is true that Luiz Reyas was killed. That much I know. But how do I know you are who you say you are, Senor? How do I know you have not just told me a clever story?"

Luiz Reyas raised his hands. "May I, Senor?"

Rivenza nodded. "I am watching every move."

"I have something to show you." Luiz reached into his jacket pocket and pulled out a wallet that opened out to show photographs at the same age of himself, his father and his grand-father. "Tell me, Senor, that we are not all called Luiz Reyas?"

The three men looked almost identical. Rivenza nodded. "I must believe you are who you say you are. But tell me, why are you with the Soto?"

"It is nothing I wanted to choose. But to overcome evil, you must be close to evil."

Satisfied, Rivenza turned his gaze towards Miles. "And the *gringo*? Why is he here?"

"He has his own reasons, just as strong as my own."

"Then let him talk."

Miles told how he'd been responsible for sending his brother's wife, Julia, to Florence where she'd been abused by the Lando family. He spoke of the anguish of the past three years when he heard she'd been imprisoned and raped. "You see, Senor, I have every reason to see the pride of my family restored by bringing down the Lando family. There is nothing to be gained in implicating you in Town Lake and everything in implicating El Romero."

Johnny Rivenza thought long and hard, holding the gun on his captives the whole time. There were moments when the gun hand twitched that convinced Miles and Luiz he'd decided to kill them there and then. But as each moment passed, it became clear that what had been offered was too good to turn down. "I am convinced, Senors. Not just by what you say. More that you have risked your lives in coming to Juarez today. No man would do that unless he had a good reason." He paused long enough to smile. "And, you are right, moving in on El Romero, taking over his business, is the *everything* you promised it to be."

He called his men in. They brought up the SUV for the ride to an outbuilding on the furthest reaches of the ranch. Inside, Rivenza prized open one of the dozen steel drums. "Plastic from Libya. From the time when you could get as much as you want, before the changes." He scooped up a handful of the explosive. "This is the material supplied to the German in Austin." He placed the sample in a linen bag and handed it to Luiz Reyas. "Use this well, Senor. If it does what you say, this will be a great day for us all. If not, I will find you and kill you."

Chapter 41

When the journey resumed and we pulled back onto the Autostrada, I returned to our conversation. "Nico, so, can I take it we trust each other now?"

He checked there were no speed cameras on the next stretch of road and powered the Alfa Romeo up to 140 km/hr. "I understand what you have been through, James. Forgive me for testing you. I had to be sure."

There was an awkward silence that I filled by asking him about his work. "Your card says *comparative religion*. That's what you study at the university?"

"Amongst friends, as now, James, I have to say it is a convenient title. It is what I teach. It is what I examine my students in. What I research is something different. I study myth, in particular the point where belief in myth leads certain people into secrecy."

"You mean secret societies?"

"Yes. I'm interested in the point where people, sometimes clever, well-educated people, cross that line. It is why I am headed for Puglia. To carry on with that work."

He continued like any academic unable to conceal his enthusiasm for his work. "Stop me if I digress, James. My work shows it is not uncommon to discover those who have crossed the line and live out as truth what I call the logic of their madness. There is a price being paid day on day for this thing that makes us what we are – the most successful creature on this Earth. Somehow, we have won the battle to prevail over a world that in its nature was, is and will remain hostile to us. In our distant past we found the will to survive when life was short and the people around us died of famine and plague and natural disaster, the causes of which we could not know. Something fundamental in holding on to that will to survive remains within us all and reveals itself in the power of myth. Think of it as natural selection at the level of a psychology that, if we are not careful, can make any or all of us into crusaders and jihadists or torturers and fanatics in the name of what we believe. An inbuilt, inherited tendency. And sometimes that leads to the crossing of the line into the inner logic of a collective madness."

When I did not reply, he continued. "Don't be shocked, James. You see, I study the extremes. Where myth strays over into madness, a madness most often hidden in secret societies where fellow travellers meet to feed their arrogance and desire for self-importance – matters that, in our weakest moments, make us all potential fodder for those who wish to exploit this fact of what we are, what we have become."

I struggled to find an adequate reply. "It's hard to take much joy from that."

He smiled and cast a boyish glance around the interior of the Giulietta. "On the contrary, James. Nothing the crusaders or jihadists have to offer could lead to a world like this. I celebrate each day the freedom from these shadows of the past that allows us to live life as we choose and as we should. And I defend to the last the fragile crust of enlightenment that allows us to do it."

"So why are you telling me this, Nico?"

He smiled again. "I think you know why. It is what I do. It is why Signora DeFrancesco sent you to me. And why I'm taking you to Puglia."

"You're saying Alfieri Lando was more than a criminal, more than a sadist and a rapist?"

"That is an assertion I do not have enough clear evidence for as yet. The early signs are clear but since the world he inhabited was so secretive, it may remain that way."

"Unless we can discover otherwise?"

"Indeed. And you arrived at a fortunate time, James. The colleague I will be meeting in Ostuni, Arndt Schreiber, may help."

"You don't know what Lando was involved with?"

"No. But I can make a good guess at a general level."

He was in danger of losing me again. "It sounds academic."

"It is. Remember, it is what I do."

"So how does that help?"

"Let me begin this way, James. This is a religious country. You will have seen the signs all around you. In the churches. In the festivals in which the people take pride in remembering the events of the past. And their religion is sometimes old. Older than you may think."

"Isn't that what people come here for?"

He smiled. "Yes. So, let me tell you about Greek and Roman religion. What it was like."

"Wasn't it pagan?"

"Yes, but that is a catchall phrase and does not say much."

He paused to consider what he would say next and then continued. "You mentioned twins. The ancient religions have a great deal to say about them."

I feared this was the start of one of his lectures but the feeling did not last long. Right from the start, what he had to say went to the heart of the problems facing me and my family.

He told me about the twins who were the offspring of Leda.

As he spoke, my thoughts went to the image of Michelangelo's *Leda and the Swan*, sent to my phone by Julia as she was being abducted by Alfieri Lando. And I recalled what Zella DeFrancesco had told me in Venice.

I needed to understand why everything happening to my family and those around us kept coming back to that painting and what it represented.

I'd puzzled about the meaning of the painting and had asked all the right questions concerning Julia's treatment at the hands of Lando. But now Ferrara began telling me about the symbolism of what happened *after* Leda had been seduced.

"You see, the ancient myths told that Zeus disguised himself as a swan and seduced Leda on the same night she slept with her husband, Tyndareus. And that had consequences. Have you seen the painting of *Leda and the Swan* by Da Vinci?"

I shook my head.

"It shows Leda after she has given birth. Da Vinci shows her standing beside the swan. They are like two proud parents, looking down on their offspring, just hatched from two eggs. There is a set of twins emerging from each of the broken shells. There are girl twins, Helen and Clytemnestra, and boy twins, Castor and Pollux. This is the important point, James. In each pair of twins, one is immortal, gaining their power from the god Zeus, and the other is mortal, blessed with this from their mortal father Tyndareus. Helen is immortal. Clytemnestra will have to die like every other human. They were worshipped as gods by Greece and by Rome, together with Zeus and Leda who produced them."

"And Castor and Pollux?"

"They are also an immortal-mortal pair and are also worshiped. In the myths concerning them, Castor dies and Pollux offers to give up his immortality if his brother can live again. Zeus agrees and places them in the heavens as twin stars in the constellation Gemini."

I was working hard to keep up with him. "The Michelangelo shows the act of seduction while the Da Vinci shows the outcome. Two sets of twins. Each pair with one mortal, the other immortal?"

"Yes. But the paintings show nothing more than what is recounted in the myth, as it was known in ancient Greece and Rome. The fact of the matter is that twins are everywhere in ancient mythology. Twins and the mortal-immortal duality run right through the religions of the world. There's a strong parallel of *Leda and the Swan* in Hindu religion. Brahma, the creator and

Saraswati, the goddess of knowledge, produced the swan Hamsa which represents the union of opposites, the mortal-immortal. The Egyptians have Isis and Osiris. The Celts have their own discoursi. The Germans have Siegmund and Sieglinde."

"What does this mean?"

"It is myth. It allows for as many interpretations as you care to make. It is nothing like our cause-and-effect take on meaning. Myth operates on the dark, subconscious level of who we only sometimes admit we are and things we do not understand, like why we must die. And at the same time it works on the level of statehood, why these people are living in this place and claim the right to call this place their own. And many other interpretations in between. It has truth value on many different levels all at the same time with no one meaning besting the others."

"You're telling me this has to do with what Lando was involved with?"

"I believe it does. You see, James, just as these ideas are old, so those that have been led to believe in them trace their origins back through the centuries. And in a world where you could be hanged for going against the prevailing orthodoxy, those ideas had to be held in secret. In secret societies."

"It's hard to believe there's anyone around today who believes this as truth?"

He disagreed. "I don't think that is a wise assumption to make."

There was a pause as he concentrated on steering the Alfa Romeo round a long bend at speed.

He resumed as soon as the Autostrada straightened out. "Let me ask you a question, James. Why do you think Michelangelo and Da Vinci painted those pictures?"

I didn't know. "I agree it's not the most obvious subject matter."

"But it was logical for them. Both were journeymen. Both produced what their rich sponsors would pay for. It's easy to forget the dark times when knowledge of the ancient world was suppressed. What happened in Florence in the Renaissance was a rediscovery of what had been denied for centuries. The availability of writing by men like Ovid ignited an imagination that fed on the myths of the ancient world. And what more natural than to celebrate such freedom in great paintings? This was an inspiration to men and women of genius. Yet, in the minds of others, it was a stimulus to cross the line from enlightenment to madness."

"But maybe no more than one in a million."

"You might think so, James, but back in the seventeenth and eighteenth centuries, hundreds of thousands joined the secret societies springing up all over Europe. Many were a cover for political and social demands outlawed by the ruling monarchies and churches but as many were involved in deeper and darker matters such as alchemy and what today we would call the occult. And though every attempt was made to keep matters secret by remaining hidden and using elaborate encryption devices for any material that had to be written down, the more we discover about these societies the more we are surprised by the real evil pursued in so many of them."

When I still didn't look convinced, he continued. "Let me give you an example nearer to your home, James. Everyone knows your Isaac Newton was a genius, though we Italians would not agree that he was the first to discover all the things you English say he did. One of the things we would agree on, as everyone knows, is he discovered that light can be separated into the colours of the rainbow. Right?"

I nodded. "Of course."

"But did you also know that Newton decided there should be seven colours of the rainbow because he wanted there to be seven? Of all the colours in the spectrum, there is no good reason to make a point of including blue, indigo *and* violet since, as we now know, the spectrum of light is continuous, but he wanted seven colours because seven was for him a magic number, an occult number. The world was arranged in sevens for him. So he established as a fact there are seven colours in the rainbow and we still hold to that today, as every schoolchild will tell you. You would not call this the action of a rational architect. The fact is Newton practiced alchemy and occult knowledge derived from the ancients. Did you know that on his death his family attempted to conceal many of the writings he had made in the last forty years of his life because what was in them would have shocked the public?"

I took that as rhetorical. "And you're implying that in thinking like this, Newton was not untypical of his day?"

"Indeed, as I was saying, there was a huge upsurge in those seeking what they saw as truths denied to them in mainstream life. In secret societies of all descriptions. And not all for the worst, either. Much of what we have discovered so far points to the societies as necessary cover for men seeking change for the better – men like Tom Paine, Benjamin Franklin and George Washington. And many more of the societies were simple vehicles for self-advancement. It is the rump, those bent on evil that my work concentrates on."

We were approaching a traffic tailback. Illuminated signs above the Autostrada warned that speed should be reduced to no more than 70 km/hr. He swore again in Italian and resigned himself to reducing speed and taking his place in the line.

I spoke next. "This is the reason why Zella DeFrancesco sent me to you?"

"You are right, James."

"She told you what she knew about Alfieri Lando?"

He nodded. "But I did not know your wife had been involved with him. You must know how sorry I was to hear that."

My head was spinning. "You're saying Lando was part of a secret society. One that ensnared Julia and her twin sister?"

"I believe it could be the case."

"And the myth of Leda is central to it?"

"It is a possibility. I can say no more than that. Signora DeFrancesco said that Lando had the painting. Michelangelo's *Leda and the Swan*. She saw it. It was part of Lando's ritual. In debasing your wife, he may have been living out the myth as his own way of crossing the line into madness. But without more evidence, it can be no more than an informed speculation. Signora DeFrancesco would add nothing more. Nothing that points to a wider conspiracy."

I took a deep breath. "Nico, I may have the evidence, or something pointing towards it. Zella DeFrancesco did tell me more than she told you when I met her in Venice. She said I would find this difficult and, believe me, I do. It's something I'd rather not talk about, even here with you."

He turned to look at me, his eyes averted from the road for longer than was safe before he returned his attention to the highway. "Then, James, let me assure you anything you say will be in complete confidence. You have my word. You can speak without fear."

My stomach tightened as I let him know Zella DeFrancesco had admitted to me her role in the rape of Julia, how she had acted as a handmaiden as Alfieri Lando had acted out the role of the disguised Zeus.

"So, Signora DeFrancesco left you in no doubt he was living out the Leda myth?"

"Yes, she was clear on this."

"Then it is indeed important we met today, James."

I thought back to what Ferrara had been saying about the importance of twins in mythology. "The fact that he raped both Julia and her twin sister, that's also important?"

"Indeed. It fits a pattern."

"I need to know more."

"You will, James. When we arrive, you will meet Arndt Schreiber. He will have more hard evidence." He paused and then resumed. "Not that this makes any of this any easier for you or your family, James. Once again, I have to let you know you have my full sympathy for the pain caused by all that has happened."

I understood his concern to be his way of making it clear he would not want to benefit from the tragedy that had led to Emelia's death and the trauma suffered by Julia. "I understand, Nico, and I thank you. But what is important now is we stop this before any more innocent lives are ruined. That's what Zella DeFrancesco wants above anything else and it's what I'm determined to bring about, with your help."

We fell into silence as Ferrara increased speed further on a clear stretch of road.

The green Autostrada sign that passed overhead announced that Bari was just thirty-two kilometres distant.

"We are getting close, James."

Ferrara pulled into the exit lane of the highway.

"We are almost there. Time to take the road to Ostuni."

We pulled up to the ticket machine at the Bari Nord exit. Ferrara poked in the biglietto he'd picked up on entering the road system and waited for the bill.

He grimaced as he caught sight of the charge. "Forty-seven euro. They rob us!" He paid with a card.

Pulling off the Autostrada, we travelled another sixty miles along a coastal road running high above the Adriatic with views over the sea before we headed back inland via Fasano. As we approached across a hot, flat plain, the White City, the medieval town of Ostuni, came into view ahead, dazzling bright in the late evening sunshine.

Day 4

September 5th

Chapter 42

We waited to meet Arndt Schreiber in a small cafe on one of the narrow streets of Ostuni where the morning sun brightened the surrounding whitewashed walls.

Before the man arrived, Ferrara had something to tell me. "Arndt will not like your being here. He is a driven man and hates the unexpected. I am afraid you come into that category."

I was not surprised. "There wasn't time to warn him?"

"No, James, I chose not to do that in case he decided not to come."

"You say he's a driven man?"

"There is something else you need to know. He had a brother, Max. He was lost to one of the societies. Schreiber drives himself hard to right that wrong."

"He works with you in your research?"

"I would like to say *yes* but for him it is more than that. He does what he does for the memory of his brother."

When Arndt Schreiber arrived and saw me seated at the cafe table with Ferrara, his first action was to walk away. Ferrara went after him and convinced him to come back.

As Schreiber sat down, he wouldn't look at me. He was still complaining. "Nico, you said nothing about another at our meeting."

Ferrara tried to calm him. "As I have tried to tell you, I have spoken with Signor Blake at length. He is someone you should get to know. He can help in our work."

Schreiber continued as if I wasn't there. "And you can vouch for him. With complete confidence?"

"Yes, Arndt. You have nothing to fear. I can promise you he is genuine. You have my word."

Schreiber relaxed as he heard more of my reason for being there. He said little but I could see he was analysing with care everything I said. His interest increased when he heard of Julia's role in art conservation and her search for hidden masterpieces. He could not stop himself from intervening when he heard what had happened to Julia at the hands of Alfieri Lando.

"She was a victim of his?"

I nodded.

He looked me in the eye for the first time. "There is much I could say about Lando. Yet, I doubt if there is anything that would take away her pain."

Ferrara could see that Schreiber was accepting me and sought to cement that by saying something about the man's background. "James, you are in the company of a brave man who shares a similar goal to you. He has a reason as strong as your own to see that justice is done. Though they have threatened to kill him, he has been working to expose the dark truth about the secret societies."

Schreiber nodded. "As every month goes by I discover more. I dig deeper into their past. And the further back I go into their history, the closer I get to understanding how one day they can be eliminated. As a German, and one who is proud of his country, none of the recent past is easy for me." He glanced at Ferrara. "But then, I tell myself the distant past there is no credit to Italy or England either."

I asked him to tell me what he meant.

He began by taking me back to what I'd told him. "You said you wanted to understand the evil of Alfieri Lando. I can tell you such base motivation is not achieved in a single step. It is passed from generation to generation, from father and mother to son and daughter."

He looked away and then back at Ferrara and me. "But there is not time for this now. There is someone I want you both to meet. Her name is Gina McKenzie."

Chapter 43

One of the Italians could be eliminated but the others, Bandini and Asputi, were right in John Hendricks' line of sight for the murders of Mark Craig and DI Reid.

Bandini had been quick to demand a lawyer to represent him. Someone from Italy. It had meant a delay while the lawyer was contacted but the wait was worthwhile. Hendricks had the men bang to rights. The interview room was ready.

He recognised the lawyer at once. It was Herbert Santoni, the smooth operator who represented the Landos in Florence. This was the man who allowed Alessa Lando to walk free at her trial when the Lando family structure was being dismantled. The kind of operator Hendricks hated.

Hendricks sat facing Bandini and the lawyer and addressed the in room recorder. "Inspector John Hendricks interviewing Luigi Bandini accompanied by his legal representative Herbert Santoni. 10.32 AM, 5th September."

He concentrated his gaze on Bandini. "Tell me, Mr. Bandini, what a man of your reputation is doing here in London?"

Bandini did not reply. Santoni had briefed him to remain silent. The lawyer answered instead. "Look at the condition of my client, Inspector. He has been beaten. You are going to tell me it was not the British police and I am going to tell you I do not accept this."

"Believe me, Mr. Santoni, it is just how we found your client. He's been as well cared for as you would expect."

Santoni laughed. "You would take me for a fool if I told you I agree with you, Inspector. I have instructed my client to say nothing until this matter is resolved. His arrest was improper. He and his colleagues, Signor Asputi and Signor Carlucci, are the victims of police brutality. I demand they are allowed to return to Italy at once."

Hendricks took his time to reply, savouring the moment. "Very well, Mr. Santoni. But be aware whether your clients provide statements or not, I'm charging both Bandini and Asputi with the murder of Mark Craig at the Allegro Hotel and the murder of Detective Inspector Martin Reid at Highgate Wharf."

Santoni seemed unmoved. "I must ask on what grounds you make such charges?"

"The forensic evidence is compelling. Let's just say your clients have been less than careful in covering their tracks."

"We will contest every shred of the evidence as being improper in the way it was obtained."

Hendricks shook his head. "Even a lawyer of your great skill, Mr. Santoni, will find that difficult."

He went through the evidence list in his mind. The security camera footage placing the pair at the Allegro Hotel. The fingerprints and DNA of both found in Room 301 where Craig had been killed. Reid's DNA on the bloodstained iron bar found nearby when they were arrested at Wapping Wall. Enough to convict them both twice over. "We have enough evidence to charge your clients. They have the right of silence. Since they wish to exercise that right, there is nothing more to be said."

There was no immediate challenge from Santoni.

Hendricks spoke once more into the in-room recorder. "Interview ended at 10.52 AM."

He pressed the alarm. Two uniformed officers and DI Franklin came in. "Take Signor Bandini away, Franklin. Read him his rights and charge him with the murder of Martin Craig and DI Martin Reid. Same charges for Signor Asputi."

Santoni protested as Bandini was muscled away by the officers. "This will become a diplomatic incident, Inspector. I trust you are ready for that. You will hear from the Italian Ambassador."

This was no more than Hendricks expected. It would be a fight but he would see them both convicted.

It could have been a piece of luck that the Italians had been delivered to him on a plate but the Inspector doubted that.

He returned to the incident room and listened again to the recording of the phone call directing his men to Wapping Wall. The voice he was hearing was not as clear as he would have liked but he was sure it was one he recognised.

Hendricks smiled. James Blake.

He knew if he was to prevent Santoni from getting the Italians acquitted, it was more important than ever to find Blake and make sure his evidence was heard.

Chapter 44

Nate Craven wasn't surprised his fears about Debbie Miller were being confirmed by Ashley. He'd seen the warning signs – the way she'd looked at him since the Intelligence Star ceremony, the way she'd tried to hide the change in her feelings towards him.

So, it had come to this.

He could have Miller dealt with. Given the right briefing, Ashley could be convinced to do it and make it look like an accident. And they'd get away with it. FBI Agent goes native, absconds to Mexico, is found dead there in some drugs-related attack – yes, it was a story easily sold. But this wasn't the priority. Not yet. The priority was to find out if she was a risk to the version of events at Town Lake that Craven had spun.

These thoughts gave Craven the idea that he required another source of information in Tijuana.

He picked up the phone and waited for the connection. "El Romero. We should talk."

The man did not sound pleased. "It has been too long, Senor."

Craven was used to the formalities burdening their conversations. He knew he would have to tolerate them in order to arrive at what he needed to say to the Mexican. El Romero obsessed about the amount of money Craven demanded for policing the shipments to the US. Craven's answer was always the same: top-level protection commanded a top-level price. It was the way of the world. El Romero didn't like it. Craven made it clear he could not deliver for less. There were payoffs to be made. El Romero complained but had no choice but to accept. It was the same each time they spoke.

As the formalities showed no sign of reaching a conclusion, Craven decided it was time to make progress. "Well, my friend, I have to tell you my call isn't about money. It's about something more important. I need your help with something that could affect our business together."

"What do you mean, Senor?"

"There are persons in Tijuana you should know about. One is FBI. The other a journalist."

"The names?"

"The agent is Debbie Miller. The journalist goes by the name of Blake. Miles Blake. I can tell you where to find them."

"You want me to remove them?"

"Not yet. We need to know *why* they are there. Blake has been investigating what he would call the drugs problem. It could be that. But I have a hunch it could be something more. Tell me what you know about Town Lake?"

El Romero was defensive. "Why would you be interested in anything I know about that, Senor?"

"Because I think it's where Miller is coming from and she's searching for a new angle. And if she is, why is she down in Tijuana?"

"I will make enquiries, Senor."

El Romero would say no more. By the time Craven ended the call, he was more convinced than ever the Mexican was hiding something.

Craven called up the FBI database and began to search for information on Wolfgang Heller, the one he knew must have been the real perpetrator of the Town Lake atrocity. The details were slight. The German had been observed breaking into the Ravitz home in San Diego before he went to Austin. And, what was this? A report that earlier Heller had been seen in Tijuana. This fact, together with the feeling that El Romero was holding something back, was a connection to cause concern. The kind

172

of thing that could explain why Debbie Miller had gone to Tijuana.

He delved further into the database. It led him to the discovery of another connection. Heller had been in Sollicciano prison at the same time as Matteo Lando. The same Matteo Lando who'd been under FBI surveillance in relation to the importation of cocaine into Europe from Tijuana. The same Lando family that did business with El Romero. No wonder the Mexican had been defensive.

Craven closed the database link. What was happening in Tijuana had the potential to expose the real cause of the Town Lake deaths and blow apart the drugs operation at the same time.

A further thought came to Craven. James Blake. It was too much of a coincidence that Blake's brother was now in Tijuana when there were known connections between both Blakes and the Lando family.

The request to Europol for the detention of James Blake had produced no response as yet. Craven resolved to put more pressure on the European authorities to deliver.

Meanwhile, he knew the next move he made in Tijuana would be crucial.

Chapter 45

With frequent stops to allow oncoming vehicles to pass, Ferrara took the Giulietta through the anonymous narrow white streets of Ostuni, guided by Schreiber from the front passenger seat while I sat in the back. When we arrived at the small central square, Piazza della Liberta, Schreiber signalled we should stop. "This is as far as we go."

He led us along Via Roma, past the small church of Spirito Santo, until we came to a narrow alleyway leading off the street and up labyrinthine stone staircases taking us higher into the heart of this part of the medieval city.

Schreiber paused at the doorway of one of the multistory houses perched on the still-rising hillside. "You can see why I have chosen this place. Somewhere difficult to find." He paused to glance up and down the narrow alleyway before continuing. "I found her just in time. In Florence. Working the streets. I had to smuggle her away. They threatened to kill her if she left."

He took a key from his pocket and opened the door. Before we went on up the steep flight of stairs leading to the apartments above, Schreiber made us pause again. "May I ask you both to understand that if the person you are going to meet appears distressed, there is a good reason. Her emotions are raw because of what she has been through. I ask you to respect that and allow her to tell you as much or as little as she wishes."

When we arrived at the top of the last flight of the stairs we came to a small apartment crammed into the uppermost floor of the building. Schreiber called out in a reassuring voice. "Gina. It's Arndt. I have some people I would like you to meet."

The room was clean but lacking enough ventilation to cope with the heat that remained in this part of Italy in early September.

She sat on a low couch facing us, saying nothing, watching as we came in. She was small, vulnerable, not long past her teens. She wore her silence as protection against a world that had turned against her.

Schreiber showed us to seats at an old wooden table beneath the solitary window and continued to try to put her at her ease. "I want you to meet Professor Nico Ferrara. He's here to help."

Ferrara smiled but added nothing.

"And I want you to meet James Blake. He has a story to tell. One very much like yours."

She took interest in this. "You will help me find my sister?"

I was trying to place her accent. It was Canadian, perhaps. No, American. East Coast. "You can trust me. I'll do everything I can to help."

We talked for over an hour. Schreiber and Ferrara remained silent as the conversation passed back and forth between myself and Gina. She was being wary. I needed to win her trust so she would begin to open up about what had happened to bring her here.

I told her I knew how she must be feeling, separated from her sister.

She responded to that. "How could you know? Have you lost a sister? A twin sister?"

I replied. "No, but my wife Julia lost a sister. It was her twin. I know what Julia has been going through coming to terms with her loss."

"So you expect me to care?"

"It was in Florence. Her sister was caught up with the Landos."

She shuddered at the mention of the Lando family. "What is the sister's name?"

"It was Emelia."

"I knew of her. I heard how she died. They used it as a lesson to us all not to run."

I nodded. "Your life and hers have parallels."

She glanced towards Arndt, recognising now he must have been talking about her before we arrived. And then she turned back to me. "That's easy for you to say. You don't know what it is like to be out there in the Oltrarno."

"I'm not second-guessing that."

"Arndt said you had a story to tell. Is this the story?"

I nodded. "Emelia was a woman very much like you."

"So you said."

"Let me remind you of her story. She was in the hands of Matteo Lando. Working the Oltrarno, unknown to her sister, Julia, my wife."

Gina flinched at the sound of the man's name. "And your wife, her twin, was also drawn to Florence?"

I nodded. "Yes. They met there for the first time. They had just a few days together."

She was beginning to trust me, knowing I had a good reason to be here. "Then she has suffered as I have suffered."

"Tell me about your sister."

"Her name is Malika. She is my twin. We grew up in upstate New York. In different families. Our parents, they were wealthy and kind and raised us as their own."

"But they didn't tell you they adopted you?"

"How do you know?"

"It's what happened to my wife. But you found out you were adopted?"

She looked away. "Yes. By accident. I needed ID for a new school. I got to see the adoption certificate."

"Did they say why they couldn't tell you about that before? Or where you were adopted from?"

"Nothing that helped. Some stuff about it being arranged through the church and some foundation that helped unwanted children, stuff I didn't want to believe. I was more concerned with the fact of being *unwanted*. I didn't adjust. I couldn't understand why my real mother had chosen to abandon me. I headed for New York. Fooled around. Did drugs. Got caught up with the street."

"So how did you get to Florence?"

"A white knight came to rescue me, to take me away from it all, to start a new life with him in Florence."

"Matteo Lando?"

"How could you know?"

"He did the same with Emelia."

"And that led me to the streets in Florence. Nothing different, just worse than in New York."

I thought again about Julia's sister, Emelia. Three years on and nothing had changed. From Sollicciano, Matteo Lando was controlling the same trade his father had established when he headed the family.

"What about your sister, Malika?"

"She adapted better than me to knowing she was adopted. Stayed in school. Trained. We found each other but our lives separated again. She worked her way up in the local restaurant business and got to manage a chain of restaurants in Saratoga Springs. That is, before she came to Florence."

"They fooled her into coming?"

"They told her I needed her to save me. From the life I'm living here. I'd kept it from her. The one bit of pride I had left and they took that away from me like everything else."

"Now she's missing."

"They have her. They took her off the street in broad daylight. Pushed her into the back of an SUV."

"You shouldn't blame yourself."

"How can you think I wouldn't? But for me, she wouldn't be there."

"It's not your fault. It's what they do. It's what happened to Julia and her sister."

I turned to Ferrara and Schreiber who'd been listening in silence. I apologised to Gina and asked them to join me on the stairs with the door closed, outside of Gina's hearing. "I have to ask her an important but difficult question. How far should I go?"

Schreiber was clear. "She is distressed, so be careful. But if I read well what you mean, she is an experienced woman. You should put away the coyness of the English."

Back in the room, I pressed on. "Gina. Please don't be offended if I ask you this and please be aware it's difficult for me."

She stared back. "Ask."

It took Julia three years to be able to tell me what Alfieri Lando had subjected her to. Now I needed Gina to tell me what she herself had suffered when the events were still close at hand. "If I told you my wife had been defiled by a man in a red cape and mask, would that mean anything to you?"

"Defiled? Are you being polite to spare me?"

"Raped, then."

She looked back with unlowered eyes. "Yes they did that to me. As you describe."

"Who?"

"A special client. After Matteo was sent to prison. A man who could not hide his age or his Englishness, no matter what the disguise."

"Where?"

"In a special apartment in Florence. Close to the Arno. On a special chair."

"And your sister? You fear the same will happen to her?"

"It has already happened, Mr. Blake. They tried to keep it from me but I found out what they'd done. And that they planned to do it again. It's why I contacted Arndt, seeking a way out for my sister. When they knew I'd spoken with him they said they'd kill me. But I know them well enough by now. They wanted to give me time to know real fear before they finished me. It's the way they treat women like me. That's why I'm still here. Their delight in making it a fearful death gave Arndt the chance to get me away."

She looked at Schreiber. "The women of Oltrarno thought he was weird. Befriending them yet not for sex. Seeking out twins. Now I know he is a good man seeking to help people like me."

I knew Gina was going to be important in helping me and she had been brave in being this open and honest when she was so concerned about her own safety and that of her sister. I didn't want to put pressure on her too soon.

I was about to turn towards Ferrara and Schreiber to thank them for bringing me to Gina when there was the sound of a commotion from the apartments below.

When Schreiber opened the apartment door, black smoke poured in and began to fill the room.

The building was on fire.

Chapter 46

Craven's call disturbed El Romero. The warnings the Mexican had given Alessa Lando about recent events bringing them all down were in danger of becoming a reality.

He wished now he hadn't indulged Matteo Lando when he'd come to him requesting help with Wolfgang Heller's visit to Tijuana. This was what came of a moment of weakness in honouring the loyalty he felt to Alfieri, Matteo's father. El Romero should have cut the ties. But it was too late. Now he must act and act at once.

El Romero picked up the phone and called Alessa Lando. "It is as I feared, Senora. The first of the Americans is here. FBI. There will be more to come if we do not stop this thing now."

Alessa did not sound pleased. "How do you expect me to help?"

"Tell Matteo that Nate Craven is our weakest link. Tell him one of the Blakes is here. The one by the name of Miles."

She could be heard struggling to hide an upsurge of anger at the sound of the Blake name. "They are a curse on this family and all we do. Yes, I will tell Matteo. But you know what he will say. No more loose ends. Remove Blake and all who have anything to do with him." Alessa Lando ended the call without saying anything more.

El Romero called Ramirez into the office. In truth, Ramirez was no replacement for Luiz Reyas, the best lieutenant he'd ever had. But Ramirez was effective enough and knew when his boss was angry. He showed this by approaching El Romero with his shirt sleeves rolled up to display the more than one hundred star tattoos on each forearm, saying, look at me, El Romero, I have killed all these men for you and I am just as good as Luiz Reyas ever was.

When Ramirez opened his mouth to speak he showed off the gold and diamond work he'd spent so much on. "You asked for me, El Romero?"

"You can see my anger, Philipo. There is FBI here in my town I know nothing about. There is an English journalist in my town I know nothing about. How many do we pay for information?"

"More than most, Senor."

"Then why do we not know about this?"

"You have the names?"

El Romero nodded. "Find them and take them to the safe place. I wish to ask them why they are here."

Chapter 47

Choose the best way to achieve the objective. This was Wolfgang Heller's firm intention, no matter what others might advise. If arson was the most dependable means, why deny it?

These old Ostuni buildings with their whitewashed walls might look charming to the eye but it didn't take much to realise they were firetraps.

Blake was naive to think he could travel anywhere in Italy and keep it secret, the more so if he was carrying a phone given to him by the Florence Questura. Didn't he know Matteo Lando had a man there? Shouldn't he have guessed he would let them know where Blake was headed?

Heller smiled. It was yet another wonder of the modern world. With a GPS-enabled phone you could determine the carrier's location to an accuracy of a few meters. That's what had enabled Blake to be followed all the way from Padova, though Heller had been forced to drive the BMW 3 Series they'd given him at speeds greater than he would have regarded as safe. That's what had led him to the firetrap in Ostuni that Blake had entered with two men an hour ago.

The good thing about arson was that the means to carry it out were always at hand. The spare fuel Heller kept in the boot of his vehicle was the ideal accelerant. The door to the building had a convenient letter box. There was no one in the narrow alleyway. It was simple to pour the petroleum in, wait a few moments for the vapor to spread and then toss in the lighted match.

It was a marvel how the flames spread throughout the staircase at such speed, how the choking black smoke billowed throughout the building.

Heller took up position at the end of the alleyway, his weapon readied to take aim when the survivors struggled out.

If they managed to make it out, he'd shoot Blake dead.

If he remained inside, he would die anyway. And with him, the girl.

Chapter 48

I grabbed Gina by the hand and pushed her towards the door of the apartment. "It's no use staying here. The smoke will kill us long before the fire has any effect."

She was crying. "We won't get out. The stairs are a death trap. I'm staying here."

I looked across the room for Ferrara and Schreiber but the smoke was so dense I couldn't see them. Ferrara was shouting, "Make for the stairs. It's the only chance."

Gina pulled at my arm, directing me towards the small window over the kitchen sink. "It's sealed and doesn't open. Smash it."

My lungs were filling with toxic gas; it was difficult to breath let alone answer.

The apartment was all of one hundred and fifty feet above street level so that even if we could get out through the window, there would be nowhere to go. But there might be a ledge, somewhere we could cling to in the hope of rescue before the flames engulfed the apartment. In any event, there would be fresh air out there. Anything seemed preferable to following Ferrara and Schreiber down the stairs.

I searched for something heavy to smash the window. I lifted one of the kitchen chairs. I hurled it at the window with all the force I could muster. The chair bounced off. The window would not break no matter how many times I smashed the chair against it.

I struggled to shout back to Gina. "It's a plastic window. It's cheaper than glass. It's unbreakable."

Her face came close to mine and I could see her features for a moment. The crying had stopped. She was calm; sure she was going to die.

Flames rushed in from the stairwell and began to advance across the apartment at speed.

I soaked a towel in water and wrapped it around Gina's face, leaving just her eyes exposed. I did the same.

She had become limp, unresponsive, as if she wanted to stay there and let the flames take her.

I took her arm and pulled her behind me through the flames and towards the stairwell.

We clattered down the stairs, holding our breath until our lungs were about to burst.

Chapter 49

Heller watched as the first of the survivors emerged from the building, coughing and wheezing, falling down onto the ground and gasping for air.

Yes, arson was most effective.

Yet these were locals, almost certainly from the lower floors of the building. No sign of his target yet. Perhaps Blake was trapped on one of the upper levels. Perhaps he would die there and save Heller the trouble of firing a bullet into his brain when he came out.

Here came two more. Two he didn't recognise but who looked more like they didn't belong in this town. Yes, the two accomplices of Blake seen entering the building with him.

But still no sign of his man. Or the girl.

Minutes passed. The building was alight. There was the sound of emergency vehicles on their way, distant now but getting ever closer.

Still no sign of Blake.

Heller was on the point of putting away the rifle when two more survivors crashed out onto the street, their clothing steaming as they met the cooler air outside.

When they removed the coverings from their faces and began coughing and drawing in lungfuls of fresh air, Heller could see that one of them was indeed the target he had travelled halfway across the world to kill. And, yes, the girl was with him.

Heller lined up the rifle sights and prepared to pull the trigger.

At this range, James Blake was an easy target.

Chapter 50

We'd made it out.

Into clean air.

Away from the blinding smoke.

My lungs were about to burst. There was searing pain from the act of breathing itself. Everything depended on that simple act you took for granted ten thousand times a day. But now the simple act of filling the lungs with air was a slow motion exercise in pain.

Yet somehow I managed to breathe and with every whooping breath, the pain lessened and I was able to realise we had escaped.

I looked for Gina. She was nearby, struggling for breath like me.

Arndt Schreiber was with her, caring for her. Ferrara was nearby, recovering from the ordeal.

I moved towards them, still in pain, moving at a slow pace.

I had a fleeting sense of being watched from afar but shook it off. I wanted to know Gina was safe but smoke inhalation had weakened me. As I struggled to move further, I slipped and fell.

A shot rang out. It missed me and continued on, hitting Schreiber in the throat.

I rolled on the ground and placed my body on top of Gina as more shots came in.

She was covered in Schreiber's blood.

Chapter 51

Heller cursed.

At the moment he had the Blake target dead and buried, the man had somehow fallen out of sight and the bullet had struck another. One of the others who had emerged from the apartment. One of the visitor types. One of Blake's accomplices.

And now in the commotion caused by the unsuccessful first shot, Heller was being denied a clear shot at Blake.

He thought back to East Texas. How he'd had Blake in his sights more than once and how events had conspired to allow the man to escape. Perhaps Heller was destined never to be able to kill this man who was so much the antithesis of himself. So weak where he was so strong. So unpractised in killing where he was so knowledgeable. So lacking in the life energy that infused Heller's mind and body.

Perhaps that was it. Something was preventing him from killing the man because he was his perfect opposite. The matter to his antimatter that would result in annihilation if the two came together.

The next three shots had missed their target.

Blake was still alive.

The girl was nowhere to be seen.

Time to leave as police and firefighters were arriving.

Chapter 52

I looked over towards Ferrara who was trying to revive Arndt Schreiber with chest compression. He stopped pumping and lowered his head. "He's lost too much blood. He's gone."

Firefighters in fluorescent red uniforms moved in and cleared a path to allow them to inspect the burning apartment block. They soon deduced there was no prospect of sending in any of their own; the blaze was so intense and so well established there was no hope of survivors inside. A second team came forward and started injecting foam into the apartment to choke the flames.

Gina stared down at her bloodstained and scorched clothes and couldn't seem to control the shaking in her limbs. "I thought I'd be safe here. I should have known nowhere is safe from them."

I tried to calm her. "You're going to be OK. You're in shock. It will pass. We can take you somewhere safe."

"What about Arndt?"

I lied. "He'll be OK. You need to think about yourself. Getting through this."

She was crying. "I know he's dead. It's no use trying to keep it from me."

Paramedics moved in and surrounded Schreiber.

He was pronounced dead at the scene.

A female medic began attending to us. I didn't want Gina to see Schreiber zipped into a body bag. "This woman is in shock. Can you get her out of here?"

"Can you both walk?"

I nodded. "We're burned and bloodied but we're OK."

"Then we'll get you to hospital."

Gina pulled at my arm as the medic walked us towards the waiting ambulance. "I can't do this. The police will have questions at the hospital and I'll be as good as dead."

"You don't know that."

"From what you told me, you should know Italy well enough by now. Nothing stays secret for long, not even for an hour. The Landos have men everywhere. They'll know where I am and they'll come for me."

"So, what do you want to do?"

"Find Ferrara and get out of here."

What Gina was saying about the police in Ostuni was a problem I shared. I would be in as much danger as her from a Lando place man.

Gina occupied the medic by pretending she was having difficulty walking further. While she received attention, I found Ferrara further back in the line of the injured. I moved up close to him. "You're OK?"

He was less affected by smoke inhalation, having escaped the apartment before us, but he was in shock over the death of Schreiber in his arms. "First time I have seen a man die like this. A good man. Such a waste."

"But you're OK?"

"I will live. You?"

"Lungs are sore, body aches, nothing more."

"And Gina?"

"She's in shock but she'll make it. She wants you to get us out of here."

"You both need the hospital."

We were interrupted by the medic accompanying Ferrara. He was saying in Italian that I should return to my place in the line. That was good. As with many in this southern corner of Italy, he didn't speak or understand much English. I took my chance to let Ferrara know Gina's fears about going to the hospital and her need to escape.

Ferrara understood. "She could refuse treatment. We could all do that."

"But the police will want witness statements. They won't let us leave."

He managed a smile. "Then can you still run?"

"I can give it a good try."

I hobbled back towards Gina, now waiting at the open rear doors of the ambulance and about to be assisted to climb aboard. The medic had gone before her and now stood on the rear step of the vehicle, waiting to help her up. When I was close enough for her to hear, I shouted, "Let's go!"

Gina turned and began moving towards me. It was clear she was in pain but she made good progress. The medic called out in Italian for us to stop but he made no attempt to leave the vehicle. For him, this was a matter for the police and at this moment they were supporting the firefighters attempting to halt the spread of the fire to neighbouring buildings. I had time to see him pull out his phone and begin calling for assistance.

By then we were on our way, joined by Ferrara. We hobbled down the narrow alleyway in front of the burned-out apartment and made it to the stone staircases leading back down to Via Roma. Each step brought a jolt of pain to my legs and back, strained and stressed by the escape from the apartment. Movement was no less uncomfortable for Gina but Ferrara was able to help, supporting her weight by placing her arm over his shoulder and neck.

There was no sound of pursuit by the police. The medic's call had resulted in no rapid response.

Ferrara's Giulietta was where we'd left it on Piazza della Liberta. It was a welcome sight. He unlocked it by pressing the key fob as we approached and showed Gina into the back seat. I looked back, fearing a pursuit that didn't come.

I took the front passenger seat as Ferrara turned on the ignition and gunned the engine. "You're OK to drive?"

He nodded. "Let's leave."

The drive out of the old town was as slow as the journey in as the Giulietta negotiated the twisting streets and made the required stops to allow oncoming traffic to pass. All the time we feared that around the next bend a police car would be waiting, blocking our escape. But there was none. The Ostuni police were still to react.

Back on the coastal road to Fasano, Ferrara pushed up the speed. We'd escaped Ostuni.

None of us noticed the black BMW following us every kilometre of the way.

Chapter 53

The turbo-charged Giulietta was a good machine, the kind Heller would have chosen for himself but they'd given him the BMW. Following Blake and the two others he'd escaped with would be a challenge.

Heller phoned the Lando contact in the Florence Questura as he chased the Giulietta onto the approach road to the Autostrada A14, heading north.

"Ranzini. I need you to assist. I am tracking a vehicle. Let me know who I am following."

"You did not ask for this before, Signor?"

Heller disliked the way he called him *Signor*. "They were not about to get away, before, *Signor*."

He gave Ranzini the number on the Giulietta license plate and waited.

The reply came back before he'd travelled a mile further. A professor, no less. From Padova University. One by the name of Niccolo Ferrara, Professor of Comparative Religion.

Heller's flesh crawled. He hated the academics who pretended to study and teach religion when none knew anything of the real belief, the real religion that men like him and his followers breathed and made into reality each day. This Ferrara was one of them. Another to mark down as one of the enemy.

The Giulietta was pulling away from him. Not only did Ferrara have no respect for the speed limit, the Alfa Romeo had faster acceleration than the BMW and a faster top speed. Heller did not like a contest as uneven as this.

He returned to his call with Ranzini. "Give me continuous updates of the location of the Ferrara vehicle. If I lose them, I need to know where they are."

The reply came back that this was possible so long as Ranzini could remain unsuspected at the Questura monitoring terminal.

Chapter 54

She didn't see them coming. Debbie Miller had noticed the three Mexican men in brand new suits that looked like they'd just been bought to get them into the hotel but had thought little of it. It was now too late. They followed her into the elevator as she made her way back to her room and surrounded her.

The biggest of them smiled at her with a mouth full of diamonds and gold. "Senora. You will come with us. You will not shout or try anything to attract attention." He showed her the gun concealed beneath his jacket. The weapon aimed at her heart. "Many have died in this town, Senora. You do not want to be the next."

When the elevator reached the floor Debbie Miller had selected, Ramirez closed the doors again and pressed the button for the lobby. "You will walk out of the hotel with us. You will act like we are together. You understand?"

Debbie protested. "You know I'm a Federal agent. Harm me and we will hunt you down."

Ramirez pushed the muzzle of the gun tighter against her chest. "You are not the one to make threats at this moment, Senora."

They walked her out of the hotel to a waiting SUV. Ramirez sat beside her in the back with the gun pressed to her heart while his two accomplices took the front seats. Ramirez flashed the teeth again. "There is someone who would like to speak to you."

They drove beyond the city limits and through the desert until they came to a farm complex that looked like it hadn't produced a crop in years.

Debbie Miller was worried. They hadn't covered their faces. She hadn't been hooded to prevent her from knowing where they'd taken her. This all pointed to the fact that they were not planning on giving her back.

An hour earlier, Dillon Ashley had observed Agent Miller leaving her hotel with three suited Mexicans. She'd looked comfortable with them, as if they were into something together.

Ashley followed the SUV at a safe distance as it left town.

Chapter 55

Ferrara became aware that the BMW was following before I pointed it out to him. "James, it has been with us for some time."

I looked behind. Gina was curled up on the back seat. Through the rear window, I could see the BMW nearing as Ferrara slowed behind a truck that would not pull over.

I'd only seen him close enough to recognise twice before, both times in East Texas, yet it was a face I couldn't forget, even though he'd sought to change his appearance. The hair was darker, shorter, but there was no doubt it was Wolfgang Heller at the wheel of the BMW.

I shouted to Ferrara, "It's Heller. It was him at Ostuni, starting the blaze, shooting Schreiber."

Ferrara stared into the rear driver mirror. "Who is Heller?"

"All you need to know right now is that if he gets close enough to us he'll kill us."

Ferrara gunned the Giulietta to 180 km/hr, and it began to pull away from the BMW. "We won't stay ahead for long. The BMW's cruising speed is not as great as ours and we can beat it for acceleration but, unless we are lucky, there will be traffic that will slow us down to a speed he can match."

The BMW disappeared from sight as we pulled further away.

Ferrara was thinking fast. "If we stay far enough ahead, we will try to lose him at the next exit, pull late off the highway and leave him to assume we have continued straight on."

The green overhead sign told us that the exit to Fasano was approaching in 2 kilometres. Ferrara accelerated further. As the exit approached the BMW was still out of sight behind us. At the last minute, Ferrara switched late across lanes and took the Fasano exit at speed. He circled the next roundabout and pulled up on the lane used to join the Autostrada from Fasano and waited.

We had a clear view of the traffic on the northward bound A14. If Heller had not observed our leaving the highway, we would see him pass below us, continuing on north.

We held our breath.

Heller's BMW passed beneath us.

It was twenty miles to the next exit. When Heller realised what had happened, we would be well on our way.

We had lost him.

Ferrara circled back on the slip road and we began to make our way into Fasano.

I was feeling better. "That worked, Nico. What do you plan next? Is there a route north not using the Autostrada?"

He nodded. "Yes, we can use the old roads between the towns that were used before the Autostrada was built. It will take longer, but it will be safer."

I told Ferrara what I knew about Wolfgang Heller, that he was the Lando henchman who had tried to kill me in East Texas.

We journeyed through the centre of Fasano and on towards Locorotondo, a twenty mile trip.

The BMW was waiting for us on the outskirts of town.

Ferrara made a sudden U-turn, risking our lives and those in the vehicles oncoming in the opposite lane.

He pushed the Giulietta to maximum speed as we headed back towards Fasano, swapping lanes, weaving between slower vehicles.

Heller followed, gaining on us as we were slowed by delivery trucks ahead.

Ferrara was shouting, "He knows where we are. How did he find us again? He must have some means of tracking us."

I was thinking. If a tracker was fitted to the Giulietta, it would explain how Heller had traced us to Ostuni. "Something fitted to the car?"

He shook his head. "That's not possible. I had the Giulietta checked before I picked it up. Something else?"

The truth was dawning. I could feel the phone in my pocket growing in size, taking on the aura of an alien object. The phone Manieri had given me to use to report back to him. The phone he was using to monitor my whereabouts.

I took the phone out, showed it to Ferrara. "The Florence police gave me this."

Ferrara took his eyes off the road for a long moment and gave me a withering stare. "James. Tell me about the phone."

As soon as I began his driving became more erratic as he realised what I was saying, causing him to remove first his left and then his right hand from the steering wheel to gesticulate. "And you did not think to tell me you are wanted by the police?"

I was trying to come to terms with my role in what had happened. If I hadn't travelled south with Ferrara and hadn't been this foolish in not realising the phone Manieri had given me could be used as a tracker, there would have been no fire in the apartment in Ostuni. Gina would still have a safe hiding place. Arndt Schreiber would still be alive. "I had it switched off. I don't see how it could be used to track us. I only turned it on when I needed to call in."

Ferrara sighed. "A pity then, James, you did not know that such a phone can be altered to give off a signal, even if as far as you know it is not turned on. It just needs a second, hidden power source; one you would not suspect was there. The Italian police do it all the time."

"We can't be sure the phone is the way Heller has been able to follow us."

He was clear in what he wanted me to do. "James, there is one way of knowing. Rid yourself of it. If Heller is no longer able to trace us, we will know it was the phone."

I had a better idea. I called Manieri.

He picked up without much delay. "Signor Blake, you are late reporting in."

"Why didn't you tell me?"

"Tell you what?"

"You're using this phone to track me."

He hesitated for a moment. "It is an operational matter. Something you do not need to be concerned about. A means to allow us to be sure of your safety. There was no need to make matters more complicated by telling you this. It was for your benefit."

I laughed but I felt more like crying. "You don't know what damage your concern for my safety has done, Inspector."

"Do I detect a sense of ingratitude, Signor Blake?"

I was overcome by his attempt to trivialise what I was telling him. "Wise up, Manieri. The Landos have a man inside the Questura, tracking me for them. A good man has died. Others have had their lives put at risk. You have responsibility for that."

I opened the passenger window and threw the phone out onto the highway.

The threat was real that Manieri would go to the international authorities now. I didn't care. I was overwhelmed by a sense of injustice.

I began apologising to Ferrara. It was futile since the one I should have been saying this to was Arndt Schreiber and I had led a killer to him. Yet this was all I could do.

Ferrara removed his right hand from the wheel and gestured me to stop. "This will not help now, James. Now the phone is gone, we may be able to outrun Heller."

I looked behind. The BMW was closing. Heller had opened the driver window and was taking aim with a rifle.

Ferrara swerved into the inside lane as the shot rang out, the bullet impacting instead the tailgate of one of the delivery trucks slowing our progress. He swerved back into the outside lane, overtook the truck, gunned the Giulietta and we began to pull away, hoping that our superior acceleration and speed would win the day.

The luck Ferrara had talked about was with us as we raced on to a stretch of the Autostrada outside of Fasano that had light traffic. As we put real distance between us and the BMW, the risk now was of being stopped by highway police as the Giulietta took us through the 200 km/ hr, barrier.

We pulled off the Autostrada at Monopoli, took connecting roads until we found a disused airport, pulled off the road and waited behind a line of trees.

Without the tracker, Heller was at a disadvantage but would be waiting somewhere near in the hope of catching sight of us if we ventured back onto the Autostrada.

Ferrara was confident he could find a route to make the journey back north without being seen. He began typing information into the Giulietta's navigation system. When he'd finished, he sat back. "It will take a little longer but I think this will be safe enough."

Chapter 56

El Romero eyed the US agent with regret.

Such a waste.

Why was a beautiful woman like this mixed up in this world where life was cheap and came and went on the breeze?

The Americans had no shame in sending their women into danger.

He knew she would have to be killed. But for now he needed to know why she was here.

It would come down to torture, he'd always known that. He would not stay in the room and watch the harming of a woman. But she would not speak.

El Romero turned to Ramirez who wasted no time in beginning to work on her. When the woman began to scream, El Romero made for the clean air outside, closing the door of the ranch house behind him.

He spoke with Moreno, the one he'd posted to keep guard. The woman's screams could still be heard. He moved further away until the noise of her suffering was cancelled by the sounds of the desert.

When Moreno came to fetch him, there was no sound coming from inside even though the door was now open.

As El Romero came back in, he could see she was unconscious. Her head was sagged forward on her chest yet the blood released from her mouth could still be seen. A darkening, spreading stain was visible on the front of her linen jacket. Ramirez had been working on her teeth with a pair of silver-plated pliers he kept for just this type of work.

El Romero inspected the pliers. Between the jaws he found a bloody tooth. "You go too far, Philipo. She will not talk like this."

He lifted her head to check she was still breathing.

"Bring her round. Let me speak to her again."

Chapter 57

Wolfgang Heller was bemused. What could a professional like him do if he was hampered by inferior hardware? For this is what had allowed the targets to escape. Once the highway had cleared for them, the BMW could not keep up no matter how hard he pushed it.

And now Ranzini from the Questura had made matters worse by giving Heller false information. "Herr Heller. They are stationary. Perhaps they are trying to hide."

When Heller went to the location just outside Fasano given him by Ranzini, the target was not there. It was a barren stretch of highway. He called back to complain. "Why would this happen?"

"I should explain, Herr Heller. The signal is strong and stationary. They should be there."

"What does the tracker comprise?"

"A special phone. It is reliable."

"Unless they have discarded the phone."

The tracker was no longer working. It would be difficult to find them now.

It was the problem of the Blake target again. Somehow he'd been informed or had guessed that the phone was being used to track him.

There was no need to be concerned. The future was his, nothing was more certain than this. Blake and his kind were the insignificant barriers that fate placed in Heller's way, more to test his determination, to sharpen his will, than to stop him.

Chapter 58

When Dillon Ashley heard the screams, he knew he had to decide.

If the Mexicans killed Debbie Miller, wasn't that what Craven wanted all along?

But there would be consequences.

It would be known that Ashley was down here. Craven would come up with some believable lie but that wouldn't help Ashley. He would be left out in the open, with questions he couldn't answer about why he'd followed Miller.

Something else. The same feelings he'd had in the bar at the hotel were resurfacing. A fellow agent was in trouble. He couldn't stand by.

This was something he hadn't suspected of himself. Because for all the years of dissatisfaction he'd endured while he did the dirty work so others could get rich, he'd never thought he would feel this. Loyalty. Something he'd given up on once and for all. Stronger than the lure of the money Craven offered. Stronger than the thought that one day he might become as rich and powerful as Craven himself.

He surveyed the ranch house. There were three of them, maybe more. He was alone. There was no one to call. If he went in, there was a good chance they'd cut him down and there would be two dead agents rather than one.

He had to believe. Believe he would prevail. He was a professional. He'd been trained to kill. They were amateurs, no matter how many they might have killed, they were no match. It was only this belief that made possible what he was about to do.

Go in and go in hard.

He checked the Uzi, making sure of the mechanism.

They'd left a guard on the entrance. He would have to be dealt with in a way that wouldn't alert those inside. Otherwise this would be a hostage situation at best.

A broken-down stone wall ran along one side of the property. If Ashley could get close enough without being seen, under cover of the wall, he would be within touching distance of the guard.

He crawled along the far side of the stone wall, stopping every few yards to listen. All that could be heard were Miller's screams. He felt guilty that the sound of her pain was cover for his approach. He was closing in on the position he'd been aiming for – a gap in the wall where the stonework had failed and had not been repaired. From here he would strike at the guard. He was just about to risk peering through the gap in the wall to sight his man when the farmhouse door opened.

One of the Mexicans came out and walked towards the guard. They spoke for a short time, something in Spanish about the noise being made by the woman inside. The Mexican who'd come out moved further away and stood staring at the desert.

Ashley cursed his luck. If he made a move against the guard he'd be seen by the Mexican who'd emerged from the farmhouse. Meanwhile Debbie Miller's screams continued and were getting louder. It was difficult but Ashley knew he had to wait.

When the screams stopped, the farmhouse door opened once more and the guard signalled that the Mexican who'd emerged earlier should go back in.

The guard remained, turning to watch the farmhouse until the door was closed.

This was Ashley's signal to act. He took the guard from behind and broke his neck with a single rotation of the head. He lowered the man's body to the ground.

The approach to the farmhouse door would be unobserved now. If he was lucky both those inside would be preoccupied with Miller.

Full on was the only way of doing this. What he was about to do would be quick and bloody.

No more thinking now.

He kicked open the farmhouse door and burst inside. In shock, the two men turned towards him, both reaching for their weapons.

Miller was slumped unconscious on the far side of the room.

He had surprise on his side.

His only concern in this frozen moment was that his fire should not injure Miller.

He fired two deadly bursts from the Uzi.

Both men fell before they could reply.

Chapter 59

I couldn't help thinking that Schreiber's death had been my fault. I should have known the Landos would have an informer in the Questura. Yet I hadn't been careful. I'd led Heller to Ostuni. He killed a good man. He almost killed Gina and Ferrara.

I felt the need to know more about Schreiber but was unsure how to raise this with the professor.

Ferrara told us it would be safe to rejoin the A14 Autostrada near Foggia. Heller was so far behind by now he would not be able to catch up with us. The risk of the police stopping the Giulietta for breaking the speed limit was ever present but Ferrara was certain his box of tricks beneath the dashboard could handle that.

"You concern yourself too much with speeding, James. Remember, this is Italy."

Yet he was concerned about something else. While Gina slept once more in the seat behind us, he confided in me. He was sure the Landos would be given the results of traces made on the license plate of the Giulietta. "They're going to know where I live, where I work, who I bank with, where I spent my holiday this summer."

"No good returning to Padova?"

"Or the university."

"So, tell the police."

He took his eyes off the road for moment to give me a disbelieving stare. "James, after your recent experience with the

Florence police, I find it hard to believe you would suggest such a thing."

We fell silent as the Giulietta sped north.

I took my chance to return to my feelings about Schreiber. "Nico, tell me about Arndt. What kind of man was he?"

He was disarmed by the directness of my question. "I can't get used to talking about him in the past tense."

"I'm sorry if I saddened you."

"No, you are right to ask. You need to understand more about him and his work. I told you Arndt's brother died because of his involvement in one of the secret societies."

"What kind of society?"

"He once told me it was something you would think had no right to survive in modern day Germany but he would say little more. They made it look like a hit and run but Arndt knew the truth about his brother's death. He confided in him a matter of days before he died that he had made a mistake and he wanted out. Arndt told me the killing was no accident. Arndt dedicated his life to righting that wrong."

"You're working with him. You know how far that dedication had taken him?"

"We have not worked together for long, I am afraid, James. Arndt was a careful man. He did not want to risk revealing anything while the information was incomplete. For him, that would have amounted to giving those who killed his brother a chance to cover their tracks. So, he guarded what he had, from me as with everyone else. He was clear he would reveal it once his investigation was complete. This is something you must understand, James. What I have told you is close to *all* I can tell you. The real detail of what Arndt discovered may have died with him."

"But he was systematic, right? He kept notes?"

"Yes, I'm sure that is the case."

"And where would he have kept them?"

"He kept an office in his home in Munich. His wife may know if he has anything stored there."

We fell silent as the Giulietta raced on.

A few hours later, we were approaching the Florence exit. Gina was awake. When she saw the green overhead sign for Firenze, she became agitated. "I can't go back there. They'll find me and kill me."

Ferrara tried to calm her. "It's OK. We are not going to Florence. Nor to Padova."

"Where then?"

"We continue to Munich."

"Over the Alps?"

"There is a tunnel through the Brenner Pass that leads on to Innsbruck. We can drive straight through. You will enjoy the scenery."

Chapter 60

By the time the Federates arrived, Dillon Ashley had brought Agent Miller round and given her first aid. She was traumatised and still in pain. She would need time to recover but there would be no lasting damage – unless you counted the missing tooth.

Police Chief Pedro Martinez arrived, a measure of the importance the FDM attached to the report that the condition of El Romero was critical. Martinez had handpicked his team, including the paramedics, and sworn them to silence in the hope that the news of El Romero's arrival at hospital and the deaths of two of his men could be contained until arrangements for the expected backlash were in place.

Martinez confided his thoughts to Ashley. "In the fight against drugs here in Tijuana, Senor, news of such events has to be presented in the right way. I trust I can depend on your cooperation."

Ashley agreed. "The reason I'm here at this moment is to protect Agent Miller. You manage this however you feel is right. Just allow me to get her out of here."

They shook hands in agreement and as a silent farewell.

On the drive back into Tijuana, Ashley was getting used to the idea that the injuries to Debbie Miller's mouth were such that she would remain silent for the whole trip but it was not long before she began to address him through swollen lips. "I want to thank you for what you did back there. It took a lot of courage."

He was not distracted by the praise. "Like telling Nate Craven you're taking a holiday in Hawaii and coming down here instead?"

"You know about that?"

"I'm on Craven's team now. He sent me."

"What did Nate tell you?"

"I should make sure he wasn't misjudging you. Was that him, at the hotel?"

"Who?"

"Miles Blake, the guy you came here to meet."

"So, what if it was Miles Blake?"

"Wanted by the Agency as a threat to State security. Why would you have anything to do with a guy like him?"

"Since you're so thick with Craven, I might ask you the same?"

"I thought you were on Nate's team?"

"I am. You know that. But I'm with the Agency. We're both with the Agency."

"Meaning?"

"Meaning what did Nate promise you? A slice of the action?"

He didn't deny it. "So, if that's the case, what's to stop me reporting back to base and getting you busted out of here?"

"That's just what I want you to do. Play the whole thing with Nate as we agree and I'll make sure the drugs thing doesn't come back to bite you."

He looked concerned. "You know about that?"

Debbie Miller knew it was a risk, yet there was no other way but to trust her instincts. She could have waited and watched yet this man had risked his life for her. That had to mean something. "You can come out of this as a hero or spend a long time in jail. It's a simple choice."

"And to be the hero I have to deceive Nate Craven. Tell me why I should do that?"

"Because what he's offering is nowhere near enough. Not when the truth comes out about the drugs shipments. And the fact you have a real problem."

"What's that?"

"How do you tell Nate you've just shot up the guy Craven is paid good money to protect? That's not going to earn you any kind of bonus, is it?"

She paused to consider how much more she should tell him. She knew she would have to avoid mentioning Town Lake in case Ashley decided to report everything back to Craven. The longer Craven thought this was about drugs and not about Town Lake the better.

She changed the subject. "Anyway, you must have doubts about Craven, otherwise you wouldn't have saved me."

"You wouldn't use that against me."

"I'd rather not."

"What is it you want?"

"I need you to do what Nate asked. Tell him you have me and you're bringing me back to Washington. If he asks what I was doing here, tell him what you want him to know."

"That you're on to the drugs connection. And nothing about the rescue?"

She nodded. "Just right."

Day 5

September 6th

Chapter 61

I was concerned Ferrara had been driving for too long. It was gone midnight. We'd been over five hours on the Autostrada getting from Ostuni to the outskirts of Bologna. The journey to Munich would take another five hours. At first he wouldn't listen. "I have driven further and for longer than this."

I tried to convince him. "But not under such stress."

"If it helps, we can call in at the next Autogrill. I'll be fine with a twenty minute break."

"Let me drive."

"You do not know well enough how we Italians drive or the Alpine roads, James."

Gina interrupted with a solution. "I'll drive. I'm fresh. I've been sleeping."

I looked at Ferrara. He stared back. His look said, *Why not?*

Ferrara spoke first. "You can handle that?"

She nodded. "I drove for two years in and around New York, didn't I?"

We pulled into the Autogrill Santerno Est to refuel the Giulietta and for much-needed food and drink. As we sat with panini and coffee, two armed State Police officers came in and sat nearby. I kept my head down, hoping that Manieri had not yet gone through with the threat of putting out an arrest warrant for me.

We left one at a time and met at the Giulietta.

Gina was a good driver, respecting the speed limit more than Ferrara ever did. He took the back seat, I was up front.

Concerns about being chased by Heller were not now at the front of our thoughts. We headed on north, bypassing Verona on the A22, making steady progress through agricultural North Italy.

It was time to make my peace with Gina.

"I'm sorry for what happened."

"What do you have to be sorry about?"

"You were listening to what I was saying to Nico?"

"Enough of the time. Was it so obvious?"

"No one sleeps for long when there's so much trouble around them."

"So, let's come out and say it. I forgive you. It's not you doing the killing. It's the Landos and their henchmen."

"I'm not going to be able to forgive myself for not knowing about the phone."

"Anyone could be forgiven for thinking it was safe if it was switched off."

"But that led them to Arndt. No, I led them to Arndt and I led them to you."

She spoke with a maturity that came from the streets. "You need to get off the guilt trip, Mr. Blake."

"My name is James."

"Get off it, James. Don't you see, it's always been the way of the Landos. Making the people they exploit feel guilt for what the Landos themselves have done. They're merciless in the way they use people's fears to gain control over them. So, look at you. Feeling all that guilt that Arndt Schreiber was killed."

I shook my head.

"Did you have any ill feelings against him? Did you fire the weapon that ended his life? No, it was the Landos. They did it."

"You're just saying that to help me."

"No, James. I'm telling you this because if you'd lived in the shadow of these people like I have you'd know every word of it was true."

"You're not on a guilt trip yourself?"

"Sure. I can agree with that. Yeah, look at me. Feeling the guilt of not understanding the parents who raised me, being on the streets in Italy, being the reason why my sister was drawn to Florence and is now missing. Being the reason Arndt went to Ostuni. Did I pull my sister off the street and imprison her? Did I shoot Arndt?"

"No."

"Then say it. It was the Landos. That's where the guilt should lie. But you know what? They're incapable of feeling guilt. They have no conscience. That's what makes them what they are. The quicker you understand that and quit blaming yourself, the sooner you might have a chance of beating them."

I thought of my brother Miles and the guilt he felt about being involved in sending Julia to Florence and how what happened to her there had cast such a shadow over his life. "Gina, you're right."

She smiled. "Who am I to talk like this? Someone who's made such a mess of her life."

"Thanks for saying it."

We had been on ascending sections of the Autostrada for some time. The flat plains of southern Veneto were behind us and we were in the more mountainous terrain of Trentino as the highway tracked alongside the Adige River and carved its way towards the white-capped Italian Alps we could see in the distance.

I was keen to discover what Gina knew about Arndt Schreiber. "Tell me, Gina, what do you think drew Arndt to Florence?"

"You mean to people like me?"

"No, I don't mean that. Except for the fact that you're a twin."

She understood what I meant. "He didn't tell me a great deal about what motivated him. He was the private type. But he was sincere in his belief he would track down those responsible for his brother's death. It made him the kind of man you want to trust even when you've met so many bad types you wouldn't want to trust another man again. So, yes, he had a thing about twins. But there was nothing sinister about that."

"He didn't tell you why?"

"As I said he was the private type. There wasn't much he wanted to talk about."

"Nor why he came to Florence?"

"I don't know why. I had the idea he was certain he should be there because he was closer to uncovering what had happened to his brother. But he would never be specific. He told me I would be safer that way."

"He must have had something to say when he heard about the abduction of your sister?"

"He was as alarmed as I was, as worried about what was happening to her. When he heard about the threats to me, he was quick to say we should leave for the South. Something told me he knew about the kind of abuse she would be suffering and what would happen to me if I stayed. I didn't need to spell it out for him. He already knew."

"And that's all you know about why Arndt was in Florence?"

"Yes. And that art was important to him. Art that had gone missing. He kept asking me if I'd seen any paintings of unusual subjects in and around the Lando properties. I told him in truth I'd seen nothing."

"You got no indication of where he might have been looking?"

"As I told you, he was protecting me. One time I looked over his shoulder as he was typing a message to someone on his laptop. He became angry, stopped typing and told me to forget what I'd seen."

"What did you see?"

"I don't recall much about the detail of the message. It was routine stuff. He was asking someone what they knew about IDDL."

"IDDL?"

"Some organisation with those initials. I asked him to tell me what it stood for and he wouldn't say, just that it was important for my safety that I knew nothing about it."

I knew it was important to discover what Schreiber had been referring to but also that it was clear Gina knew no more and I should not press her further.

I thanked her for being so open in talking about a man who died in her full sight just a few hours ago.

I needed to concentrate on what was coming next. We were passing through Trento. Soon, we'd be arriving at the Austrian border. Later we would be crossing into Germany.

I didn't know what to expect. Would Manieri have alerted them to look for me?

I turned my head so Ferrara could hear. "Nico, what kind of checks will there be at the Austrian and German borders?"

He called back. "You should have nothing to worry about, James. They are both Schengen countries. There are no border restrictions."

"But they could be alerted to look for us? For not remaining at the scene at Ostuni?"

He agreed. "Of course it is possible. But I suspect the only people who know about the Giulietta are Heller and the Landos. They are not going to want to allow their contact in the Florence Questura to be known and broadcast that elsewhere with the authorities. They will want to use what they know to take us out, if and when they please."

"If they find us?"

"Yes, *if* not when. As to your own prospects of arrest, James, I suggest the only way to know about that is to cross the borders. My guess is the system is so slow that even if the Florence police have sounded the alarm about you, there has not yet been time to set anything up to detain you."

He was right. The road at the border at Brennero looked no different from any other stretch of the highway, except there was an exit lane at which vehicles could be asked to stop.

As the Giulietta swept through unchecked, Gina was reassuring. "Welcome to Austria!"

The A14 Brennerautobahn opened up before us and provided a quick ride along the Brenner Pass to Innsbruck.

After another quick stop for coffee, Ferrara resumed the driving as we sped on towards the Austria-German border near Kufstein.

I shouldn't have been concerned about being stopped. As at Brennero, the Giulietta sailed through, unimpeded.

Ferrara looked at the onboard timer. "Not bad. In another hour we will be in Munich."

The feeling of relief was evident.

We had escaped Italy.

Chapter 62

When Miles Blake and Luiz Reyas made it back to Tijuana, they decided to split up. Miles would go to the Anglia Hotel to let Debbie Miller know they had the sample of the explosive. Luiz would make sure his cover with the Soto cartel wasn't blown by any wash-back from the trip to Juarez.

It was a surprise for Miles on entering the hotel to be taken to a back room where Police Chief Martinez was waiting.

Miles took this as a bad sign. "Tell me why you're here."

Martinez tried to calm him. "We tracked your progress back from Juarez as soon as you entered the Baja. I came here to meet you because we need to talk."

"About what?"

"About Agent Miller. Don't worry. She will be OK. There was an incident."

"What kind of incident?"

"She was captured by the Soto."

"I need to see her."

"Not yet. There are matters we need to agree. Agent Miller was rescued by a fellow American, a Federal Agent. Mexican lives were lost. I need you to be aware of the sensitivities involved. If this is known, it would set back our fight against the cartels by years."

"Who died?"

"Two Soto foot soldiers. But more important is the one who was wounded. El Romero, the cartel head. He is in Hospital Centenario, in a coma. They are saying he might not regain consciousness."

Miles was thinking fast, trying to work out how this might affect the plans. "So, if it wasn't the FBI, who are you saying rescued Debbie Miller?"

Martinez's eyes sparkled. "Who else, Senor, but the FDM, my own specialist unit."

"And why are you telling me this?"

"Because you are a journalist, Senor, and because we have an agreement to assist each other."

"You're not asking me to report a false story?"

"Indeed not. You report nothing of the incident. Nothing that Senora Miller tells you."

Miles had no choice but to agree. The police chief thanked him. When he was let into the room, Miles saw at once that Debbie Miller was still in pain. The right side of her face was swollen. Scratch marks covered her neck.

Miles sat on the edge of the bed. "Debbie, you're all right?"

She spoke through swollen lips. "I'll live. They tortured me. Ripped out a tooth. But I didn't tell them anything they wanted to know."

Miles held her hand. "Who saved you?"

"Agent Ashley. Dillon Ashley."

"How come?"

"He was sent here by Craven to follow me but he laid his life on the line for me."

"So, where does Ashley stand? It's important because I have the sample from Rivenza."

She was pleased but because of her injuries found it hard to show it. "Then the plan goes ahead. If we play this right we can keep Ashley on side. He'll feed Craven the news that we're on to the drugs shipments. That should keep Craven thinking."

"And put you in danger."

"It's just until the analysis of the explosive comes through."

"You're sure about this?"

"Yes. Martinez paints us out of the picture. Craven and the rest of the world will get to know the Federales shot and captured El Romero. No need for us to be involved."

"It doesn't matter if Craven gets to know the truth about who killed El Romero?"

"Ashley has every reason to keep it from him. But even if Craven does find out, it's all connected to the drugs racket. Something that will throw him further off the trail."

"So what's next?"

Her voice was weakening. "We need time to get the right report back to Craven. Nothing to alert him to what we're doing. I'll arrange to get the sample analysed. Then I head back to Washington and stall Craven until the results of the analysis come through."

"You'll need a courier to get the sample to the lab. Someone we can trust."

"I'll speak with Bill Maynard in London. Ask him to find a courier."

Chapter 63

Agent Marvin Bryce was clear about the instructions. *Get yourself to London. Get the mess cleared up. Get out clean.* It sounded simple the way Craven had put it. Yet it was true. Their future depended on getting this right.

The pretext for Bryce arriving in London was good enough. Craven's team was alarmed to discover that one of their key targets, James Blake, had exited the US and, when last heard of, was on the loose in London, communicating with men like Adam Weston who were themselves under surveillance for breaches of security. What was left unsaid was that the real mission was to eliminate Maynard and Bedford and to close down anything that might lead to the drugs operation out of Tijuana being compromised.

When Bryce arrived at the London office and showed his credentials, Maynard was not welcoming. "I can't see why Craven needs men on the ground in London when he has so much to do back there after Town Lake."

Bryce tried to keep the man calm by making his reply sound matter-of-fact. "It's just procedure. We've lost Blake. We want him back."

"Then why not just *ask* us for him?"

"Of course, Chief. It's just what we've done all along. We all want the same thing. To keep the country safe. It's just that we need to take a more personal interest in Mr. Blake. And we'd heard your men are thin on the ground right now."

Maynard banged the table. "It's still damn close to saying we can't be trusted here to deliver. And I won't have any operation of mine criticised."

"Think of it more like we're sure you do a great job but I'm here as some extra help. An extra man on the ground in recognition of what's at stake."

"And just what do you think is at stake?"

"Blake's the link in the chain that can lead us to his brother. And as you know, Chief, brother Miles is one of those liberal journalists ruining the security of the country, encouraging whistleblowers to divulge state secrets we're pledged to protect. We have to take an interest in bringing Blake in and getting to the bottom of what his brother is doing."

"No need to spell it out, Bryce. We're on the case."

"So why turn down an extra pair of hands?"

Maynard didn't look any more convinced but was sounding more accepting. "OK, Bryce. You may have a point. Let's say you're here to help. Join our team for a while. I can go with that. But if I get the slightest indication you've got any other kind of agenda, you're out. You get me?"

"OK, Chief. Where do I start?"

Maynard called in Agent Bedford and introduced the two men. "Bedford, we have reinforcements, all the way from the U S of A. Agent Marvin Bryce will be joining the team."

Bedford shook the man's hand. "It's a great honour, sir. I've followed your career. You don't know how much it means to me to be able to work with you."

Bryce was pleased this young agent was overawed and his reputation in drugs enforcement had preceded him. This would make it easier. "Just doing the job."

Maynard reddened. "OK. We don't have time for the mutual admiration society. Bedford, give us a heads up on your take on the Weston–Blake association. And keep it brief."

Before Bedford could begin, the phone rang. Maynard picked it up, listened for a while and swore. "Look, there's something else I have to deal with, and it won't wait." He turned to Bedford. "Take Agent Bryce to your office."

Back in Bedford's office, Bryce gave a smile. "Is he always like that?"

"Every day. All the time. He's on my back twenty-four seven."

"Kind of grinds a man down."

Bedford nodded. "I was a happier man when I was back room. It's what I came into this business for. You know, tracking hackers, cracking down on Internet fraud. But Maynard has me out on the street and is making my life hell. That's the top and bottom of it."

"So it's true. The man is the devil to work with."

Bedford didn't know how to play this. He knew Bryce was part of the Craven team. But given the man's reputation, he couldn't believe Bryce had anything to do with the trade out of Tijuana. Craven wouldn't have told Bedford anyway. It was the way Craven played it with everyone. No one knew where they stood. It gave him his power over them. Bedford decided he would have to play it straight. "OK, here's the briefing."

He told Bryce about the surveillance carried out on Adam Weston and James Blake.

When he'd finished, Bryce had a question. "You have the recording?"

Bedford stalled. "You know about that?"

"Craven briefed me. You have it logged at a secure location?"

"Somewhere safe. That's between Craven and me right now."

"You don't have Weston or Blake under surveillance. Why are you so confident you can run them down?"

Bedford looked down. "Blake has escaped, could be somewhere in Italy. But we have Adam Weston and once we get him to talk, I'm sure he'll lead us to Blake."

"It must have been tough when you told Maynard?"

"You don't want to know."

Bryce smiled. It was possible, just possible, there was a way of closing this thing down before it was too late.

Chapter 64

There was a week to go before *Oktoberfest* began and the hotels were not yet full. The *Condor Hotel Munchen* on Sparkassen-strasse had rooms.

There was no scrutiny of our passports and no questions about our dawn check-in. All three of us booked in under false names.

Ferrara used his university credit card to take care of the costs. "I should not be doing this. It is meant for conferences when I am away from the department. But this won't be traced to me and I can pay the money back when I return."

We had a room each on the fifth floor. Time to shower and rest after the long journey from Ostuni, but my first thought was to phone Julia.

I used the hotel room phone and placed a collect call.

There was a long wait for the connection to be made.

Then, the unmistakable warmth of Julia's voice. "Yes?"

"It's me. It's early. I was worried you weren't going to pick up."

"Just finished feeding Simon."

"He's OK? You're both OK?"

"We're fine. Mark Stone is making a good job of keeping us safe."

"That's what I wanted to hear."

"And you?"

"I'm OK."

"Where are you?"

"I'd better not say."

"You mean you're in trouble."

"No. We shouldn't mention locations, here or there, just in case."

"What if they trace this call to you or me?"

"That's why we need to keep this short."

"OK. Tell me you're all right."

"I'm fine. I wish I could stay on longer."

"You should go."

"I'll call again tomorrow."

I told her I loved her and closed the line.

I showered and rested on the bed. It had been a long night. My eyes closed and I slept until I was woken by the ringing of the hotel room phone.

It was Ferrara. "Good morning, James. You slept well?"

I struggled to reply. "What time is it?"

"Don't worry, James, both Gina and I did the same. Join us for breakfast."

By the time I dressed and made it down to the hotel restaurant, Ferrara and Gina were already seated and had started their meal.

Ferrara was upbeat. "You look better than you did at dawn, James. The rest has done you good."

I took a seat with them. "I might say the same for you, Nico. I wouldn't want to go through another day like yesterday."

I knew what Ferrara was doing, trying to make us unwind after having escaped unscathed from southern Italy, but I couldn't shake the feeling that nothing had changed. Heller was out there, searching. The Landos were a continuing threat to me and my family. And Gina's sister was still missing. No wonder I didn't want to relax for too long.

I needed to move the conversation on. "Tell, me Nico, when can we meet Frau Schreiber?"

He smiled. "She has agreed to meet us this morning, at eleven. Enjoy your breakfast. We will be there in good time."

It was a meeting I was dreading. Without my mistake over the phone Manieri gave me, Arndt would still be alive. I now had to make my peace with his widow.

Ferrara recovered the Giulietta from hotel parking and took us out into the Munich suburbs to a neat apartment surrounded by trees overlooking the Englischer Garten. Elise Schreiber, dressed in black, was waiting for us. She showed us into a high-ceilinged drawing room of the formal German style.

Ferrara took the lead. After giving her his condolences, he introduced us. "This is Gina McKenzie. And this is James Blake."

She was finding it difficult to come to terms with what was happening. "You must forgive me. It is only a few hours since I heard what happened to Arndt. That he would not be coming back."

I offered her my heartfelt condolences. "I'm sorry for your loss, Frau Schreiber. I know it's too soon and we shouldn't be here but we need your help."

"What could be more important than the loss of a husband?"

I knew we were intruding on private grief and should not be here. It made me feel all the more guilty about my involvement in her husband's death. "You must forgive us, Frau Schreiber."

Her look told me she was in no doubt I had much to hide. "The police brought me the news. They will be returning to ask questions of me. You should leave if you do not want to be here when they come."

"We don't plan to trouble you for a moment longer than necessary."

She was as distressed as I'd feared. "Nothing will bring him back, I know, but if you know anything, anything at all about the circumstances of Arndt's death, you must tell me."

I wondered what Ferrara had told her to get her to see us. "I'm not sure I can add anything to what you already know."

It was clear she didn't believe me. "Isn't that why you are here?"

I glanced at Ferrara. He took her by the hand. "Frau Schreiber. We were among the last people to see your husband alive. What we're here to tell you is he died as he lived, fighting for the truth. We are all proud to have known him. We are so sorry for your loss. When the police come back they will take you through the detail of what happened. Right now, we need your help to continue Arndt's work. It's what he would have wanted."

I clung onto Gina's words of the night before. I had not pulled the trigger and I should not be overcome by self-blame. This is how the Landos and their kind dominate those they exploit. This gave me the strength to reply. "Your husband was a brave man, Frau Schreiber. He died fighting for what he believed in."

She turned to face me. "You know who killed him?"

I nodded.

"Then, tell me."

"He was killed by the same men of evil who ensnared his brother and threaten me and my family."

"You've told the police?"

"As soon as we can find the proof we will tell them what we know. But, Frau Schreiber, I'm sure you know enough about Arndt's work to see that the people we are talking about are beyond the law."

"And you cannot do this now?"

"Because we are under threat from the same men who killed Arndt. We need to act now and talk to the police when the time is right."

She requested we should all sit. "I tried to warn Arndt that he was placing himself in danger but he would not listen. He told me he would not stop until he had found and exposed those responsible for his brother's death. And now Arndt is dead. So, yes, Mr. Blake, I *do* know what you mean and you need to know it is no consolation to me."

I said it again but the words were empty. "I'm sorry for your loss."

She was so bereft, I could say no more.

Gina moved closer to her to offer what comfort she could. "There's another reason why we're here, Frau Schreiber. My sister is missing. They have her. I need to find her. I'm begging for your help."

Frau Schreiber wiped the tears from her eyes. "And that's the real reason why you are here?"

Ferrara joined in. "Yes, we need your help, Frau Schreiber. We need access to Arndt's work."

She did not reply at once.

Ferrara prompted her. "You know this is what he would have wanted."

She looked at each of us in turn, seeking to be sure we were genuine. But it was Gina who had moved her. "Yes, I will help. Arndt's computer is in his study. All his work is on there. But you can't take anything away. The police have already said they want to look at it."

Ferrara showed her the pen drive he'd removed from his jacket pocket. "There is no need to take anything away, Frau Schreiber."

It took time but she agreed to allow the files from Arndt's computer to be copied to the pen drive.

An hour later, we left with the results of Schreiber's work.

Back at the hotel in Ferrara's room he showed us the laptop computer and small-form printer he'd retrieved from the Giulietta. "I need to work when I travel. This is my portable office."

He began printing out the files we'd recovered from Schreiber's computer. "There is so much information here. We need to share it out and get reading."

With the printer still running, Ferrara left and returned fifteen minutes later with ten reams of printer paper. "We are going to need this, down to the last sheet."

By mid-afternoon we'd produced three neat piles of printout, each close to a foot high. I'd been glancing through the pages as they'd emerged from the printer. The material looked relevant but it was dense and detailed. "We don't have enough time. This will take days."

Ferrara smiled. "Then we will work all day and into the night."

Chapter 65

Deceiving Bill Maynard was the last thing Debbie Miller wanted. But she'd given Miles Blake her word and she intended to keep it.

A small lie to out a bigger lie.

If Blake was right and the chemical signature of the explosive brought back from Tijuana matched that of the residue found at Town Lake, there would be proof Craven was lying.

She opened the secure link to Maynard in London. He would see from the incoming signal that she was in Tijuana.

He picked up. "Debbie, what can I do for you?"

Her mouth still ached. She formed her words with care so he would not be concerned about her. "I have a sample, Bill. I want it analysed."

"So, send it to the lab in Virginia."

"I can't do that. I want to send it under your name."

"Now, why would I do that without knowing what kind of sample it is?"

"Plastic explosive. A possible match with the material used at Town Lake."

Maynard's interest peaked. "And where's it from?"

"It's from a known trafficker here in Tijuana. He goes by the name of El Romero, real name Alvaro Gutierrez. If I tell you there are those who say Nate Craven is an associate of his, you'd understand why I don't want to send the sample to the lab under my own name."

"Because Craven would get to know about it?"

"You're with me. If the signature of the explosive matches what was found at Town Lake, Bill, it's fair to say your warnings about Craven will be proven."

"Get the sample to me and I'll send it on to Quantico Virginia."

"Can't do that, Bill. Can you send someone out here to courier it there?"

"It's as urgent as that?"

"This all depends on Craven not getting to know this is coming."

"OK, I'll get an agent from the San Diego office onto it. You can hand it to them on your way back into the States."

Chapter 66

For Marvin Bryce the way to do this was to keep it simple.

He invited Bedford for a lunchtime drink in the *White Feathers* in Fulham, a bar he knew from an earlier visit. Bedford's smile showed he found it difficult to hide that he was flattered a man of Bryce's experience had chosen to drink with him. He preened when Bryce said, *Call me Marvin*.

Three whisky sours and Bedford was on the way to becoming drunk. Two more and he would be just about incapable. The dose of Rohypnol added in secret by Bryce to the fifth drink was the finishing shot.

Bryce ordered a taxi. "We'd better get you home, Michael."

Back at Bedford's room in the apartment in Kentish Town, chosen by the Agency to allow Bedford to come and go without notice, Bryce made a point of going inside to help his colleague out.

"No need, I can manage."

"It's no problem. No more than a colleague would do."

In the room, he helped Bedford remove his holster and pistol. "Need to check you have this somewhere safe."

Bedford looked surprised to see the Glock-23, staring at it as if it belonged to someone else. His words slurred. "You know, I've arrived now. No longer the backroom boy."

Bryce handed him the holster. "Better check the safety."

"Of course, check the safety."

Bedford passed out.

This was going to be easier than Bryce thought. He removed a small sample envelope he had been carrying in his suit pocket.

He then smeared gunshot residue over Bedford's hands and right arm and wiped some onto the sleeves of Bedford's jacket. Once you knew the forensics, it was simple. Whenever a gun was fired, powder residue was propelled along with the bullet. What they checked for on clothing and skin was lead, antimony and barium along with nitrites. That was enough to determine who had fired the gun.

Bryce prized his own Glock-23. It was the weapon offered to all Agents on qualifying and with few exceptions they all bought one. So much more concealable than the standard issue assault rifle. The gunpowder residue Bryce had just deployed on the comatose figure of Bedford was from his own G-23, collected earlier. But its residue would have the same profile as that produced by Bedford's.

Bedford would be out for at least four hours. Time enough to complete the plan. More than enough time to make it over to Maynard's apartment and kill him using Bedford's weapon. Time to return to Bedford's apartment and replace the G-23 in the man's grip. Time to make the anonymous call that gun shots had been heard in and around Maynard's apartment. When Forensics analysed the markings on the bullet casings and compared them with those fired from Bedford's weapon, they would match. Time to get the story straight. Bedford had got drunk and threatening towards the boss who would not let him be.

Bryce put on latex gloves. He pocketed Bedford's G-23 and the man's room keys. He let himself out and walked half a mile to a taxi rank, enough distance away to be unconnected with the Bedford apartment. He left the taxi half a mile from Maynard's apartment and walked to it.

Once Maynard opened the door, there was no time for the bureau chief to expresses surprise at seeing Bryce here in the evening. Bryce pushed the man inside and, without speaking, drew Bedford's G-23 and shot Maynard twice in the heart.

That was when it all went wrong. Maynard staggered back but did not fall. He was wearing a bulletproof vest. Before Bryce could raise the Glock and fire again they were on him. Two agents in maximum personal protection gear, one with a Taser. Bryce fell to the ground, convulsing. A steel-toed boot stamped on his hand and the Glock fell away.

Maynard's face loomed over him. "You should have known, Bryce, that I'd be keeping a close watch on you."

Chapter 67

It wasn't easy reading through Arndt Schreiber's research notes. It was the work of a man seeking to answer the single question of who killed his brother but who had produced multiple leads that each spawned their own sub themes and agendas. Schreiber stored everything he came upon in the expectation it might be relevant. He'd given little priority to the information collected; as presented, everything carried equal weight. It was up to us to work out the significance, if any, of what we found. I was grateful to have Ferrara to advise.

We were set up in Ferrara's room, each with our own pile of printed notes. Ferrara took the small desk. I lay on the bed. Gina sat in the single armchair. It was cramped but workable.

There were long periods of silence as we read, punctuated by one or the other of us calling out if we thought we'd found something of interest. Ferrara did his best to explain. If he didn't know, he used the laptop to search for more information.

The first breakthrough came when Gina found paperwork relating to Alfieri Lando's father. "Benito Lando. Charged with crimes against humanity in 1947 and later released owing to lack of evidence."

Ferrara was keen to see what she'd discovered. "Let me see."

He read in silence through the four or five printed sheets that Gina handed to him.

When he'd finished he told us what he'd discovered. "He called himself Benito Lando, though it was not his given name. He changed it to Benito in deference to Il Duce, Benito Mussolini, the fascist, whom he idolised. Mussolini brought fascism to Italy. Benito joined. When fascism spread to Germany, Benito was part of it. He rose high in German Nazi ranks, was inducted into the SS. Made it all the way up to *Obersturmbannfuhrer*. He was useful to them because of his knowledge of mysticism and art."

I recalled what Schreiber had told me when we'd met in the cafe in Ostuni. "Arndt knew about the Landos when I mentioned the name. He also said you couldn't explain the evil of a man like Alfieri Lando in a single generation. Perhaps we're beginning to know now what he meant."

An hour later, I found a bundle of papers referring to Heinrich Himmler. "Why is there so much on Himmler here? Seems he was a local, from the countryside near Munich. This town was his power base."

Ferrara stopped reading. "Yes, it is true. A shadow hangs over this place. A shadow so long it makes hollow the joviality they pretend to today. Just ten miles from here is Dachau. Himmler's brainchild."

Ferrara told us that Dachau was Heinrich Himmler's own special creation, the first Nazi concentration camp, the place where they modelled the atrocities they would carry out at Auschwitz, Buchenwald, Treblinka and Majdanek. "It started as a place to intern political prisoners, anyone who showed opposition to the Nazi regime. The first inmates were trades unionists, socialists, anarchists. Then came the painters and the poets and the university academics. Then the criminals. Then the Catholic priests and the Freemasons. Then the Jews. Then the Slavs. They told the remaining population they had nothing to fear if they had nothing to hide, even as the numbers interned continued to rise. The locals had a saying: *Dear God, make me dumb, that I may not to Dachau come*".

"They knew what was happening?"

"I don't think there is much doubt. The concentration camps were meant as a deterrent. Over three million Germans were interned in them, how would those who avoided that not know?"

Ferrara told us Himmler didn't stop there. Every detail of each inmate was recorded with precision. Prisoners were categorised according to type. A different colour badge for each. Green for politicals, red for criminals, yellow for Jews. The more he interned in Dachau, the more Himmler realised the possibility of using the inmates as slave labour. "The lie *Work Will Set You Free* was set out in the ironwork of the camp gates. Satellite camps were set up in and around Munich so the forced labour could be close to the factories. They worked as slaves and they starved. When they died they were cremated and that presented a new opportunity – the grisly economics of what the components of a human body are worth. The blueprint for Auschwitz. The true horror of the century. It is a crime against humanity that must not be forgotten or forgiven. But what I think Arndt Schreiber is asking us to do is to begin to understand the state of mind of a man like Himmler, how he and others like him crossed the line."

I struggled to understand what Ferrara meant. "So you're saying something about Himmler is key to understanding what happened to Arndt's brother?"

"Yes, I think it's clear from the importance Schreiber has given this. We are walking in Arndt's shoes, here, where he is leading us, trying to piece together what he knew from the notes he left. This takes us a few steps further, I am sure."

"And Munich itself is central."

"Yes, James. I think that's right."

Gina called out again. "There's a photo."

She handed it over. It was a group photograph taken during one of Himmler's visits to Dachau. Arndt Schreiber had annotated the image, drawing identifier rings around the faces. One of those present was Benito Lando.

I stared at the remorseless face that looked back. "There's no doubting the family resemblance. Alfieri Lando was a dead ringer for his father."

Ferrara cut in. "Proof enough that Benito Lando was an integral part of Himmler's operations within the SS."

Gina had a question. "So they executed Himmler, right?"

Ferrara shook his head. "The English captured him in 1945. He took a cyanide pill and avoided trial."

The work continued into the early evening. There were false trails, all dismissed by Ferrara as not relevant, at least as far as he could tell at this time. The *Ahnenerbe* section of the SS, the myth of Hyperborea, the underground world of Shambhala, The Thule Society – all aspects of Nazi mysticism that Schreiber had found a passing interest in – were all given the same summary treatment by Ferrara. "These are dead ends unless we can establish a meaningful link to them and so we should place them on one side until we have need to refer to them. They are the subject of so much speculation and myth-making in their own right that I think we should leave it to others to speculate about their importance or otherwise. I am concerned that considerations such as these will deflect us from our search. Like so many others, these are matters Arndt strayed into that took up his time with no guarantee they would lead anywhere. The key to this lies in the art. I am certain."

Gina nodded in agreement. "As I told James at the Swiss border, Arndt was concerned with missing art. It has to be important in what he discovered."

I was less convinced. "So why was he so concerned to point us in the direction of Benito Lando and the Second World War?"

"Of course, that is relevant, James. I am not saying it is not. We have the photograph of Alfieri Lando's father with Himmler at Dachau. But neither can we be certain at this stage that what we are looking at is anything as simple as the mythology of fascism. If I am right, the type of secret society Lando was drawn into has existed here for a long time and has seen fascism come and go. To survive all those years, to weather the wars and plagues and famines that have beset it through its long history, it has adapted, or seemed to adapt to suit the times."

"And during the Second World War, fascism was where it found a home?"

"Yes, when it came to power it is likely it was nothing more than the vessel that Benito Lando's distorted beliefs could be poured into, doing what he and his antecedents had always done, shifting the focus, the modus operandi to survive and prosper at that given moment in its long history, all the time retaining its secrecy. For the Landos, the SS became that vessel and the reason why Benito Lando was a part of it."

"And that was sixty years ago."

"Yes. And the kind of secret society Arndt's brother, Max, was drawn into will also have moved on. What we are looking for is the reason why Arndt was so determined to look for what that connection might be."

I was still not clear. "So where does it take us?"

"To places we would rather not go. To understand we must know and by knowing we run the risk of corrupting ourselves if we do not remain strong. And if we are not careful we may shine a light into dark places that should forever remain in darkness and are best left forgotten. Yet to defeat this evil, we must take this upon ourselves. We must focus, remain clear in the direction we need to pursue and not get diverted by the multitude of theories and inventions surrounding criminals like Himmler."

Gina brought us back to earth. "Bring it on. I can be as strong as you need if that helps find my sister."

Ferrara leaned back and stretched. "We need a break. Let's see something of Munich."

Chapter 68

Holding Bryce in interrogation was a problem Maynard could do without.

The facility was not supposed to exist. As far as the world out there was concerned the Agency had finished with torture. It would have been bad enough in the Middle East or Indo-China but here in the Haymarket in a quiet corner of London it would be a tough number to explain.

As if that was not enough, the prisoner was one of their own. It was distasteful to contemplate using any of the techniques at his disposal. Yet Bryce had planned to kill two of his fellow agents including Maynard himself and whatever had led him to this point was unknown. He was refusing to talk despite two long sessions of questioning.

Maynard knew there would be consequences if he didn't find a way of unlocking Bryce. There could be a wider conspiracy threatening the lives of others in the Agency. There could be wider infiltration leading to a full-blown security threat. The do-nothing option was no option at all.

Despite these concerns, Maynard decided to give it one more try.

Bryce was waiting in the interrogation room, shackled at hands and feet.

Maynard went in and began. "Tell me, Bryce, what makes an Agent like you with twenty years of exemplary service lose it like this?"

Bryce remained silent.

"Can't you see it's going to be easier for you if you make a clean breast of it? Tell us what you know. It's going to be a whole lot less painful that way."

More silence.

Maynard told himself he should not underestimate the resolve of the man before him. As part of the training they'd all been through, Bryce was practiced in the kind of displacement that would allow him to endure days if not weeks of interrogation.

Maynard decided to act like a friend. He moved closer and spoke in quiet tones. "This doesn't have to be ugly, Marvin. You know this is your last chance. You will tell us, sooner or later. But it doesn't have to be that way. Think of your wife and kids. How much they need you. How they're going to be devastated when they hear you're MIA."

Bryce shuddered. "You wouldn't?"

"What, snuff you out? Like you tried to snuff out Bedford and me? Think about this with great care, Marvin. There are a million and one ways you might not make it out of here and every one of them is a believable accident."

Bryce lowered his head. It was clear he was composing his thoughts, preparing to confess. "I shouldn't have been taken in by him, Bill. I guess it's too late now. You have me and there's no way back."

"You can tell me, Marvin. I promise I'll do my best to get you the best possible result."

Bryce began. "Nate Craven." He paused to take a deep breath. "He received information that the Blakes were involved in the Town Lake bombing. They were there in Austin when the bombs went off. They were there for a reason. It's why I came to London, to track them down. You know I told you that when I arrived."

"So, why the attempt on Bedford and me?"

"It was James Blake. I found him from the leads Bedford made. I had him cornered. But he got to me. I was weak, I

246

have to admit it. He offered me money. A million. More than I'm going to see in a lifetime with the Agency."

Maynard leaned forward. "So, why would Blake want Bedford killed? How would he even know I exist?"

"Because they have contacts inside the organisation. Miles, the brother, has someone feeding him from Washington. They know you're after them. They want you out of the way. He was definite he wanted you both."

"And where would he get that kind of money?"

"I don't know, Bill. The Blakes are linked with Italian organised crime. I guess the money comes from there."

"OK, Marvin. I've heard you. I'll keep to my promise. I'll report this in the best light I can. Meanwhile, I need to raise the priority level on bringing the Blakes in."

"And what about me? Maybe there's something I could do to make amends?"

"If you mean you have any chance of getting away with this, you can think again. But you could start by telling me what you know. Everything you know."

"Like what?"

"Like Nate Craven. Is he straight?"

"Why would you ask?"

"Things I'm hearing I don't know if I can believe. And the fact that he sent you here."

Bryce looked back and didn't blink. "I can tell you Nate is straight. He's one of the best. He lives the job twenty-four-seven. He's determined to close down the Blakes. That's why he sent me. He had no idea I was going to let them get to me."

"So tell me about McGraw?"

"What do you mean?"

"He's missing. He wasn't on the hit list you got from James Blake?"

Bryce shook his head. "No and no again, John. I don't have anything to do with that."

When Maynard left the interrogation room he had one thing on his mind. What Bryce had told him was believable and meant Bedford was the one he needed to talk to.

Maynard called Bedford into his office.

"No need to look sheepish, Bedford. Mark it down to crass inexperience. There are no heroes, get me? Just a bunch of damaged guys trying to make the best of a flawed world. You got that?"

Bedford was still the worse for wear. "I get it, sir. I shouldn't have allowed myself to be taken in by Bryce. I want to thank you for doing what you did."

"Don't think I did it out of anything more than saving my own skin, Bedford. I could smell it on Bryce the moment I cast eyes on him. I knew he was set on some kind of betrayal. I just didn't know that would come from the direction of a low life like James Blake."

Bedford showed no surprise. "Is that who he named, sir?"

Maynard nodded. "That's right. And you have no idea where Blake is?"

"No, sir. But we have Weston. We can use him to find Blake. I'm sure we can."

"It's all too little too late. But it's not why I called you in here. Tell me about McGraw?"

"He's missing."

"I know he's missing. Tell me *why* he's missing. You were targeting Weston as a team. You were tailing him. What happened?"

Bedford looked guilty. "There were two traces on the RFID tracker app. We split up. The one I took was Weston. We have him back on board. McGraw took the other trace."

"And you saw fit not to tell me?"

"Yes, sir."

"So, tell me about the second trace."

"That's just what it was, sir. Someone else who picked up the dust from Weston's apartment."

"But you don't know who it is?"

"No, sir."

Despite what the young agent had been through, Maynard was finding it difficult to control his impatience. "Better find out where James Blake is."

"Yes, sir. And thanks again for what you did."

Maynard realised he had been wrong to ease up on his disapproval of Bedford. Just look where that had led.

It was a mistake he was not about to make again.

Chapter 69

The next hours focused on aiding Debbie Miller's recovery.

She was as strong-willed as ever and rebuffed all attempts to tell her to slow down. "I'll be all right. Concentrate on the strategy. Let's make sure we get this right. We'll only get one shot at it."

Miles and Luiz Reyas were seated around the table in the living area of Debbie Miller's hotel suite. The TV was on with the sound turned down so they could monitor the local news.

Both Miles and Luiz had found it difficult to conceal their real intentions when they'd met Dillon Ashley for the first time. The easy part had been to thank him for rescuing Debbie. He'd responded to that with a welcome modesty. The difficult part was knowing that Ashley had been sent by Nate Craven and having to be careful each word didn't give anything away that might get back to Washington.

Luiz Reyas showed concern. "How do we know we can trust him?"

Debbie was in no doubt. "Because I believe him when he agreed with me he has too much to lose if Craven gets to know he shot El Romero."

Miles cut in. "So where is he now?"

"Just so you know, he's in his hotel room. Says he needs some down time to get over the fact that he's just killed two men and placed another man in a coma."

Miles agreed. "I guess after what he's done we have to trust him."

Luiz Reyas did not have time to reply. His gaze shifted towards the TV. "Turn up the volume."

It was Martinez addressing a news conference. He was surrounded by a dozen or more reporters thrusting fuzzy-cover microphones his way.

He was claiming credit for the capture of a key member of the Soto drugs cartel, saying this was a breakthrough in limiting the power of the cartels, as he'd promised when appointed. He was making it clear that while two cartel members had been killed when they refused to surrender, the prize was the capture of El Romero, the cartel head. One of the most feared men in all Mexico was now brought to book.

Martinez did not get to finish the news conference.

A hand reached out from the press pack to reveal a gun. The barrel of the weapon was placed on the back of Martinez's head. The assailant fired as the journalists scattered.

In the hotel room, all three were silent as Martinez was seen falling to the floor.

Debbie Miller was first to say it. "If Martinez is not safe, then no one is safe in this town. We need to leave."

Miles agreed. "With Martinez gone, there's going to be no one in authority to keep the word getting out that the FBI was involved in the El Romero shooting. And that's going to lead straight to us. But what about Maynard's courier?"

"Shouldn't be a problem. We'll hand the explosives sample over to someone Maynard trusts from the San Diego office on our way back home. They'll ship it out to the Quantico lab under Maynard's name."

Miles looked down. "I won't be with you, Debbie. My plan is to get back to the UK and to do that I need to go to the British Embassy in Mexico City to get an Emergency Passport."

Debbie looked down. "In normal circumstances, I might be able to help, Miles. But it would alert Craven if I did anything to help."

Luiz Reyas interrupted. "Be careful, Senor. There are as many in the power of the cartels in Mexico City as here."

Debbie Miller turned to the Mexican. "What will you do, Luiz?"

"I will stay here, Senora. I have family to protect when the drugs war comes, as it must now that El Romero is finished and Johnny Rivenza is coming. You will all be wise to be far away from Mexico when the killing starts."

They fell silent. Each knew this might be the last time they would see each other when, in the next few hours, they went their separate ways.

Miles felt the need to make his feelings clear to the young Mexican. "Luiz, don't think this means you will not see the fulfilment of your mission to right the wrongs. If what we've discussed comes to pass, it will bring down those that have done wrong against the Reyas family."

"I hope with all my heart that you are right, Senor."

Chapter 70

Bedford took a deep breath.

Marvin Bryce had remained loyal to Nate Craven.

Maynard had accepted the lie he'd told about James Blake. So, things were bad but perhaps not irredeemable. Bryce had kept Craven in play.

For Bedford, that meant he himself was still in play. If Craven had gone down he would have taken Bedford with him.

Bedford dialled the secret number.

There was no delay. Craven picked up. "Bedford. Good to hear from you."

"Don't play me for a fool, Nate. I know what you sent Bryce here to do."

"I don't know what you mean."

"I knew you'd deny it. But I'm still here. Bryce is in lock down. And you know what, he's talking."

Craven chuckled. "Nice try, Bedford. But I have Maynard's report. Bryce named James Blake. Looks like Maynard believes him. He wants to raise the priority on Blake's capture. So, don't think you can hold this over me."

"Beats me why a man like Bryce would remain loyal."

"Because of what you will never know. We go back. Right back. Understand?"

Bedford gathered his thoughts. "OK, Nate. This is how it is. I told you I had you dead to rights with the recording I made of Blake and Weston. You still sent Bryce after me. What's stopping me going ahead and turning you in?"

Craven chuckled again. "Two things, Bedford. First, the chances of anyone believing any claim made by James Blake just went down by one hundred percent now he's become a Class 1 target."

"And?"

"Oh, yes, something I almost forgot to mention. Your encryption is nowhere near as good as you think it is."

"Meaning?"

"Meaning don't you dare threaten me again with anything like that. Oh, and watch your back, Bedford. You won't always have Maynard to protect you."

Craven closed the line.

Bedford didn't understand what Craven was implying until he logged in to the secure site he'd used to store the Weston-Blake recording.

It was gone. The file had been removed.

Chapter 71

I met Ferrara and Gina in the hotel lobby. We'd spent long enough cooped up in Ferrara's room and needed natural light and fresh air.

It was a short walk to Marienplatz where, in the square fronting the ornate Town Hall, a city was at peace with itself. A jazz band played cool music from a dais placed close to the ornate archway of the building. Long trestle tables were set out on the grey flagstones of the square. Munich beer in foaming glass steins glowed amber in the late summer sunshine as young and old sat and drank together. We joined them.

Ferrara was thankful. "Next week all hell breaks loose once *Oktoberfest* gets started. It's become a cross between a beer festival and a pop concert with six million visitors piling in. Not much like it was."

Gina joked, "And not even in October."

"That's right. Much of the celebration takes place in September. But no one cares. *Oktoberfest* was always meant to be about escapism so who cares about breaking a few rules of common sense."

We drank beer and ate pretzels. Ferrara and Gina ate wurst. We tried hard to get into the prevailing feeling that life was good, uncomplicated and to be lived for the moment. But it was no good pretending. There was too much at stake.

Ferrara was first to break the spell. "You're not enjoying this, James? Not just for a moment?"

"I don't believe you are either, Nico."

"Does it show that much?"

"You're worried about Heller?"

He nodded. "Aren't you?"

"Yes, I'm concerned being out here on Marienplatz makes us more visible to him or the Landos. But it's more than that. It's about what you said, Nico. A dark shadow hangs over this place. I can't tolerate the joviality. Not when the past hangs so heavy."

Gina joined in. "If it helps, I don't buy it either."

We made it back to the hotel and reassembled in Ferrara's room, out of sight from the prying eyes that would have been on us if we'd stayed at Marienplatz. Away from the contrived joviality. Immersing ourselves once more in Schreiber's research notes, searching for the answers we hoped would be there.

Ferrara was clear. "Concentrate on the art. It is where the answer lies."

I needed to know why he was so sure. "Nico, why the art?"

He paused to think and then continued. "James, we need to keep the connection with the reason your wife came to Florence."

"To search for missing art?"

"Yes, and why so many of those masterpieces are missing. Did you know the original of the Da Vinci *Leda and the Swan* I told you about is lost, and what we have left is the copy made at the time by Cesare Lesto?"

I thought back to my visit three years ago to the National Museum in London to view Rubens' copy of Michelangelo's *Leda and the Swan*. "Just as the Michelangelo version is also lost and replaced by a copy."

"Would you call that a coincidence?"

"Maybe not. Julia has her own view of why so many masterpieces are lost or missing. She's convinced that in a number of cases their existence had been concealed by overpainting. Her career's work is to use her conservation knowledge to discover one of these hidden masterpieces and give it back to the world. That's what her visit to Florence promised."

He nodded in agreement. "Yes, but why conceal them?"

I replied with what Julia had always believed. "Because of their content. The subject matter can be offensive to many."

"Agreed. But overpainting may not have been the only way to conceal them. Do not forget, these paintings were commissioned by wealthy patrons for their own needs. They could decide on their own interpretation of morality so long as they kept them hidden, so long as no one knew they were there. And simple hiding was another, effective means of concealment from the demands of orthodoxy."

"So, another way of concealing them?"

"Yes. And there is a simple enough conclusion to be drawn about such paintings that made it *necessary* to hide them. There are those who believe the reason why the paintings had been commissioned at such great expense was they were the vehicle for the concealment of secrets that, if they had been spoken of in the open, would have led to prosecution, even the deaths of those that uttered them."

"The secrets were hidden in the art as a means of preserving them?"

"Indeed. What better place could there be? Much else perishes with time, including people's memories, but precious works of art, like myth itself, survive the centuries, survive war, famine and disease."

"You have evidence for this?"

"We know the Church condemned many to death for far less. And we know that Da Vinci and Michelangelo and a large number of the other artists of the time were skilled in concealing secret messages in their work."

"That's not going to stand up in a court of law."

He nodded. "Agreed. And in my profession we are not allowed to speculate for too long without firm evidence. But bear with me for awhile. Let me point to a few moments when the line was crossed and the madness surfaced in the world of art. You know about the *Bonfire of the Vanities*?"

I told him what little I knew.

He had more to add. "Yes, in Florence in 1497, Savonarola, the Dominican priest railing against the corruption of the Vatican, encouraged his followers to demand that the wealthy should publicly burn their precious objects, their books and paintings, to show they had turned their back on the sin of avarice. But, did you know such bonfires had been going on in Italy for half a century before Savonarola?"

"Which means?"

"So many masterpieces, by Botticelli, by Bernini. No longer hidden, destroyed in those fires. Yet, just as your wife Julia supposed, what a convenient way for clever people to intervene and acquire the paintings for themselves."

"You're saying those in the secret societies acquired them?"

"I am saying that a number of those great works and their secrets have disappeared and that what was concealed was the very stuff of the intrigue fuelling the secret societies. It would be surprising if they had not been involved. But hard evidence is always going to be difficult to find because the whole idea of such societies is they operate in secret. That was what impressed me about what Signora DeFrancesco had to tell me."

"Alfieri Lando was in possession of the Michelangelo. It doesn't matter to you that the painting he had was shown to be a contemporary copy?"

"I do not think so. It follows that an object of such importance would be protected by having copies made. But the desire to devour the secrets in the original remains."

"How do we know the copy contains all the secrets of the original?"

"We do not. And there lies one of the drivers to recover the originals."

"No doubt there's a good rival explanation for each and every missing masterpiece?"

"I do not doubt it. But with so many missing, it appears more as if there is a pattern over a long period of time. The disappearance of so many key art works may be evidence in itself for the existence of the secret societies right the way back to the days of Savonarola."

I looked down at what remained of the print out of Arndt Schreiber's research we had yet to consider. My pile, like that of Gina and Ferrara, was going down fast. I could only hope the breakthrough we were seeking was to be found somewhere in the remaining pages.

It was getting late and becoming difficult to keep focused yet I knew I had to keep questioning. "Nico, what you've told us about the importance of art in all this means we need to know more about Benito Lando's activities."

Ferrara held up handful of papers he'd selected from his pile of notes. "Agreed. We need to return to World War Two. You've heard about the *Fuhrermuseum*? It was one of the largest projects proposed by the Nazis. The art works of Europe in all the countries occupied by the fascists were stolen. Paintings, sculpture, by the train-load, was sent to Austria where plans were drawn up for a vast museum in Linz, the town where Hitler was born. Well, the paperwork I am holding in my hand right now shows Benito Lando was involved. Except he was working for Himmler rather than Hitler."

"We know why he was useful to them. He knew about art. But, Nico, I thought it was well-known that the fascist looting of all those art works was down to simple greed?"

"Yes, it's true, much of what the Nazis did was the kind of gangsterism that comes with unbridled power."

"So, theft, the grabbing of personal wealth, self-aggrandisement. There's nothing more?"

"Don't you see, James. It *was* about greed. But at the same time it was something else altogether. If Benito was a member of a secret society that believed there were secrets in the art, think what occult secrets he could discover. What if there were more like him? That would be as much the reason for the obsession with stealing art as any simple grabbing of wealth."

"So, Nico, what had Arndt got to tell us about Benito Lando and Himmler?"

He held up another of the pages. It was an order issued by Himmler in the closing years of the War. Ferrara read it out. "*Use every means of transport to get all works of European art out of Florence except works of art from English and Americans... get anything away that you can get hold of. Heil Hitler.*"

Gina was quick to understand the significance of this. "And Benito Lando was close enough to the action to play a part?"

Ferrara gave a nod of agreement and continued. "We know he was part of Himmler's inner circle." Ferrara read further through this section of Schreiber's notes. "Here it is. Lando was part of a specialist SS group called *Nibelungen* detailed by Himmler to protect the art he was stealing unopposed in the ruins of war. And Himmler, like Goering, was a serious collector of art, in competition with the official policy of looting for the proposed *Fuhrermuseum.*"

I was beginning to see where this was going. "So, Benito Lando had access to art works on an unprecedented scale."

Ferrara seemed sure. "Indeed. The Nazis looted over six hundred thousand works of art from right across Europe. Hitler for the *Fuhrermuseum*, Himmler for his own SS world centre in Wewelsburg Castle. Vast schemes. And, you know, many of those stolen works have still not been returned to their rightful owners, even today. But you are right, James. What an ideal cover for a determined man like Benito Lando to be following his own agenda amidst the chaos and disorder."

I waved a sheaf of papers from my share of Schreiber's research notes. "So maybe this is relevant." I held up a thick batch of print-out sheets that were all concerned with art. "There's so much material here. There has to be a good reason why Arndt attached such importance to it."

Ferrara walked across to look over my shoulder. "What kind of art?"

I leafed further through. "Your instinct was right, Nico. It's missing art. Classic paintings, lists of masterpieces believed to be lost, stretching right back."

And then I stopped. I turned over the next page and was presented with the image that had started the whole chain of events that had engulfed my family, first seen when Julia had sent it to me by phone as she was being kidnapped by Alfieri Lando's men – Michelangelo's *Leda and the Swan*.

Gina now appeared concerned. "You look like you're in shock."

I steadied myself. "I'm OK. It's just the first time I saw this picture I thought my wife was dead. Each time I see it, I get the same feeling of dread." I held up the page. "The Michelangelo."

Ferrara spoke next. "Once again we follow in Arndt Schreiber's footsteps. He is taking us back. He is saying: don't get trapped into thinking this is only about Benito Lando and World War Two, also look back. At the same time that Benito Lando was serving Himmler he was using his position to serve an older cause."

I leafed further through the pages. "Yes, there are dozens of images of missing masterpieces."

Then I found the list.

It had been produced on a manual typewriter during WWII and scanned from surviving documents by Arndt Schreiber.

182/NI/SS Lorenzo Monaco – Madonna mit Kind und Heiligen Johannes dem Taufer und Nikolaus und Engel, inthronisiert 1402

238/NI/SS Andrea Mantegna – St. James fuhrte zu seiner Hinrichtung 1455

419/NI/SS Fra Angelico – Jungste Gericht 1456

421/NI/SS Sandro Botticelli – Portrait von Cosimo Di Medici 1478

533/NI/SS Luca Signorelli – Das Gericht Pan, 1490

619/NI/SS Giovanni Bellini – Das Abendmahl in Emmaus, 1494

655/NI/SS Ghirlandaio – Jerome und Johannes der Taufer, 1496

711/NI/SS Fra Bartolommeo Himmelfahrt der Jungfrau, 1508

724/NI/SS Leonardo da Vinci – Leda und der Schwan, 1508

749/NI/SS Michelangelo – Leda und der Schwan, 1530

*758/NI/SS Veronese – Apollo und Juno und Saturn Hilft Religion
zu uberwinden Heresy, 1580*

821/NI/SS Caravaggio – Matthaus und der Engel, 1602

I handed the list to Ferrara. He looked at it with care. "It is a copy of a document found in Benito Lando's possession when he was arrested by the Allies. It is incomplete. It is the start of a much longer list. We do not know how many paintings there were on the full list. Arndt has notes in the margin making that clear."

Gina chimed in. "Looks like a shopping list."

Ferrara nodded. "That's just what it is. Or more like an accession list. It is Benito Lando's list of the masterpieces he acquired under cover of looting for the Nazi cause. It shows the SS obsession with recording and numbering everything. Just as the internees in Dachau were recorded and numbered."

He began to take us through the list, translating from the German.

*182/NI/SS Lorenzo Monaco – Madonna and Child Enthroned
with Saints John the Baptist and Nicholas and Angels, painted
in 1402.*

"Look at the accession number. NI/SS could refer to the *Nibelungen* group of the SS, the group we know Benito Lando was attached to."

He paused to check details on the Internet. "As I recalled, it is one of many masterpieces known to have been lost to Allied bombing in 1945 when a storage tower in Berlin in which they were hidden, the Friedrichshain Flakturm, was destroyed. But if Lando had stolen the paintings on the list for Himmler, I doubt they were ever sent to Berlin, despite Hitler's order to send all stolen art there. The paintings on this list would have gone to Wewelsburg Castle."

I wanted to be sure I understood. "Nico, you're saying these are all masterpieces that were stolen and then supposed to have been destroyed in the Allied bombing?"

He nodded again. "Most of them. Mantegna's *St James Led To His Execution*, Fra Angelica's *East Judgment*, Botticelli's *Portrait of Cosimo De' Medici*, Ghirlandaio's *Jerome and John the Baptist*, Fra Bartolommeo's *Assumption of the Virgin*, Veronese's *Apollo and Juno and Saturn Help Religion to Overcome Heresy* and Caravaggio's *Saint Matthew and the Angel* are all listed as having been destroyed in the bombing of the tower."

"And the others?"

"Signorelli's *The Court of Pan* and Bellini's *The Supper at Emmaus* are thought to have been lost long before that."

"Are you saying they were found by Benito Lando and taken to Wewelsburg?"

"Why else would he have given them an accession number?"

"You haven't mentioned the two paintings of *Leda and the Swan*."

"If we are right, and this documentation suggests that is the case, both the Da Vinci and the Michelangelo versions were part of the consignment, with an SS accession number."

"If the whole consignment went to Himmler at Wewelsburg Castle rather than Berlin, what happened to it?"

"That is what Arndt Schreiber was trying to discover. We know that by the time the Allies realised what had been happening with the Nazis plundering so much art, Himmler was dead. And because he was dead, his treasure trove of stolen works was not investigated. Nothing was done until 1998 and by then too much time had passed. Benito Lando was not in custody for long. It is altogether probable once he was released he found a way to recover the paintings from wherever they were being hidden."

"But we have no proof."

"That is true. As the years pass it is ever more difficult to have certainty."

I looked again over the list. "It reminds me of the list Julia compiled before she set out to Florence in her own search for a hidden masterpiece. Except, the Lando list is shorter. And that brings us back to *Leda and the Swan*. Everything comes back to that single image. Leda being raped by Zeus. It's always been what this is all about."

Day 6

September 7th

Chapter 72

Ferrara ordered coffee from room service as we fought against sleep, determined before dawn broke to complete our search through Arndt Schreiber's research papers.

We were running out of time and material. Schreiber's research notes were revealing much, yet the answers we were seeking still remained out of reach.

My pile of papers was almost finished. Then I turned over the last page but one. It was about Isaac Newton.

Ferrara came to look over my shoulder.

I was ahead of him in reading Schreiber's note. "It's about speculation that Newton was involved with the Rosicrucians. Why would Arndt take time and trouble over him?"

Ferrara paused before speaking. "They were one of the most influential secret societies of Newton's day. Knowing Newton's interest in alchemy and what we would today call the occult, it is perhaps not surprising. But there is a school of thought that says Newton was involved because he was trying to find the *Elixir of Life.*"

"A way of living forever?"

"Yes, and that he was close to Rosicrucians because they claimed to have found it."

"But it still doesn't explain why Arndt was so interested."

"James, you know we have had the feeling since we started that Arndt is guiding us even though he is no longer with us. I think he may be pointing us to look again at the mythology with which Lando and those before him surrounded themselves."

"You'll need to explain."

Ferrara continued. "Let me take you back, James, to what I was telling you about my work, about those who cross the line from myth into madness. What if you were to allow yourself to enter into the mind of a man like Alfieri Lando, a man for whom the myths about Leda had become so real he may have come to believe that aspects of those stories conceal literal truth? Once you cross that line, you ask the question, why did Zeus disguise himself and seduce earthly women? As a swan with Leda. As a white bull with Europa. You might deduce that even for him, pleasure was everything. And that might lead you to another conclusion. What if when Zeus came to Earth to seduce those women some of his immortality was lost to mortals? And, if that is the case, it is only a short step to believing his immortality had been left behind in children, twins like Helen and Clytemnestra, and over time there must be descendants. Some mortal, some immortal, just as in the myth."

I was working hard to understand what he was saying. "But men like Lando were mad?"

"Yes, but within their madness, ideas that are crazy to us could be believed as truths by them. Only them. What if, for them, it was just another short step to believing it was now a provable fact that the essence of immortality, the *Elixir of Life* that men like Newton and so many craved, had been distributed throughout this select number of mortals on the Earth. As a result of the past folly of Zeus and the accidents of their birth, certain twins had come into possession of some part of the immortality that was in the first place all his own. And, of course, if you were a true adherent, you might find it easy to take a further step along the way to madness – to come to believe that if you could find such mortal-immortals by some means, you might become like Zeus."

"And have your own chance of immortality. To somehow gain it from the women?"

"I am afraid it could be so. It would be knowledge worth any amount of effort to keep hidden; something to conceal in a secret society."

I had to interrupt the flow of his argument. "I'm sensing what you're telling me is more than speculation."

He nodded. "You are right. I think it is the terrible truth that Arndt has been pointing us towards all along."

"But we still don't have hard evidence. This is all still *what if*."

He pointed to the empty pile of unread papers before him. "And I have arrived at the end of Arndt Schreiber's evidence."

I gestured towards my pile of papers. "Me, too."

Gina agreed. "And me. All I have left is this. Doesn't look like it's going anywhere."

She handed over her last bundle of papers. Ferrara speed-read them. "It is Arndt's work on trying to trace further back into the history of the Lando family. He has the genealogy, pieced together from Church records. It must have taken months. He traces the Lando line back to before 1400. But there is nothing more substantial here other than what we know; the Lando family has been in a position of power for centuries."

I was disappointed. "So we still don't have a convincing lead on where to go next."

Ferrara was trying not to be downbeat. "We have discovered much. What we seek will come, I am sure of it."

We sat for some time, staring at the upturned piles of paper, trying not to admit we had exhausted everything that Schreiber had researched.

It was Gina who broke the deadlock. "Arndt knew about the importance of twins and the importance of Florence. It's where I first met him, on the streets of Oltrarno, seeking out the women there who were twins. He must have discovered more. Are we sure we've looked at everything?"

Ferrara checked the documents. "I am sure I printed them all."

He looked again at the hundreds of icons on the laptop screen. "Except. We have not considered the audio files."

Chapter 73

Instinct had told Bill Maynard not to delay, to head straight for Washington.

It had been too long since he'd been here. It made him realise how much he was losing influence while in Europe running the London office.

There had never been any question before about who to call. But every year key personnel moved on. As he searched his list of contacts, he found it difficult to choose, now that he needed someone with influence to get things done.

The name that caught his eye was Vincent Carnegie. They'd been recruited by the Agency at the same time, trained together, but never got on. Something between them didn't click. There was no real reason for it, unless Carnegie disliked Maynard for being so up front. Now Carnegie was Deputy Director of Surveillance. Authority enough for what was needed.

The sample of explosive from Mexico had been delivered at San Diego by Debbie Miller as arranged and fast couriered to Quantico Virginia, where the tests were positive beyond any doubt. The explosive used at Town Lake was a one hundred per cent match for the material supplied from Tijuana. The results, delivered to him on arrival in Washington, had shocked Maynard.

Craven had questions to answer and Maynard was the man to ask them.

The appointment with Carnegie came sooner than expected. The man seemed pleased to meet an old colleague.

"It's been too long, Bill. How's London treating you? I'm hearing you've lost none of your get at 'em approach."

Maynard was surprised by how time had mellowed their relationship and how well Carnegie had come to terms with Maynard's take on life. "You've done so well, Vincent. I wasn't sure you'd be able to see me."

"Anything for an old friend. What can I do?"

When Carnegie was told about the Quantico tests, he was surprised. "You sure, Bill? That's one hell of an accusation. Nate Craven has just been given the Star. You know he's something of a hero round here. Some say he's the future of the Agency."

"It's more than an accusation, Vincent. The tests prove Craven deceived the Agency over Town Lake. The attack couldn't have been the work of East Africa terrorists. And that means he's had the Agency looking in the wrong place for the perpetrators."

"Craven has a motive?"

"To prevent knowledge coming to light of the kick backs he's receiving from the drugs trade out of Tijuana."

Carnegie was shocked. "You can prove this?"

"Agent Miller has been investigating this. She has the proof."

"So, what are you asking for, Bill?"

"Authorisation to investigate Craven."

"I'm not sure I can agree without hearing what Craven has to say."

"There's no time. I'm sure Miller is in danger."

"From Craven? Isn't she in his team?"

"That's just it. He's in a position to know she's on to him. I'm sure you can understand my concern, Vincent. Given her evidence, he has reason enough to harm her."

"You're saying she may be in imminent danger?"

"I believe that's the case. So, let's be precautionary. Let me investigate, internally. Sort this thing out once and for all."

"What do you need?"

"Half a dozen men, armed, from outside of Craven's team."

"I can do that. What else?"

"Authorisation to go as far as is needed."

"You have that also." Carnegie paused. "Listen, Bill, I'm trusting you with this. Don't make me regret it."

Chapter 74

Dillon Ashley was delivering. That pleased Nate Craven. More important was the fact that Craven had chosen well. Ashley could expect rapid advancement in the Craven team.

So, Debbie Miller had been convinced to come back to Washington.

Ashley was almost apologetic when he'd called. "I had to use some force, Nate. Enough to make her see sense."

"Regrettable I know, Dillon, but you're doing your duty. It's going to be better for her and for the security of us all now she's coming back to set the record straight, if you get me. Great job."

Craven gave a smile as soon as the call ended.

Ashley must have roughed her up more than he cared to admit.

Chapter 75

We gathered round Ferrara's laptop as he played the first of the audio files taken from Arndt Schreiber's computer.

Ferrara explained, "Arndt's embedded notes tell us that each file is a recording of a phone call with a *witness*, as he describes them. He does not say if the other person knows the recording is being made, but perhaps that should not concern us too much. The first recording is a call from eight months ago with a school friend of Arndt's brother, Max, here in Munich."

He started the playback. The school friend was called Dieter.

"Herr Schreiber?"

It was the voice of a frightened young man. Arndt Schreiber could be heard encouraging him to be calm and accept Schreiber's word that whatever was said would go no further.

"Dieter, I want to bring you to the reason why I am calling."

"It is about how Max died?"

"Yes. I know it was a shock to you but time has passed and I am asking for your help."

"I can only tell you this, Herr Schreiber; I am glad I did not follow Max in joining them. It was something I was close to doing."

Schreiber's voice was calming. "And why was that, Dieter?"

"Because of the change I saw in him. In a few months he lost all the good nature and humour we liked in him so much. He became a different person."

"And who are they? Were they active in searching for recruits at your school?"

"Yes. It began with extra tuition in German history through the after-school club. Then we were invited to a meeting in town, outside of school. Max joined. I spoke to my parents. They forbade me to have anything to do with the Ancestral Heritage Society. They told me they were fascists."

Ferrara paused the playback. "*The Ancestral Heritage Society*. Sounds like a throwback to the *Ahnenerbe* Group set up by Himmler within the SS to investigate the occult madness that fuelled so much of the Nazi atrocities. It is of concern in itself that anything like this could still exist in modern Germany. As far as the outside world is concerned such organisations were closed down and banned after the War. Yet here they are again, signing up naive schoolchildren to poisonous beliefs."

Ferrara recalled the section of notes assembled by Schreiber on the *Ahnenerbe*. "Arndt spent a great deal of time seeking to understand just what kind of society his brother had become involved with. So the *Ahnenerbe* has relevance after all. But perhaps it has more relevance for Arndt than for us. We have to show tough love here. What happened to Arndt's brother Max was the tragedy that drove Arndt Schreiber. What is driving us is the need to uncover what lies behind the madness of the Landos, to rescue Gina's sister and end the threat posed to your wife and family, James. It would be a great mistake to give equal weight to both."

I was satisfied we should depend on the clear thinking of the professor, on his ability to retain focus on what was relevant to our discovering the truth behind the Lando menace and take his advice to not get diverted by the background noise within which they had hidden themselves. "It's a tough conclusion to come to, Nico, and one that may be necessary. But where does it take us? What do we have so far to use against the Landos?"

Ferrara, like all of us, was looking tired. "Yes, James. There has to be more."

There was little to be learned as we ran through the remainder of the playback. The young man no doubt felt he had risked enough in what had been already said.

"We may return to this one later. Here is the second file. Arndt's note tells us it is the recording of a phone call made with Herman Schmidt, now a Lutheran pastor but, during the War, a member of the SS."

Gina was curious about the man's age. "Must be well into his nineties."

Ferrara agreed and began playing the recording.

Schreiber's voice came first.

"Dr. Schmidt, thank you for agreeing to speak to me. I know it must be difficult to return to those days but, as you know, I am grateful for your help in finding the truth of what happened to my brother."

It was the voice of an old man but with the assurance of one who had no regrets about his past. "I am here to help, Herr Schreiber. But I am puzzled why you would want to return to those dark days for Germany."

"Let me say, Dr. Schmidt, l take no pleasure in returning to events long forgotten and best kept that way. But my investigations show this is where I need to go in order to find truth."

"So long as you place light over darkness, truth above deceit, I am prepared to assist in whatever way I can."

"I give you my word."

"What is it you need?"

There was the sound of paper rustling as Schreiber referred to his written notes. "You served in the Waffen SS, with *Obersturmbannfuhrer* Benito Lando."

The old man's voice hardened. "Where did you get that information?"

"You deny it?"

There was a long pause. Schmidt's voice became quiet, close to inaudible. "I have refused to deny it all my life. And I have made a new honourable life for myself. If you are a true friend of Germany you would not want to expose me now and ruin all I have achieved, the reputation I have in my closing years for being an honourable and caring man."

Schreiber was quick to respond. "No. This is not why I am calling. I need the answer to specific questions. About matters of fact. I trust you will tell me. Then I promise to preserve your anonymity."

"Is this not a threat? If I don't answer your questions you will expose me?"

"No, it is nothing like that. When you hear my questions, you will realise that nothing you tell me will jeopardise what you have now."

"Though you do not leave me much choice, I agree I must trust you. What is it you want?"

"I have an accession list of paintings, great works of art, acquired for Himmler and taken to Wewelsburg Castle."

The old man sighed. "So, it is about the art?" There was relief in his voice.

"That is all I am interested in."

"And this will help you find out what happened to your brother?"

"I believe it will. Tell me about Wewelsburg."

"How do you know about that?"

"I do not believe the paintings on the list ever went to Berlin, as was ordered. Neither do I believe they were destroyed there by the British and the Americans."

"We captured many items on Himmler's orders. You will need to be more specific."

Schreiber began reading from the list. "Mantegna, *St James Led To His Execution*, Fra Angelica, *Last Judgment*, Botticelli, *Portrait of Cosimo De' Medici*, Ghirlandaio, *Jerome and John the Baptist*, Fra Bartolommeo, *Assumption of the Virgin…*"

Dr. Schmidt interrupted. "I understand. You know about the paintings."

"I can give you the SS accession numbers."

"There is no need. I believe what you are saying."

"What happened to the art?"

Schmidt cleared his throat. "You are right. The paintings you mention and many more were taken to Wewelsburg Castle. They were about to be shipped to Berlin under the Fuhrer's orders. But Himmler knew the end was near. He knew the British were within a few hundred miles. He instructed *Obersturmbannfuhrer* Lando to take them instead to Italy. To find a safe hiding place for them there."

"Do you know where in Italy?"

"Lando suggested Florence. He told Himmler he knew places where they could be concealed and he would keep them there until the Reich established victory. Himmler agreed."

"Do you know where in Florence the paintings were taken?"

"I am sorry. This is all I know. I saw the paintings being crated and loaded ready to be sent. But I was not instructed to accompany Lando to Florence. I do not know where he took them."

"You saw them leave?"

"I did."

The conversation between the two men continued but offered nothing more than closing remarks, Schmidt still concerned his involvement would not be revealed, Arndt Schreiber checking to make sure the pastor knew nothing more of value and reassuring the man his past would remain secret.

Schreiber was about to sign off when he asked one more question. "I almost forgot, Dr. Schmidt. Why was Himmler content for Lando to take the paintings to Florence?"

"Himmler knew the War was lost by then. He would not admit it to his men but we knew that was the reality. His mind had turned to the future. The distant future. A way to ensure that what he believed in might endure."

"Lando promised to feed money from the sale of the paintings back into Germany after the War?"

"That is right. He agreed to pay the money into a holding company charged with keeping the ideology going, albeit now as a secret organisation."

"You know the name of the organisation?"

"I do not. It was some sort of umbrella to fund new far right societies in a new Germany. That is all I know."

Ferrara stopped the playback. "We now know one of the reasons Arndt was drawn to Florence. And we know how the theft of the paintings could have played a part in funding the kind of organisation that Max was drawn into, membership of which led to his death."

Gina cut in. "It would explain Arndt's interest in Florence. If he could expose what was happening there, if he could discover the source of funding for the far right in Germany, it would in the end lead back to *Ancestral Heritage Society* in Munich and those who killed his brother."

Ferrara agreed. "Indeed. The more so since Arndt was an intelligent man who knew about art. He knew about mythology. Enough, anyway, to know the significance of paintings like *Leda and the Swan*."

I wanted to get this straight. "So, Benito Lando was able to take the Wewelsburg paintings to Florence on the promise he would use their wealth in the future for the support of fascist groups in Munich, like the one that ensnared Arndt's brother Max?"

Ferrara nodded. "Yes, James, I think that is right. Benito Lando was an ideological fascist as much as anything else. It would have appealed to him. And he would have been credible in this role in the eyes of Himmler."

"He would keep his word?"

Gina cut in again. "If you can say such a thing about a madman like Benito Lando."

I agreed. "But I don't see Benito Lando ever having the need to sell those paintings. Everything I've learned about the Landos in the past three years points to the fact they make as much money as they need through drugs, extortion and the sex trade. It wouldn't have taken Benito Lando long to re-establish the family business once the War ended. If he wanted to keep his word about funding the fascists in Germany, it wouldn't have been difficult to find what was needed through the criminal activity. And when Alfieri Lando succeeded him, he would have done the same."

This appeared to make sense to Ferrara. "It would have been difficult then, as now, to find a buyer for masterpieces of such quality and such importance. It may be possible to find private collectors who would want to own one of them in secret, but they would demand a hefty discount. I agree, James, it is altogether possible those paintings have not changed hands. They would have much greater ritualistic value to the Landos."

"Which means they may still exist and have not been destroyed as so many are certain is the case."

"It is a possibility."

"So where does this leave us?"

"It means we have one more audio file to listen to. Then we will know the full extent of Arndt Schreiber's research and we will be on our own."

He read over Schreiber's note that accompanied the file. "It says it is a recording of a phone call from last year with a Dominican priest called Fra Finasi. There is no other information."

He pressed play.

Schreiber was speaking. "Father, you can tell me. There will be no comebacks."

The father's voice was unsteady. "You do not know what you are asking."

"I only want to know their name. What is there in a name?"

"Everything. You ask for everything."

"Without the name I will never be able to honour the memory of my brother."

"You promise anonymity."

"I guarantee it."

The father's voice was almost too quiet to hear. "*I discendenti di Leda.*"

"What was that?"

He repeated the name. "*I discendenti di Leda.* That is who they are."

"They seek the Elixir?"

"I am bound by oath not to say it."

"But since I say it for you, it is true?"

"Yes, it is true."

The recording ended.

Ferrara spoke first. "No doubt it was a longer conversation, but this fragment is all that Arndt retained."

I wanted to know if I'd heard the name correctly. "The Descendants of Leda. Is that what the secret society is called?"

Gina couldn't wait. "IDDL. *I discendenti di Leda.* It's the name I shouldn't have seen on Arndt's computer. The one he wanted to keep me away from."

Ferrara leaned back and rubbed his eyes in tiredness. "Yes, there is everything in a name. This is what I have feared. Men like the Landos involved in a secret society that has become a cult. Proof enough that they created their own world of madness. Something I have long suspected but which I hoped would never be shown to be true."

I could feel my heart sinking as I could not help thinking once more about what Julia and her sister had been put through at the hands of Alfieri Lando. "When you say they are a cult, Nico, what do you mean?"

He was trying not to alarm me but his words had just that effect. "I mean a grouping not just formed around the notion of secret knowledge but one believing its rituals offered them superior powers."

"Like immortality."

"Yes, and beyond that power over us all."

"By seeking out twins and turning them into victims."

"More than that, James. Taking the life energy of others so those in the cult could satisfy their deluded ambition to live forever."

"Yet Benito and Alfieri Lando died."

"Yes, they both died, like those before them, no matter what they believed. But that is never enough to stop the madness once the line is crossed. It is the real tragedy history seeks to hide. The truth that still will not speak its name."

"So where does this leave us?"

"Arndt has guided us as far as he can. We are now on our own."

"And what does that mean?"

Ferrara gave us both a look that said we should know what was coming next. "Everything leads back to Italy and Florence. There is nothing more for us here."

I knew I wouldn't be able to go anywhere without sleep.

Gina voiced my concern. "It's too far to drive without rest."

Ferrara was forced to agree. "OK. We take four hours sleep and then we set off."

Chapter 76

Retired Chief Superintendent Giles Cleary congratulated himself. He had a result. Something to make up for the debacle over DI Reid.

He knew where the Blake woman was.

Cleary prided himself on his contacts and his knowledge of how to employ them. That's what had continued after his early retirement from the Force. Business as usual.

He'd used the method that had paid such handsome dividends so many times in the past. He circulated images of the Blakes, all three of them – James, Julia and Miles. He let it be known there was a handsome reward for anyone who could let him know where they were. Nothing as inflated as what was offered by Matteo Lando. That sort of money produced problems in itself. Problems like DI Reid. Problems he'd had to work with. No, he offered something much less noteworthy, a few thousand, something more likely to produce reliable results. If in the end Matteo wanted to pay a million for each of the Blakes, so be it. He'd take the balance for himself.

It was more than luck, then. It was inevitable that no matter how careful the Blakes had been in leaving London, they would be found. Constable Eric Morgan's wife Clarissa had been the one. She worked in the maternity unit at Ambleside Hospital. Clarissa had recognised the woman from the photograph sent to her husband by Cleary. When Eric Morgan went to check he found the woman had given a false name and address that no one in the hospital had bothered to question. Yet, knowing the woman was still in Ambleside in all certainty, Eric began asking locals if they'd seen the woman in the photograph. It hadn't been difficult to discover that Julia Blake was staying at the farmhouse at the top of Rook Lane. She'd been seen with Faith Webster who lived there. When Eric Morgan went to check he heard that a young woman with a baby was staying in the farmhouse.

Cleary was in no doubt whom we should call.

Not Matteo.

He dialled and waited for the call to be answered.

He smiled when he heard the voice on the other end of the line. "Herr Heller. I have some good news for you."

Chapter 77

The journey back to Florence was long and troubled for Gina. The worry of not knowing about her sister was eating away at her. Yet the threats to her own safety in returning to Florence were as real as ever. Nothing had changed in that respect since she'd run south with Arndt Schreiber.

We'd crossed into Austria at Kufstein and were heading for the Italian border at Brennaro with Nico Ferrara pushing the Giulietta ever harder along the Brennerautobahn.

He sought to comfort her. "Gina, you can stay with my sister in Padova. No one will know you there. We will go on to Firenze and search for your sister. You could do no more if you were there yourself and you will be out of danger in Padova."

Gina was still conflicted. "It doesn't feel right. I should be there for her."

"It's going to be another three hours before we get close to Padova. Think it over, Gina. You can decide then."

I was in the back seat of the Giulietta. I was missing Julia. I had not spoken to her for days. The prospect of returning to Florence with no clear idea of how to bring to an end the threats to my family brought back again doubts that I'd done the right thing in being here, in leaving Julia and young Simon back in Ambleside. But I knew there was never a choice. The Landos were intent on destroying us.

We fell silent as we crossed into Italy at Brennaro. The fear that Manieri would have men waiting for us at the border was real but as on the journey north to Munich, we sped through unhindered. Yet we should have heeded those fears.

When we stopped at the Autogrill at Trento for coffee and food, Ferrara and Gina were approached by two State Police.

I'd separated from them for a few moments to wait in the line to order coffee and panini and was about to return to the table when I realised something was wrong. The questioning by the police was serious. It was clear they'd been watching for the Giulietta. Ferrara was unable to deny he was the owner. Then, to my dismay, I could only watch as Ferrara and Gina were led away. I could do nothing to stop them. The only consolation was I'd been able to remain out of sight and avoid being picked up with them.

I was alone again, over a hundred miles from Florence, in need of a lift.

Once the State Police left, taking Ferrara and Gina with them, I approached one of the drivers in the nearby truck parking area. I said I needed a ride. I hadn't expressed this well but he shrugged and gestured me to climb aboard.

I didn't know how to respond to the loss of Ferrara and Gina. I'd learned much from the professor. I would miss his level-headed advice on problems that for me were often overwhelming. I would miss the depth of his knowledge. And I would miss Gina's resolve to stand up against the odds.

Maybe they were better off in the hands of the police. Ferrara had his academic career to think about. He didn't belong out here, in the criminal world. If he could find honest police to deal with in Padova, he had a good chance of returning to a life away from danger, his career intact, teaching his students, examining them in the philosophy of religion. What did it matter that he was a witness to a shooting in Ostuni? He was no fugitive. Being arrested was the best thing that could have happened to him.

Or so I told myself.

The same went for Gina. She needed to find her sister and get away from the grip the Landos had on her. She had a better chance of help with Inspector Manieri. The more I told myself this was the case, the more I began to believe it myself.

I was the real fugitive. I was the one out in the cold, where I'd always been, seeking a key to bring down an enemy that had me outnumbered and outgunned. That hadn't changed.

As the truck lurched along the highway towards Florence, through a gathering storm that reduced visibility, I was distracted by the pulses of light from the oncoming traffic in the adjacent lanes piercing the gloom, playing across my face, dazzling me. Perhaps it was the aftermath of losing Ferrara and Gina and the feeling of being alone once more. The humming of the truck engine became ever more distant.

My mind began to wander, trance-like.

I was back with Alfieri Lando three years before, in the mausoleum at San Berado, staring down at his face distorted by death. Outside, his son Matteo was being arrested for the murder by Manieri's men. As I pressed on further into the stone cold labyrinth, I found Julia, lying there, drugged and abused. I was overwhelmed by the joy of seeing her again, of holding her close, knowing it was only the belief that I would find her that had sustained me and made this moment possible, finding her alive. In that moment, in my waking dream, the whole of my attention was on her, on taking her away from the stench of death down there and carrying her out into the clean air outside.

Yet in the dream I was seeing something more, something I had discounted then, something I could see now, as if for the first time.

In the periphery of my vision there was a movement.

Someone was closing a doorway.

One that led deeper into the hillside on which San Berado stood.

As I replayed the scene, I realised it was more like the closing of a secret compartment. When it was closed, it no longer looked like a doorway. It looked like any of the other mould-covered stone walls of the mausoleum.

I saw now what I hadn't seen then when I'd been overjoyed at finding Julia alive and taking her to safety.

I wanted to talk with Ferrara. He would be able to help, to put this into perspective. But as I came out of the dream and jerked back to attention, I remembered that, like Gina, he was no longer with me. I would have to work this out on my own.

The truck made good progress on the journey to Florence. The driver agreed to drop me at the railway station in the centre of town.

As I thanked him and stepped down onto the street, I knew where I should go next.

Chapter 78

What bothered Nate Craven most was he couldn't quite be sure he could read Agent Ashley. He hadn't been on the team for long and in the normal run of events there would be time to understand why. But too much of what had happened in Tijuana was outside of what Craven had expected.

First there were the reports that El Romero had been taken and all but killed by the Federales. It wasn't just bad for business. It was close to the end of the protection operation that had earned so much good money over so many years, not just for himself but for all those he'd moved over to the black side of his team, including Ashley. So why was he showing so little concern that Craven couldn't help thinking the man was hiding something?

Craven called Ashley into his office for debriefing. "Dillon, good work in bringing back Miller. I guess we'd call it mission accomplished."

"Well, Nate, she took a little convincing but let's say I persuaded her to understand the logic of coming back here and facing up to what she'd been doing down there."

"Nothing too rough, I hope."

"I think you'll find I got it right."

"So, tell me, what was she doing?"

"You need to ask her, Nate."

Craven scrutinised Ashley's face, seeking any indication he might be hiding something. "You heard about El Romero?"

"I saw the news reports, if that's what you mean?"

"And you know nothing more?"

"Like what, Nate?"

"Like it happened when you were there?"

Ashley shuffled in his seat but his expression did not change. "I was concerned with what you sent me there for, with Miller. I wasn't there to have any dealings with El Romero or anyone else in the cartels. The news says it was Martinez and the Federales who brought him in. I can't add anything more. Except it's no surprise Martinez is dead, after what he was doing."

Not a flicker. Not a sign that Ashley was hiding anything. Either he was a good liar or he was giving back just what he knew.

This brought into focus the second matter Craven couldn't square. When Debbie Miller had left for her supposed holiday in Hawaii, Craven had been certain she was on to him over Town Lake. It was hard to believe that hadn't been her purpose in meeting the Englishman in Tijuana.

It was a risk involving Ashley in anything to do with Town Lake but Craven decided this was merited by the situation. "Tell me, Dillon, in the time you were with Miller, was there any mention of Town Lake?"

"Why would there be, Nate?"

"Just another line I'm working on. Was it ever mentioned?"

Again, not a flicker. "No, Nate. I can tell you it wasn't and I can't think of a single reason why it would be."

Craven tried another approach. "You saw Miller with the Englishman, Miles Blake?"

"Yes, and from what I saw, I'd say they were close."

"You didn't seek to detain Blake or report his whereabouts, knowing that he is one of our prime targets?"

"My mission was about Miller. Bringing her back here."

"And what do you think Blake told her about the drugs business we have with El Romero?"

"She wouldn't say, Nate. But I think it's most certain we now have a problem."

"With Miller?"

"Yes. If she's now on to us."

Craven smiled. "Leave it with me, Dillon."

As the debriefing ended, Craven wanted to believe that the Tijuana events were all about the drugs business. As far as he could tell, this was what Ashley believed. He was playing his part as a team player, warning about Miller as far as he should. So, why did the nagging thought keep returning that Town Lake was still in the picture?

Craven ordered Ashley back to his workstation. "I'll run what you said past Miller and let you know how it plays."

Chapter 79

The cemetery behind the church at San Berado had changed little in the three years since I'd last been there. The multitude of marble monuments, clustered together, still vied for attention, overshadowed by the more substantial family mausoleums, small buildings in their own right, standing nearby.

I found my way to the Lando tomb. I had a plan of how I would gain entry. I'd stopped in Florence to buy a flash lamp and a crowbar from the old ironmonger store on Borgo la Croce where there had been no questions asked. If the wrought iron door to the tomb was locked, I would break in.

I glanced around. I was alone in the cemetery but I was concerned that any noise I might make would carry as far as the church and be heard by one of the monks who from time to time crossed the cobbled apron between the church itself and the outbuildings. I shouldn't have worried. When I pushed against the door it gave way and I was able to enter the tomb.

I used the flash lamp to pick my way past the small religious shrine with its cross and image of Mary that filled the entrance area. Pressing further inside, I squeezed past the stone coffins of the Lando ancestors. The stale, sweet smell of death made me catch my breath.

A new stone coffin had been added. It bore the name *Alfieri Lando* and the dates of his birth and death. Nothing more.

I pushed past, deeper into the mausoleum, into the small chamber where I'd found Julia.

Recalling my waking dream, I shone the flashlight around the walls, searching for the secret doorway I was now certain must exist. But there was nothing to indicate that my dream had been anything other than a product of my imagination.

Then I heard noises coming from outside. The sounds of someone checking the entrance to the tomb. I held my breath and turned off the flash lamp. I stood in the dark and trembled at the thought that the entrance door might be locked from the outside and I would be trapped inside.

When silence returned and I ventured back towards the entrance, I found my worst fears confirmed. I couldn't reach the entrance door. The door separating the chapel from the stone coffins of the Lando ancestors had been shut tight and I was on the wrong side. As I peered through the gaps in the wrought iron lattice of this doorway, I could see it had been barred and padlocked and could only be opened from the other side. There was nowhere to go but deeper into the tomb.

Had it been an act of fate that when I arrived the entrance to the tomb had been unlocked and someone had then come to close it? Or had I been seen approaching the churchyard and been taken in by a deliberate plan to trap me? It didn't matter which. I was here in this cold, damp, death-filled place with only the light of a flash lamp to find my way around.

Why had I been so foolish as to allow myself to be trapped like this? Why had I staked everything on a dream?

If I couldn't find a way out, I could die in here.

Chapter 80

When Wolfgang Heller received the message from Cleary he was in a hotel room in Innsbruck. He was in the city to rest for a few days, find available women and gain from them the energy that would allow him to overcome the disappointment of losing Blake.

Cleary's message changed all that.

He made his way to London on a scheduled flight. In a further few hours he was in the English Lake District, stepping off the train on to the platform at Windermere Station. He marvelled at this wonder of the modern world. That he could pass through countries with such ease as this.

He decided to wait until nightfall to make his move on Rook Lane.

The intelligence received from Cleary told him that the Blake woman had rudimentary protection. Nothing to delay him for long but something he needed to take care of if he was to achieve his goal in being here. He spent the hours he needed to wait in the Internet cafe in Argyle Street, using his tablet computer to keep in contact with Matteo Lando.

He messaged him from their chosen social media site.

> *My friend, I have good news. There is no need for me to come to meet you again as soon as planned. I have a lead on the woman we have the most interest in.*

The message came back by return.

That's no problem. Send her my best wishes for a long and trouble-free life.

Heller knew this was Matteo's way of granting permission for the Blake woman to be killed.

Heller closed off the conversation.

OK. I will wish her the best from you.

He logged off the site.

Another two hours until darkness fell.

Time to meditate on the success of his plan.

Chapter 81

He was surprised to be called in to see Bill Maynard but Agent Ashley soon realised what was required.

"Just tell me where she is, Ashley."

"Don't get me wrong, sir. I'm with you on this."

"So, where does Craven have her?"

"I can show you."

Ashley took Maynard and the six armed agents Carnegie supplied to the basement area of the FBI building. At the end of a long passageway on a level that could only be reached down an unmarked staircase and hence did not exist as far as anyone using the elevator was concerned, they were faced with a guard who sat behind a locked, roof-high lattice steel barrier.

The guard looked up as Maynard and his men approached, weapons drawn. "It's no entry. There's an interrogation in progress." Maynard waved the authorisation paper given him by Carnegie. "This says open up. And if you don't, in comes the pepper spray and the CS gas. So, let us in."

The guard looked once more at the six weapons pointed at him and pressed the button to open the door. "This is down to you. I just follow orders."

Beyond the next door, the interrogation was in full flow.

Debbie Miller was staked out on the downward-sloping wooden board and was choking on the water that had been drawn into her lungs as she'd fought for the last breath of air that might save her life.

Craven was enjoying his work and for a moment was unaware of what was happening behind him. "Tell me, Miller, what was the real reason for your trip to Tijuana? Tell me and this can stop."

When he realised what was happening, Craven turned and eyed Maynard and his men. "What do you want? This is a secure zone. What allows you to come bursting into here like this?"

Maynard said nothing. His look of disgust said it all. While Maynard's men surrounded Craven, Maynard pushed Craven aside, undid the leather restraints that pinned Debbie Miller to the board and lifted her in his arms. He carried her away from the interrogation zone and began administering first aid. "Got to get the water out of your lungs. Give you a chance to breathe."

Debbie began to come round with violent coughing and gasping as the water was expelled and clean air was taken in.

Craven was still protesting when Maynard called in medical support for Debbie and she was taken from the room on a trolley to the sick bay to recover. He was pointing at Maynard and shouting, "I told you I need to know who you are and what gives you the authority to come in here like this."

"The name's Maynard and I'm here to make your life hell."

Craven shuddered at the sound of the name. "I know you're thick with Miller. You don't think any of the lies she tells about me will be believed, do you? She's implicated. Compromised. No one's going to believe you're not just doing this to help her."

Maynard came up close and looked deep into the man's eyes. "Guess we'll see about that."

Maynard had never imagined he would do what he was about to do to a fellow agent. Someone on his own side. But then he'd never imagined someone like Craven could rise so far within the Agency and exert such a perverse influence on all he touched, nor that Craven would sink so low as to waterboard Debbie Miller. To do the same to Craven was nothing more than effective and appropriate.

Craven did not want to believe what was about to happen. "You're out of order, Maynard. You're not going to get away with it. This will finish your career."

"Like you tried to finish Debbie's?"

"Just see sense. I'll face my superiors. Our superiors. I'll give them my motivation in doing what I did. I'll explain. I'll take what's coming. Whatever they decide."

"Except you don't get the chance to do that, Craven. You see I know about the lies you served up about Town Lake. I know what you did and how you're the last man on the planet to deserve the Intelligence Star when all those people died. And I know about the drugs out of Mexico. It's all up for you, Craven. I just need to find out what else you know."

Maynard dragged Craven towards the waterboard.

Craven tried to fight back but Maynard was too strong. He appealed to the men with Maynard. "You're not going to let him do this. This is Nate Craven. Agent Nate Craven."

When Maynard nodded, two of them forced Craven onto the sloping wooden board and fixed tight the leather straps at his wrists and ankles. Maynard placed the thin cotton sheet over Craven's face and turned on the flow of water. The man's complaints soon stopped as he struggled to find the air to breathe.

Maynard knew this was a form of drowning. Except the process could be halted by stopping the water flow and allowing the victim to recover long enough to answer the questions put to him. And then it could be repeated again and again until every last secret was revealed. The Japanese had used it in World War Two. It was said they'd picked it up from the Spanish who'd used it during the Inquisition. Now it was part of Agency training to prepare field operatives for what might happen to them if they were captured.

They all talked. With Craven it was no different. Before the fifth drowning he'd told Maynard everything.

Maynard dismissed the men who were with him. "Stand guard outside. Close the door."

With Craven still struggling for breath from the last immersion, Maynard took the man by the throat and began to squeeze.

"I could strangle you, Craven, for what you've done. For who you are. But it would be too good for you."

Craven's eyes pleaded. "Let me go. There's nothing else you need."

Maynard covered Craven's mouth and nose with his big hands and waited as the life in the man began to be snuffed out. "This is the only release you deserve."

Craven struggled for longer than Maynard expected. He was a tough man but the leather ties at his wrists and ankles meant that all the strength that remained would be in vain.

At the last moment Maynard released him and stood back as Craven fought once more to fill his lungs with air. "Know this, Craven. I should have finished you. But I've let you live on to face the shame of what you've done. You're going to find your hell on earth."

Maynard called in the guards once more. "Better call the medics back. This man's suffered a relapse. Get him seen to. Then lock him up."

Chapter 82

The dankness of the tomb seeped into my skin. It was cold in here. I was shivering.

The battery in the lamp would fail if I used it too much. Without it I was lost.

I sat on the edge of Alfieri Lando's coffin and thought through how I'd arrived at this worst of all outcomes. It was a cruel irony that my best attempts to root out the evil of this family had led me here. To the place they were brought when they died. To the place where Julia had been abused.

I tried not to think about what Alfieri Lando had put her through. I had to keep my mind from returning to the way he'd drugged her and imprisoned her here and done with her as he wished. I tried to keep these thoughts at bay but they kept returning, fuelling a burning anger that was going to consume me if I didn't overcome it, sapping my resolve to find a way out.

I had to concentrate on what had brought me here. I had to trust myself if I was to have any chance of surviving.

In my waking dream I'd seen a doorway closing. Someone had closed it from the other side. It meant there must be something on the other side. A way out if I could find it.

I returned to the chamber where I'd rescued Julia and ran my hands over the surface of the walls. Cold, mould-covered stone. No notable features. Nothing protruding that could be pushed or pressed and could allow a secret doorway to open.

The lamplight was beginning to flicker. I was running out of time.

I turned off the lamp and stood shivering in the darkness. I fought against the growing feeling that I would never get out of there.

I told myself that a secret doorway was no use to anyone if it only opened from one side. There had to be a mechanism of some kind to open it from this side.

I used the lamp in flashes to return to the Lando ancestors. I sat again on Alfieri Lando's coffin. The next coffin belonged to Alfieri's father, Benito. I recalled the conversations we'd had about Benito Lando and the role he'd played in World War Two. Something told me to look in more detail at his coffin, using up precious lamplight as I searched.

There were scratch marks on the stone base the coffin rested on. Those marks suggested the coffin had been moved. Or could be moved. Why would that be needed for something this heavy?

I pushed hard against the coffin. It began to rotate. I pushed harder until it had moved through almost ninety degrees.

Then I saw it. A lever, set into the stone base, revealed now the coffin had been moved.

I pulled the lever.

In the chamber next door there was the sound of a mechanism being activated. Something like a weight supported on a chain being dropped.

I made my way back into the chamber.

A doorway opened.

Chapter 83

Bill Maynard sat at Debbie Miller's bedside waiting for her to come round.

He was holding her hand when she opened her eyes. "Bill. How long have I been out?"

"Not long, Debbie. You made it. That's what matters."

"You got me out of there."

"Promise me Debbie, you won't take risks like that again. Craven would have killed you."

"It was the only way to keep him from discovering how we were going to stop him."

"Yes, and you were so good at it you almost got yourself killed. And if the test hadn't shown a match?"

"But it did. You got the truth out of Craven?"

"All of it. The whole pack of lies. You were right, Debbie. Town Lake had nothing to do with East Africa. Craven blamed terrorists to cover for his own involvement in the drugs business in Mexico. He's been offering protection to the Soto cartel for the past five years. While we've been chasing the wrong people in East Africa, cocaine has been flooding into the US, mining lives. If he went down for that alone it would justify all I've just done. But that's just the beginning."

"You got more out of him?"

"By the time I'd finished with him I'm sure he'd held nothing back. Did you know he sent one of his men, Marvin Bryce, to London to try to kill me and Michael Bedford? And to make it worse he colluded with Bryce, once I'd stopped him, to name James Blake as the one behind Bryce's attempt to kill us, making Blake a key target. Another false trail Craven led us along."

"You accept that James Blake is innocent?"

"The more I look into the database, the more it looks like it. Craven's actions in renditioning him to Austin were way out of line. Another part of Craven's cover up."

"And his brother, Miles?"

"Same story. OK, he's been tapping contacts in the State Department to get information on the drugs traffic out of Mexico. So what? It's no capital crime. It's what journalists do. Though you know I'd stop most of them doing any of it if I had my way."

"You never were the touchy-feely type, Bill."

He smiled. "OK, Debbie, you know me too well. But you get the point. Making Miles Blake public enemy number one, making him a prime target, was all part of Craven's cover up of his own involvement in the drugs business. Miles Blake could have blown apart Craven's operation. No surprise that Craven was prepared to go to such lengths to stop him."

"And that's all, Bill?"

"I wish it was. Craven had Joe Franks killed, one of the most respected and loyal agents the Agency has ever seen. Removed by Craven to cover his tracks. And setting off more false trails in London. Everywhere you look, Craven's muddied the waters. All for his own gain. The more we look the more we find."

She sat up in the bed and stretched. "So, where does that leave us on Town Lake? Who was it if it wasn't East Africa terrorists?"

"I was hoping you'd know the answer, Debbie. Who was Craven covering up for? Who was it who used the explosive that came up from Mexico?"

"I couldn't be sure before this, Bill. Before you got the truth out of Craven. Now I'm more certain than ever that the Blakes know the answer."

She told Maynard what Miles had said about the Lando family. "They had a grudge against Elmore Ravitz. About a stolen Picasso. They sent an assassin to have the Ravitz family killed. A German called Heller. Wolfgang Heller."

"So Craven was hand in glove with this Lando family? That's why he covered for them?"

"I don't think so, Bill, I think Craven and the Landos are more like enemies brought together by circumstance. Craven had to cover for them because they were involved with the same cartel as Craven in Mexico. If they went down, Craven went down with them. So he covered for them at the same time as he worked against them."

"So little honour between thieves. Tell me, Debbie, what do we know about the German, about Heller?"

"He almost killed me and James Blake in Austin."

"You've seen him. You'd recognise him?"

"Yes, he's one I'll never forget."

"Where is he now?"

"We have no idea. What you say about Craven's false trails is so right, Bill. We haven't been looking for Heller."

"Or taking any special action on the Landos?"

"That's right."

"So, we need to find them. Take them down. Where do we begin?"

"With Matteo Lando in Sollicciano prison."

"I checked. The Italians are saying he's escaped."

"Then we need to start with Miles Blake."

"Where is he now?"

"When I left Tijuana, he headed for Mexico City. For the British Embassy to get travel papers. I guess he's still there, waiting for them."

"We can expedite the documents but we need to get someone out there to him."

Debbie sat up in the bed and swung her legs over the side. "I'll go."

"You need to stay here. You need time to recover."

"No, Bill, when I say I'm going, I mean it. I need to see this thing through. You know I'm not about to settle for anything less."

"Then if you won't listen to sense, I'll have to go with you."

Chapter 84

As the mechanism I'd activated from beneath Benito Lando's coffin clattered to a halt, the opening was waiting. I stepped through. It led into an unlit passageway just wide enough to shuffle along.

I tried the flash lamp. The battery had failed.

There was no choice but to keep moving forward into the darkness before me. I began to think this was a dead end and I'd be trapped here. Then I saw it. A faint glimmer of light in the distance ahead told me there was something at the end of the passageway. As I got nearer and my eyes adjusted to the light, I could make out another doorway. The light from whatever was on the other side was diffracting from the narrow gaps between the door frame and the doorway itself.

As I approached I heard noises coming from the other side. If the door could be opened, I knew I'd have to be careful not to step straight into whatever was waiting on the other side.

I listened. It was the sound of two men talking as they walked past. I could make out only a few words – *Our time is fast approaching* – before they were lost in the distance.

I pushed against the door. It opened and I stepped through into a wider passageway. The light, normal by usual standards, burned my eyes. I crouched down and waited for my vision to adjust.

I was in a clean, well-maintained space with an institutional look of its time. It reminded me of the Italian public buildings built during the Mussolini years and still in use in many parts of Italy. Grey steel and glass, utilitarian, featureless.

I knew I had to get out of the passageway. I didn't know where it led but the voices I'd heard were proof enough the area was peopled. It was vital I was not seen.

Moving along the passageway, I opened the first large steel frame door on my right. I entered a large room, an art gallery.

It was bigger, much bigger, than anyone would suppose when looking at the entrance to the Lando tomb in San Berado churchyard. This room was on a scale that belied any idea of a simple extension of the tomb. Though I had yet to explore further, the thought was forming that this was just one part of a major development, an underground complex hollowed out from the hillside beneath San Berado.

There were paintings, but they were not secured to the walls as in a conventional gallery. Each was stood on a gilded easel, allowing each painting to be picked up and moved when needed. There was an engraved plaque at the top of each easel with the initials IDDL.

I discendenti di Leda. The Descendants of Leda. The secret organisation.

I walked the length of the gallery, looking at each painting. They were all here. The priceless paintings on the itinerary set up by Benito Lando, the record of which we'd discovered in Arndt Schreiber's research papers. The paintings that were believed to have been destroyed in World War Two but moved here to Florence with the blessing of Himmler. Each was a masterpiece in its own right – Mantegna's *St James Led To His Execution*, Fra Angelica's *Last Judgment*, Botticelli's *Portrait of Cosimo De' Medici*, Ghirlandaio's *Jerome and John the Baptist*, Fra Bartolommeo's *Assumption of the Virgin*, Veronese's *Apollo and Juno and Saturn Help Religion to Overcome Heresy*, Caravaggio's *Saint Matthew and the Angel*. There were other masterpieces I did not recognise, ones not on the list, over fifty in all.

At the end of the line, set apart on more ornate gilded easels as a sign of their importance, stood the two paintings of *Leda and the Swan*, the Michelangelo and the Da Vinci, side by side.

What I was seeing was remarkable in its own right. I thought of how overjoyed Julia would have been to know such masterpieces had survived. But I knew the existence of the paintings here meant something more. They were proof that the conclusions we'd struggled to recognise as certainties when going through Arndt Schreiber's research papers were just that.

Certainties.

I discendenti di Leda was a reality. IDDL was a cult that had survived down the years and had prospered even as wars and plagues and natural disasters had passed by them. And I knew now why Arndt Schreiber had attached so much importance to understanding the occult fantasies of a madman like Himmler, the weird beliefs used to justify genocide and the hatred of mankind. Benito Lando had convinced Himmler to develop the San Berado site as a secret underground centre.

Nico Ferrara had been right to follow the art. Here it was. But he had been wrong to say Arndt Schreiber had spent too much time on the *Ahnenerbe*. There was a reason why Himmler had been content to allow Benito Lando to take the looted paintings to Florence. There was a hiding place in Florence far superior to anything offered at Wewelsburg Castle. The underground complex beneath San Berado where I now stood.

The connection we'd missed was that the secret society in Munich that was responsible for the killing of Arndt Schreiber's brother, Max, was itself linked to the *Ahnenerbe*, to the same fallacy.

The more I thought about this, the more I recalled what I'd learned from Arndt Schreiber's research, the more I was convinced this was what Benito Lando had all along been aiming at. To use the madness of Nazi mysticism as a vehicle to establish his own secret centre at San Berado. The whole hillside beneath the church was a vast labyrinth, a secret centre for *I discendenti di Leda*, IDDL.

Ferrara was right that Benito Lando had used the crazy self-delusional beliefs of Himmler for his own ends. But Ferrara had not dared to consider the scale of Benito Lando's ambition. It was certain now that Lando had convinced the Germans to develop San Berado as one of the *Ahnenerbe* underground sites. Himmler believed in the literal existence of a superior race living underground in secret locations, possessed of superhuman powers drawn from the energy of the earth and who would one day be released and rule the world. Benito Lando had convinced Himmler to develop San Berado as one of those sites, to search for that energy, while all the time serving the interests of his own cult.

How much suffering had gone into the construction of this place? How many of the inmates of Dachau, or concentration camps like it, were shipped here and worked until they died? How many local Florentines were killed to preserve the secret of its existence?

My thoughts were interrupted by voices approaching from the passageway outside.

I looked around the gallery. There was nowhere to hide. But there was another doorway at the far end of the room. If I hurried, and if the door wasn't locked, I might be able to make it to the next room before those approaching came in.

It was a close run thing. As I tried the door to see if it would open, the newcomers were just entering the gallery. The door opened. Just in time, I entered a small room, set up for meetings, with a white board and audio-visual equipment. I closed the door behind me and sank to the floor, out of sight.

In the gallery there were two men talking about the paintings. I recognised one of the voices. It was a voice I could not forget. It belonged to Matteo Lando. There was a window that looked onto the gallery. I risked looking in, being careful to not show too much of myself. It was him. He was giving instructions to an elderly, well-dressed man. "Bring in the Fra Bartolommeo first. Then, when I signal it, and not a moment before, bring in the Ledas."

"Both of them?"

"Yes, we need them."

They hadn't seen me. I breathed again as they walked away from the paintings and left the room, still talking.

What was Matteo Lando doing here? He was meant to be in Sollicciano prison. Yet he was here and there was no doubt he owned the place.

I was powerless but I had one strength on my side. If I could escape I could let the world know what was down here. Yet I had no clear idea how I might find a way out other than to explore and risk being discovered.

Before leaving the gallery, I removed both of the Leda paintings from their easels and concealed them in the room where I'd been hiding. How light and unsubstantial they felt as I lifted them down. There was a space between the audio-visual unit and the adjacent wall wide enough to drop the paintings in where they would be out of sight. I did not know if this was much more than a gesture of defiance. When they discovered the Ledas were missing and a search was launched, how difficult would it be to find the masterpieces? My hope was the panic caused by the thought that the paintings had been stolen might provide a diversion as I tried to find a point of escape elsewhere in the complex.

I ventured back out into the passageway, hoping I would not be seen before finding another place to hide. I opened the next door and found myself in a large amphitheatre. At the centre was a raised dais with an altar illuminated by spotlights from above. Some kind of ceremony was about to take place here and the start was imminent. Perhaps that was the significance of the conversation about the paintings that I'd overheard in the art gallery.

The periphery of the amphitheatre was in darkness. My plan was to skirt round to the far side to search for an exit.

I didn't make it.

From out of the darkness I was grabbed from behind. A gun was placed to my temple by one of them while the other placed a large hand over my mouth.

I was powerless to resist as they dragged me away.

Chapter 85

They were Lando men. Burly, strong, Italian. They dragged me out of the amphitheatre, along another passageway and into a small room with no windows where I was left to sit and wait as the door was locked behind me.

Time passed. My eyes searched the room for any possibility of escape. It had been chosen well. There was no way out.

There was a sound behind me. The door being unlocked and then opened.

I turned.

There was Inspector Manieri.

I thought for a wild moment he'd come to rescue me, that he'd been interviewing Ferrara and Gina and come to the same conclusions as I had about what was under San Berado.

But his expression told me I was wrong.

"Signor Blake. This is not the way I had hoped we would meet again."

There was an elderly, tall man with him. The same man I'd seen talking with Matteo Lando in the art gallery. If this man was with Matteo, it meant Manieri was also part of what was happening here.

He could see I was staring at the elderly man. Manieri smiled. "James, I see you have not met. Chief-Superintendent Cleary is a compatriot of yours, I believe."

Cleary showed no emotion. "We need to find out how he knew we were here."

Manieri held up a hand. "There will be plenty of time for that. First, I want to renew my acquaintance with James and let him know the real meaning of what he has done."

I looked hard at Manieri's face, seeking the intelligence and compassion I'd always assumed to be there but could find none. "Why did you do it?"

"Do what?"

"Join them. Join the Landos."

He offered Cleary a seat and took one himself. "You see, James, when I prosecuted the Landos and, with your help, began to tear down their empire, I could not help discovering there was more to them than mere criminality. They made me an offer. As you say in your movies, one I could not refuse. And I think you know what that offer was now, James."

"They told you there was a way to live forever."

"Yes. And there is."

"So you became part of this?"

"That is right. And I discovered what you should now know. The damage you did three years ago when you came here to rescue your wife had a significance you could not have understood."

"I did it for her. To save her life."

"And took away Alfieri Lando's chance of immortality. You see, none of this comes easy. To gain the gift of immortality from the mighty god Zeus, everything has to be in place. Mercury, the messenger, the Earth and the Sun had to be in special alignment. And the women have to be ready."

I was struggling not to vent an uncontrollable anger welling inside me. "You mean for him that meant Julia and her sister, Emelia."

"Alfieri Lando searched the world to find them, these descendants of Leda. They are two in a million and it's a one in a million chance of finding them. And you and your wife took that away. Your wife helped Emelia escape to London. She got Emelia killed."

"It was Ridley."

"He would not have been involved if Julia had not interfered."

"You helped me capture Matteo Lando here at San Berado."

He smiled. "I did not know then what I know now. It would be different now."

"You were doing your job. Upholding the law."

"And that meant more to me then than it does now. Think about it, James. To live forever. To not have to die."

"Why are you telling me this?"

"You have used so much initiative to get here, James. I would have expected no less. But you will never leave this place and you should know what you have done. And when the moment of transformation comes you will know how we triumphed despite all your attempts to stop us."

There was madness in his eyes and a childish enthusiasm in his voice that told me he was lost to normal reason. If he felt the need to talk, I was prepared to listen and learn. "So why did you arrange the meeting with Zella DeFrancesco?"

"Because I wanted to draw you in."

"Into what?"

He licked his lips. "Again, I think you know the answer, James."

He was playing with me, delighting in telling me how he'd succeeded and how I'd failed. And I knew where this was going. "*You* wanted Gina."

"*Yes*. We have her sister, Malika. Like your wife and her sister, Malika and Gina are special. They are the new daughters of Leda at this special time when Mercury, the Earth and the Sun are again in special alignment. They are another of those one in a million outcomes that Alfieri worked so hard to achieve. And, of course, it is only if they are together that they are of value to us. Gina had escaped. Just at this moment, when destiny was approaching, we had lost the key to the transformation."

"So, you used me to find Gina?"

"Yes. You've been as naive as we could have hoped, James. DeFrancesco led you to Ferrara, as we expected. You were believable enough for the professor to trust you. He took you to Ostuni, to Gina."

"That's why you bugged the phone."

"Indeed."

"And why Heller was sent after us."

"He was supposed to kill you and Ferrara and bring back the girl. Once again you got in the way."

The hard truth dawned on me. "But you now have Gina."

He smiled. "Of course. It was a matter of time. The State Police knew to bring her to me. She is here. Being prepared."

"For what?"

"For the transformation."

"And Ferrara?"

"He is also here. It is fitting. Where else to keep him where he cannot talk?"

The madness had not left Manieri's eyes. His belief in the certainty of imminent deliverance meant he had no reason not to enjoy telling me over and over how he'd bettered me.

If I was never to leave this place as Manieri foretold, I knew I should at least discover as much as I could. "I've seen Matteo Lando here. What changed him?"

Manieri adopted his most paternal stance. "This is beyond what you should know, James. But since you will never leave, I will tell you. Matteo Lando is our leader. What you might think of as our high priest. But that did not come about for him with ease. Matteo knew his father expected he would one day take his place as a leader of men. Matteo thought that meant becoming head of the Lando family. He listened too much to his mother, Alessa. As you know, Alfieri died before Matteo knew that what was planned for him was much more than a criminal career. He had been so estranged from his father as a result of Alessa's influence that he did the killing himself. A killing made inevitable by you and your wife. Yet even this was not enough

314

to deny him the chance to fulfil his destiny. It took time, but we were able to groom him. It was impossible not to send him to prison. The public demanded it. But I was able, with Cleary's help, to make sure Wolfgang Heller was sent to Sollicciano to protect Matteo. And, as you also know, Sollicciano is suitable in being near to Florence."

"Heller was there for more than protection."

"Yes, he was there as much for spiritual guidance, to make Matteo aware of his destiny."

"So you got him out of Sollicciano."

"He's been coming here as he wishes for over a year. He has a private way in and out of the prison. At night. We had to allow things to be hard for him in the beginning. We needed to make sure he understood how he should depend on Wolfgang Heller. So he would trust him."

"And the authorities turn a blind eye."

"The right people have been bribed. This is Italy. It is as simple as that. Now, since the FBI has increased their interest in him, Matteo spends all his time here." Manieri paused. "Oh, I was forgetting, there is something you do not yet know about."

I pressed on. "Heller is here?"

He smiled once more. "Nothing so simple, James. And something that brings us closer to the point of letting you know all this. You see, we have not forgiven you or your wife for what you did three years ago. How you squandered the chance for Alfieri to achieve immortality. Heller is not here. He's gone to find Julia, to make her pay, just as you will now pay for what you did."

My heart pounded. "You're demented. You don't know where she is."

He glanced towards Cleary. "That's where the Chief Super-intendent comes in. Tell him, Giles. How you found her."

Cleary stood and stared into my eyes. I could feel the hatred. "You thought you were clever hiding her away in Rook Lane but I have contacts, Mr. Blake, and I used them well. Wolfgang Heller is on his way to Ambleside as we speak."

The thought that Julia was in such danger made me want to take Cleary by the throat and squeeze the life out of him. But I was powerless. There were Lando men outside who, if summoned, would restrain me. I bided my time.

Manieri smiled. "Yes, James, these are the things I wanted you to know. We want your agony to be complete when we kill you. After we show you images of your dead wife and son."

I spat in Manieri's face. "That's what I think about your immortality. You will die, Inspector, just like all the others who've chased the same illusion down the years. You'll be no different. I'll find a way to kill you if anything happens to my wife and son." Manieri wiped his face. "We will see, Signor Blake. We will see."

I realised then I had made the mistake of my life in leaving Julia. All I had succeeded in doing was getting myself trapped here inside the labyrinth under San Berado, unable to tell her that Wolfgang Heller knew where she was.

Chapter 86

I knew there was no merit in continuing to blame myself for the mistake I'd made in leaving Julia and our son. If there was any chance of saving her, I had to find a way out of this place.

The Lando man who'd been placed on guard duty outside the room came in every thirty minutes or so to check on me. I didn't know how they thought I was about to make my escape but he must have been told to keep a close watch.

The more I thought about it, the more I realised there was a way but I had just one chance of getting it right.

When the door opened and the Lando man came in I was hiding in the concealed space behind the door and the wall. As he noticed I was no longer sitting at the table and he came further in to find me, I kicked the door shut and brought down on his head the steel framed chair I'd been holding high above me. I used all the force I could muster.

He was big and for a moment I thought the blow had bounced off him. But after a second his knees buckled and he fell to the floor.

I was back as a youngster in Birmingham, facing up to my father, Danny, all over again. His endless rage at the unresolved conflicts in his life had made our family a violent place. My response had been to stand up for my mother and brother, Miles, but to disavow violence. I'd found a better way then and for the rest of my life. Through education and reasoned argument, problems could be dealt with without the need for aggression. But since the threat of the Landos had come into my life I'd learned there were times when violence was the only way, no matter how much I'd tried to distance myself from it and how much that invalidated how I'd struggled to be different from Danny. This happened first when I confronted Clinton Ridley and demanded he tell me about his involvement with Julia. Now here was another moment when only violence would do. The Lando man was reaching for the pistol in his trouser belt and preparing to get back to his feet.

I smashed the chair down onto his head again and drew blood. A gaping wound opened in his bald skull and he sank back to his knees. I swung the chair again and he was forced lower. He tried to shout out. I didn't know if he had an accomplice outside. I only knew I had to silence him. I swung the chair again and again. More blood. He fell silent, unconscious.

I took the pistol and waited, listening for any sound coming from outside that might alert me to the arrival of his accomplices. Then I heard it, the sound of onrushing footsteps. One, maybe two, men arriving.

They would not expect me to be armed. This was the element of surprise I possessed. I knew I could not afford to waste it.

I had a moment to look down at the pistol, to slide over the safety catch.

I shot the first one between the eyes as he was about to enter the room. He fell, revealing a third man behind him, who, seeing I was about to fire, turned and tried to run. I hit him in the back with two shots and watched him collapse before he could cover four or five more paces. I picked up the pistols they'd been carrying. I'd used three bullets. With the three weapons I had fifteen shots left. Was this enough to kill everyone in the place and allow me to find a way out?

I returned to the room where I'd been kept. The man I'd battered with the chair was starting to move. I shot him through the base of the skull and didn't wait to watch him die.

Somewhere in the midst of this carnage, I had the fleeting image of my father, Danny, giving a knowing smile, as if to say that if he'd taught me anything, he'd taught me this. Somehow, in this moment, I'd been forced to abandon a lifetime of reason and argument. It wasn't just the thought of what might happen to Julia and our son that drove me. It was my revulsion at the sick fantasies about to be played out in the amphitheatre.

I couldn't stay here. The sound of the gunshots would have been heard echoing down the passageways ahead. Others would be coming. I had to act and not stop to think about the consequences.

Chapter 87

It was a short run back to the amphitheatre. I wasn't sure what I'd find there but at least I could visualise the layout.

Inside, preparations were being made for the ceremony that was going to take place on the dais. Overseen by Cleary who was seated beneath them, two men in red robes were rehearsing the wording of the ritual.

I slipped into the dark periphery of the amphitheatre, keeping out of sight.

The rehearsal was interrupted by the arrival of another man in red robes. He was agitated and shouting, "The paintings. They're missing."

Cleary tried to calm him. "Slow down. What's happened?"

"When I went to collect the paintings from the gallery, they were gone. Both Ledas. The easels are empty."

Cleary became angry. "Find them." He pointed at the two men on the dais. "Take these two with you."

I didn't know how long it would take them to find the paintings I'd hidden but something important had resulted. Cleary was now alone. I approached from behind and, before he could turn, held the muzzle of the pistol to his temple. I clamped my free arm around his neck. "Cleary, if you want to live another minute, tell me where the prisoners are."

He stiffened. "What prisoners?"

"Gina and her sister. Ferrara. You know who I mean."

"This won't do you any good. In a few minutes our men will be everywhere."

"And that means no immortality for you. Not with a bullet in your brain. Take me to the prisoners. This is your last chance." I squeezed harder on the trigger.

There was a risk that Cleary's words might come true but I was prepared to gamble. Any secret society that promised so much to its adherents would be tempted to keep the numbers small, just as in those churches for whom there are only so many places for the Elect in Heaven – they are all now empty with a vast graveyard outside. If that was the case, my fifteen bullets might be enough.

Cleary relented. "OK. OK. Don't shoot. I'll take you there."

He led me along a passageway that began on the far side of the amphitheatre and ended at a set of metal doors. I pushed him through and we descended a short flight of steps to a floor below that was less well-lit than what was above. It smelled of decay and the unmistakable odour of human suffering.

I pushed Cleary further along the passageway, all the time keeping the pistol pressed hard against his temple. He stopped at another door. "They're inside. There's a guard."

I pressed harder with the pistol. "So, when we go in, you tell him not to shoot or you'll be gone."

He stammered. "OK. OK. I understand."

The door opened and we entered a confined space. There were prison cells to the right and an observation position to the left. Another of the Lando men, large and suited, was on duty there. When he caught sight of Cleary with my pistol held to his head, the guard reached for the gun before him on the table. Cleary shouted. "Don't shoot!"

The guard hesitated for a short moment. That gave me my chance. I drew the pistol away from Cleary's temple and fired at the guard, hitting him in the chest. As he fell, I shot him through the heart. Within ten seconds, the pistol was back at Cleary's head.

I could feel Cleary trembling, fearing he was next. "You don't have to do this. I can help you get out of here."

I pushed Cleary toward the dying guard and, using my free hand, searched for the keys to the prison cells. They were on a chain attached to the guard's belt. I removed the bunch of keys and turned toward the cells.

Ferrara was in the first cell. His face was bruised and he had the distracted look of a man who'd been tortured. Yet he managed a pained smile when he caught sight of me. "James. I did not think I would live to see you again."

I gave the keys to Cleary. "Unlock the cell."

He made the task of finding the right key as difficult as he could and I suspected he was delaying in the hope that help might come. "Cleary, open the door or you're gone like your friend over there." Cleary found the right key and opened the door. Ferrara came out and I pushed Cleary in and locked the door. "He'll be safe in there while I release the others."

Ferrara hugged me. He was weakened by what they'd done to him since he'd been brought here but he had enough strength left to give me an emphatic embrace. "We need to get out of here."

"Where's Gina?"

"With her sister, further along, I think."

We found them in the last cell in the block. Gina was with her twin sister, Malika. They were drugged and incapable of registering who we were. I recalled how Alfieri Lando had used heroin to drug Julia when he'd held her here three years ago. And I recalled how in the myth of Leda and the Swan, as Zella DeFrancesco had reminded me, Leda had been seduced by Zeus, under the mesmerising influence of Hypnos. The women had been prepared for the ceremony that was about to take place upstairs. It would not be long before men would be coming here to collect them.

I turned to Ferrara. "Are you strong enough to help? We need to get them away from here."

If he was unsure how well he would cope he didn't admit it. "James, I am with you."

We helped the twins, cussing and complaining, from the cell. They were so much under the power of the drugs they'd been given they wanted nothing more than to stay where they were.

I placed Gina's arm over my neck and shoulder. "Gina. It's me. James."

Her eyes flickered. The sound of my voice was enough for her to recognise me at last. "James. What are you doing here?"

"Getting you out before it's too late."

"What about Malika?"

"Don't worry, she's right here."

Ferrara supported Malika as we made our way back to the cell where I'd left Cleary.

I looked over at the guard. There was a large pool of dark blood under the table where he'd died.

I turned towards Cleary and shouted to Ferrara. "What shall we do with him? He says he can show us a way out."

Ferrara replied through clenched teeth. "I would like to do more than talk to him."

"Was he one of your torturers?"

"Yes. They wanted to know where you were and would not believe me when I told them I did not know."

I didn't know how long it would be before more Lando men made it here. I judged that if the diversion caused by the missing paintings disrupted them as much as I hoped, we should have a few minutes with Cleary.

As I took out the bunch of keys and began to unlock the cell door, the first of the foreshocks hit. It lasted just twenty seconds but its intensity was surprising. The ground under our feet shook so hard we were almost thrown off our feet.

I steadied myself and turned to Ferrara. "What was that?"

He grimaced. "It could mean the beginning of a major earthquake. They say there hasn't been a big one in Northern Italy for over four hundred years."

"Let's hope that isn't about to change."

Chapter 88

Though the foreshocks had lasted just a few seconds, their ferocity filled me with foreboding. The next shocks would be worse. A full blown earthquake was on the way. It was not something I had to reason about. It was something I felt.

The situation was bad and about to get worse. When I thought this through again, I realised Gina and Malika were in no condition to move at any reasonable pace. Ferrara was able to help but had been weakened by the treatment he'd been given here in the cells. We needed as much time as possible for all three to recover. Yet time was what we lacked. It wasn't just that the earthquake was approaching. Matteo Lando and his men would soon find us.

I gave one of the pistols to Ferrara. "If they come, you'll know how to use this?"

He nodded. "And you?"

It was counterintuitive but in this moment it was the only thing to do. "I'm going to find Matteo Lando and Manieri. Get to them before they get to us. Nico, do what you can to bring Gina and Malika round so we have a better chance to run for it when the time comes."

Ferrara gestured towards Cleary, still locked in the cell. "What shall I do with him?"

"If you're attacked, threaten to shoot him. Otherwise leave him as he is. We need him to deliver on a way out of here."

Ferrara seethed with anger. "This man has no integrity. No soul. Nothing is left but a vain hope of immortality that he would do anything to satisfy. What makes you think you can trust a man like this?"

"I don't need to trust him. I just need him to know I'll kill him if he doesn't deliver."

I left Ferrara and the others and climbed the stairs back to the upper level. The passageway leading back to the amphitheatre was deserted. I crept along with the pistol raised and the second pistol in my trousers belt.

When I entered the amphitheatre they were waiting for me. Matteo Lando and Manieri were together on the dais and saw me as soon as I came in.

I decided darkness was my best ally. I retreated into the periphery of the amphitheatre and continued to move round the chamber, crouched, watching.

Matteo Lando called out. "Blake. You should give up now. Your battle is over. Our time has come."

While Lando tried to hold my attention, Manieri was on the move, coming after me.

I shouted back. "You're deceiving yourself, Lando. I have the paintings and I have the twins. Without them you have nothing. There will never be enough time for men like you. Your day will never come. Your dreams will remain what they are – nothing but self-serving illusions."

Lando climbed down from the dais and began to circle the amphitheatre from the direction opposite to Manieri. They planned to trap me in a pincer movement.

Lando shouted back. "Think what's happening to your wife and son right now, Blake. Why you are not there to protect them? Whose dreams are illusions now, eh?"

I'd lost both men in the darkness. I pulled out the second pistol from my waistband. I kneeled down and waited, listening for the inevitable sounds of their approach.

There was the slightest sound to my right. I turned and fired. It was Manieri, closer than I expected. I must have hit him. A lucky shot. The light was too dim to see him, but I could hear the moans of a dying man.

Before I could turn, Matteo Lando was on me. He held a gun to the base of my skull and wrapped a giant arm around my neck. "Put the guns down, Blake."

I dropped the pistols.

He smiled. "You know it was always going to end like this. I hoped to see your face when I showed you the photographs of the corpses of your wife and son. I hoped to smile as I placed the agony of knowing that in your mind. It would not have been enough to repay you for the trouble you and your kind have caused my family, but I would have enjoyed it all the same. Now, I will have to kill you and forsake that pleasure."

He was about to squeeze the trigger. I prepared for the end. A last fleeting image of Julia came to my mind and with it the terrible fear I would not see her again.

The earth shook as the second wave of foreshocks, stronger than the first, hit.

Lando was thrown off his feet and sent crashing into the nearby seating. I was rolled along the floor in the opposite direction until I was stopped by something. I lay there, face to face with Manieri. I stared at his vacant open eyes and knew he'd died.

As suddenly as they had begun, the shocks stopped. I crawled back towards where I'd been hiding before Lando had overpowered me, searching for one of the pistols.

I could hear Matteo Lando coming towards me but could not yet see him in the darkness. He was close. I could hear his breathing. It told me he'd been injured by his fall but was still strong.

I reached down. It was one of the pistols. I picked it up.

Lando fell on me. He had lost his gun but he had the ferocious intent of the mad man I knew him to be. He took me by the throat and began to squeeze. I could feel the tremendous, mindless power of those hands, draining the life out of me.

With the last of my retreating strength, I pushed the pistol into his chest and fired. When the first shot didn't cause his hands to be removed from my neck I fired again. And again.

The energy drained from his hands.

I pushed him away. I struggled for breath, wheezing and gulping at the air.

I touched my chest. It was soaked in the blood that had flowed from him as he'd lain on top of me.

Chapter 89

I waited, expecting a further onslaught but it did not come. The amphitheatre was silent. I was right after all. The vanity of those who supposed they were about to become gods had led them to trust few with the knowledge of their madness. Yet I knew there were at least three of the cult members left. The two who'd been dispatched by Cleary to find the missing paintings and the one who'd reported the paintings were missing. I had the feeling there weren't many more.

Matteo Lando lay face down where he'd fallen after my gunshots. I turned him over just to make sure I'd killed him. Desperate anger was frozen in his face. He was a long way from the immortality that just a few minutes before he'd thought was his. In death as in life, his was a story of expectation unfulfilled.

A strange compulsion came over me. Despite everything, I wanted to remove the painting of *Leda and the Swan* from where I'd hidden it and find a way of getting it out of here. There was no sense in it. The painting had been at the centre of everything bad that had happened to me and my family and here was this urge to protect it. Maybe I wanted it as evidence of what had taken place. Maybe I felt the only way to be free of its influence was to possess it. Or perhaps it was about delivering something that would mean so much to Julia as a way of mitigating the fact that I'd abandoned her. I recalled that the Da Vinci *Leda and the Swan* was hidden with the Michelangelo. My plan was to rescue both.

I left the amphitheatre and made my way towards the gallery. The shocks had caused permanent damage. Deep cracks streaked the floor, walls and ceiling of the passageways that I ran along.

As I neared the gallery, I saw at the end of the passageway the three of them coming towards me. They'd found the paintings in the room where I'd hidden them. They paused as they saw me. One of them reached under his robe for a weapon. I levelled my pistol and prepared to fire. "I just want the paintings. Hand them over and I won't shoot."

My words were lost. There was another intense shockwave as the earthquake hit again. I fell as the floor beneath me undulated like a cresting wave. Between me and the three initiates, a massive section of concrete roofing came down, blocking the passageway so I could no longer see them. They'd either been buried or entombed, I didn't know which. The paintings were lost with them.

I waited. The shockwave had passed. Another would soon be coming.

The passageway behind me was still open. I hoped there was a chance to get back to Ferrara, Gina and Malika before the next shocks hit.

It was like a birth in reverse. As the shocks came closer together the result was inevitable. But this would be destruction not new life.

When I made it back to the cells, Ferrara was waiting. "James! We thought we had lost you."

I surveyed the damage. This part of the structure had escaped the full impact of the shocks so far. "Gina and Malika, are they any more able to move?"

Gina called out. "I'm here, James. I can help Malika if you can find a way out of here."

I unlocked the door to Cleary's cell and walked in. He trembled as I levelled the pistol at his head. "I'm not about to shoot. Not yet. But you need to show us the way out."

He held up his hands, making sure I wasn't about to fire. "There's an exit out onto the steps near Pizzale Michelangelo.

It's another way out if the entrance in San Berado churchyard is closed."

I pushed Cleary out of the cell holding the pistol to the base of his skull.

We would have made easy targets as we left the prison area and climbed the stairs back to the upper level. But there was no one left to threaten us. The real fear was we would not make it out before the next shockwaves hit.

Cleary went first with the barrel of my pistol pressed against his head. At the same time, I supported Gina with my free arm. Malika, with Ferrara all but carrying her, brought up the rear.

When the next shockwaves came it was like an eruption. The whole structure, carved out of the hillside below San Berado with such cunning, was about to collapse down on itself, the hollowing out having introduced fatal weaknesses the earthquake was about to exploit.

The walls and ceilings in the passageways through which we were moving were falling in on flooring that itself was in constant flux.

Cleary began to run ahead. "The exit is just here."

I didn't shoot. He may still have secrets to reveal on how we could escape.

Yet we couldn't run. Gina and Malika were still in need of support. We were moving at the best speed we could but Cleary was getting further away.

Then it hit me.

If Cleary could get to the exit, escape through it and close the exit from the outside, we'd be trapped in here.

I shouted to Gina. "Can you walk unaided?"

She shouted back, "I'll be OK. Get after him."

I sprinted after Cleary. I should never have allowed him such a head start. He was now out of sight, around a bend in the passageway. As I rounded the bend, I caught sight of him pulling back the bolts on an antique wooden door and preparing to open it.

There was another huge shock. The earthquake had peaked. The structure was imploding.

I kept my feet and continued to run until my lungs ached.

Cleary had drawn back the last of the bolts and was opening the door.

As he stepped through, I threw myself at him, landing on top of him, knocking the wind from his lungs.

I stunned him with a sharp blow of the pistol to his head and he lay on the ground, moaning.

Looking back through the open doorway, I could see only dust and falling masonry as the full violent impact of the earthquake took its toll.

There was no sign of Ferrara or Gina and Malika. I was sure they were lost.

There was no choice. I couldn't leave Cleary as he was. When I went back into the passageway to look for Ferrara, Gina and her sister, I could not run the risk of Cleary coming round and bolting the door.

I pulled out the gun and pressed it to Cleary's temple.

He whimpered. "You don't need to do this. You can trust me."

I squeezed the trigger and watched as his eyes opened wide, pleading.

I didn't fire.

There was a hand on my shoulder. It was Ferrara. "Much as I would want you to, James, there is no need. We are out."

Gina and Malika were with him.

There was an immense crashing and splintering of stone and metal behind us as the labyrinth collapsed, bringing down much of the hillside with it.

We began to run as best we could, fearful we might yet get sucked down into the boiling earth.

When the tremors stopped there was a sudden silence that was louder than any sound I'd ever heard.

We'd reached an area of made-up roadway on Pizzale Michelangelo and were at the base of one of the lesser statues of David that are common in Florence. Though the hillside had collapsed on itself throwing up a pall of white dust, the statue and the area around it were distant enough to have survived. We lay down exhausted at the base of the David.

Ferrara gave a weak smile. "I think it's over. There will be no more shocks."

I was breathless with the strain of running and supporting Gina. "I think you're right. The annihilation of San Berado is complete. There's nothing more to destroy."

We checked Gina and Malika. They were groggy and in need of medical care but had survived.

Cleary was getting to his feet. I reached for the pistol but he did not respond. "You can put it away, now, Blake. It's all changed now we're out here. If you shoot me, what are you going to tell them when they arrest you for killing a well-respected retired British police officer? You had to shoot me because I'm a danger to the world? That's not going to stand up in court and you know it. Not when all the evidence is buried under San Berado."

Ferrara was angry. "You know, Cleary, in all the years I've studied mythology, I thought I understood the madness of men like you. I thought I understood the depths your blind vanity could take you to. But I was wrong. Until I saw it with my own eyes, until I felt the pain and suffering brought about by men like you, I couldn't have known what a danger your kind pose to the future of the world."

Cleary sneered. "I'm walking away now. Neither you nor Blake will stop me. You need to know that the dream of men like me lives on, despite the damage you have done. There are others like me all over the world. I'll be joining them to pursue the dream. You'll never stop us."

He turned and was gone.

Ferrara looked angry. "You didn't try to stop him."

I whispered back, "He was right. How was I going to explain it? We've escaped with our lives. Isn't that enough?"

The sirens we'd heard in the distance were closer now. The first of the emergency response teams was arriving.

When Gina and Malika were seen by the paramedics they were assumed to be earthquake survivors in shock. We said nothing to change that.

I said farewell to Gina as she and her sister were loaded aboard the ambulance. "You did it. You rescued your sister."

She raised her eyes. "We'll never forget you."

As the ambulance pulled away I turned towards Ferrara. "No hospital for you?"

He smiled. "I don't need them. I need to find my own way back to the life I knew." He paused. "But you, James, you are still disturbed?"

I told him about Julia. "While we were trapped here, Matteo Lando and Cleary sent Wolfgang Heller after my wife and son. There's no joy in anything for me now. Bringing down the Landos is as nothing compared with losing the ones I love."

He placed his arms round me and gave me a bear hug.

As he stood back I couldn't help but stare at the blood that now covered his shirt. It was Matteo Lando's. I looked down and took in for the first time the significance of my own clothes being soaked with the same blood. One thought and one thought alone came to my mind, as if in that moment I'd been released from a trance. "Nico. What have I done?"

Chapter 90

Miles Blake was certain the delays at the British Embassy in Mexico City were deliberate. Each time, the story was the same. His application for an emergency travel document was being considered. There was a growing backlog of applications. The Embassy was short staffed due to holiday leave.

He'd made his way to Mexico City by train from Tijuana without difficulty and was lying low while waiting for the travel papers. He was ever vigilant of the possibility he would be located down here by the Soto cartel or its supporters and this meant going against his natural instinct to concern himself with what must be happening back in Tijuana following the killing of El Romero and send copy back to his paper's newsroom. He'd spent too much time alone in the hotel room watching TV reports of the deaths caused by the turf war that had broken out as the Rivenza cartel had sought to move in. He didn't know if Luiz Reyas had survived but he'd kept to the agreement not to try to contact the young Mexican, for the sake of the safety of them both.

When Miles approached the Embassy enquiries desk again he expected the excuses for delay to be the same. But instead of the expected invitation to join the long queue of those waiting to complain, the desk officer asked Miles to follow a uniformed member of Embassy staff.

He was taken along marbled corridors to a private area at the rear of the building. The uniformed officer knocked on one of the polished wooden doors and ushered in Miles.

Seated at a long boardroom table was Debbie Miller. She smiled as she saw Miles' look of surprise at seeing her here but any hint of informality didn't last long. She gestured towards the large American seated beside her. "Miles, this is Agent Bill Maynard. He's been looking forward to meeting you."

Miles had so many questions in need of answers. What had happened when Debbie and Dillon Ashley took their plan to Washington? What had happened to Craven? But the formality of this meeting and the fact that he didn't know what to make of the man beside Debbie meant those questions would not be the first to be answered. He offered his hand. "Miles Blake."

Bill Maynard squeezed Miles' hand. "I have a present for you, Mr. Blake." He took a document from the file before him and placed it on the table. "It's the emergency travel pass you need to return to Europe. The staff here are good at honouring a request from a trusted ally."

Miles stared at the document. "A gift, just like that?"

Maynard smiled. "Not quite. There are a few ways we need to help each other."

"So, conditions then?"

"Let's say there are a number of matters we need to discuss," Debbie Miller interrupted. "Before we get into that, Miles, there are some things you need to know." She gestured towards Maynard once more. "I have clearance to tell him this?"

Maynard nodded.

Debbie told Miles that Nate Craven had been detained in an internal FBI investigation. His black ops had been exposed and much of the credit went to the man sitting beside her, Bill Maynard, her boss from way back. "So, you see, Miles, the situation has changed now the Agency knows what was happening in Tijuana. There's room for you and us to be on the same side from an official Agency point of view, but we require certain safeguards."

Miles could see what was coming next. "You're saying I can't have my story?"

Maynard weighed the travel documents in his hand. "You have your story. But you report nothing about Craven and his dealings in Tijuana. You report nothing about Dillon Ashley's role in the killing of El Romero. You report nothing about Town Lake. And you give us a day during which you tell us everything you know about Agent Craven."

"And in return?"

"You get to leave here."

"And if I say no?"

"I've heard the British authorities would have no objection to withdrawing the permission to travel if they had a request from us."

Miles knew what he would be giving up. "I'm going to need a little more from you."

Maynard sat back. "Try me."

"I need you to understand the claims about me threatening state security through my contacts in the State Department were inventions coming out of Craven's black ops."

Maynard nodded. "OK. What else?"

"And since that's accepted, I need the Agency to withdraw any charges against Adam Weston. He's helping me. He's played his part in exposing Craven and deserves a break."

"We can go with that. And?"

"Help me find my brother and his wife. Help me save them from the Landos."

Debbie Miller cut in. "Miles, I can assure you, tracking down the Landos is a number one priority. But there are problems."

"What kind of problems?"

"When we sent out a request to the Italians for access to Matteo Lando, the reply came back he couldn't be found."

"And his mother?"

"There's no trace of Alessa Lando in any of the records."

Miles had gained most of what he could to recompense him for giving up the chance to tell the world about Craven. "So we have an agreement?"

Maynard nodded and offered his hand once more. Miles took it.

Chapter 91

Julia rocked her baby in her arms. She spoke to him in a quiet whisper. "Listen to the sounds of the countryside. The animals are all around us."

It was true. Before she spent time here, Julia had been unaware how much the simple presence of the surroundings of the farmhouse would come to mean to her. Swallows, come all the way from Africa, darted low across the fields feeding on the abundance of insect life. A pair of house martins had nested in the eaves of the old building and returned throughout the day with food for their squawking young.

Although the farmhouse was in private hands, the remainder of the holding functioned as a working enterprise. Farmer Ted Richards didn't interfere in the daily life of the farmhouse but he could be seen once or twice most days moving sheep from field to field, using his collie dog to help with the herding. When the sheep were out in the field, they spent most of their time feeding. It was so quiet up here at times that if you listened carefully you could hear the sound of their teeth tearing at the blades of grass.

Further down the hill, at the huntsman's cottage, once or twice a day there was the sound of the dogs being fed. Or if they were alerted by some unexpected event, there was the much louder sound of incessant barking. But such events were infrequent; the more regular sound of their presence was reassuring and did little to disturb the peace and tranquillity of the place.

None of this made up for the absence of James.

It was a strange contrast that she could be here surrounded by such serenity, holding in her arms their beautiful son, when James was somewhere she knew nothing of, facing dangers she could only imagine.

There was a knock at the door. It was Mark Stone, the huntsman, on his evening round, shotgun at his side.

He didn't plan to stay long. "Just calling by, Julia. Making sure everything is all right."

Julia felt secure in the countryman's presence. "Everything is fine." She looked down at her baby. "He's disturbed for some reason today. Crying more than usual. I hope it's something that will pass."

"Never knew of a baby that didn't want to cry."

"Thanks for calling by, Mark. You know how much I appreciate what you're doing for us."

He smiled. "It's nothing more than any neighbour should do." He paused. "No sign of Faith tonight?"

"She's visiting her cousin. She won't be back 'til late."

"No need to be concerned about being on your own here. We'll keep a close eye on any intruders."

Julia thanked him again as he left.

She listened as his footsteps faded as he returned down the lane to his cottage.

She spoke once more to her baby. "No, we're not here on our own. We have each other for company."

Chapter 92

Wolfgang Heller had been briefed well by Cleary. The farmhouse at the top of Rook Lane was defended by three locals – a close neighbour and two volunteers. The neighbour was the local huntsman who kept a pack of beagles. All three men and the dogs would have to be dealt with before any action in the farmhouse could be considered.

Heller made his way slowly up the steep rise of Rook Lane. The route was popular with walkers who used it to gain access to Sweden Bridge from where there are first-class views of the Ambleside Valley. Heller was dressed as one of those walkers. He would arouse little attention, even though the light was now fading.

Approaching the huntsman's cottage without alerting the dogs was not going to be possible. The only option was to deal with the men first. He knew they would be patrolling, seeking to protect the Blake woman from harm.

He hid behind the dry stone wall facing onto the lane and this gave him a view of both the farmhouse and the huntsman's cottage. From here he could observe the comings and goings of the men. One of them had just been seen leaving the farmhouse and walking back in the direction of the huntsman's cottage. Perhaps this was the huntsman himself; it seemed that way. The dogs made no sound as he approached.

A few minutes later, Heller observed another of the protectors. He was standing against the wall of the old barn close to the farmhouse. He'd stopped to smoke a cigarette. Heller approached from behind, put his arm around the man's throat and broke his neck. He cradled the body so it fell to the ground without a sound.

When Heller located the next target, there was a problem. There were two men together. The huntsman had emerged from his cottage and was talking to the last of the remaining protectors outside on the lane, pointing towards the farmhouse and surrounding fields, planning, no doubt, how to provide protection overnight. The danger was that one or both of them would discover the body he'd left near the barn. Heller decided only immediate action would do.

A lesser man might have delayed to find a more suitable time to launch the attack but he was not like other men. He knew the powerful effect of sudden, undisguised terror. It was what had served him and his kind so well over all the years.

He retreated down the hill under cover of the dry stone wall and emerged lower on the lane and began to walk up it, towards the two men. They would see him as just another walker, setting out for a late-night visit to the bridge.

As he approached, he gave a smile and a nod, a silent good evening.

Before the two men could respond, he struck. He pulled a silenced pistol from under his jacket and shot the accomplice between the eyes. As the man fell and the huntsman sought to find a response to the shock of seeing his partner dying, Heller aimed two sharp blows, one to the eye with two outstretched fingers, blinding the man, and the second, before he could level the shot gun he had assumed would be his protector, a kick to the leg breaking it at the knee, sending the huntsman collapsing into unconsciousness.

Heller picked up the collaborator and placed the body in a ditch beside the lane. He then picked up the huntsman and draped the body over his shoulder, fireman's lift style. Heller entered the huntsman's cottage, using the key he found in the unconscious man's pockets. He tied the man to a chair using cabling ripped from the dining room. The man was not dead. When he recovered consciousness he would have a use.

The dogs were barking louder now he'd entered the cottage. Perhaps they were responding to the attack on their master or perhaps they were responding to Heller's alien presence. Either way, they would have to be silenced.

He walked into the compound and faced the first of the animals. The fact that he did not back down as the dog charged gave him a great advantage. As the dog leapt, he grabbed it by the neck and spear-tackled it to the ground, breaking its skull as he drove it deep into the sandy floor of the compound. Two more dogs came at him and received the same treatment. The remaining eight dogs drew back, whimpering and trying to run away but there was nowhere for them to go. One by one he found them and broke the neck of each with a swift twisting action. The compound was now silent.

He returned to the cottage to inspect the huntsman. He was still unconscious, still breathing.

It was a satisfactory start to the action against the farmhouse but no more than would be expected of a man whose power and status was as well-established as his own. After all, if these people insisted on deploying amateurs to do a professional job of protecting the Blake woman, what else could be expected? He would have been foolish not to demonstrate that supremacy. So much was self-evident.

Heller listened to the silence of the countryside all around him.

He felt calmed by its serenity.

It was a short distance across the fields that surrounded the farmhouse but he wanted to do this right. To maximise the shock to the Blake woman there should be no signal of his approach. This was nothing more than the professional way. Professional since it would allow no time for the Blake woman to phone for help.

As he neared the centre of the field an unexpected confrontation took place. A ram stood in his path. To order, the clouds above parted to reveal a full moon that bathed Heller and the animal in a bright, steely light, as if a spotlight had been shone on them to illuminate the encounter.

The ram, large and horned, stood in his path. It stared straight at him with unrelenting green eyes.

Heller fell to his knees and stared back. He spoke in a quiet voice. "Just like me, dear friend, you have fathered many."

He moved to touch the animal's massive head but drew back as the ram lowered its head in preparation to charge. He was impressed by the animal's soulless intensity, by its complete absence of reason and feeling.

Heller understood what was at stake. The ram sought to protect his progeny, his right to reproduce and shape the future. His DNA, the life source, would be eternal. He spoke again. "Yes, my friend, we are the same, you and me. We demand and get the same."

It was stalemate. The animal stood as solid as stone. There was no thought. There was no fear. There was nothing but the absolute determination to take the future and make it its own. Something handed down through the millennia. Ancient, unyielding, ever present. This animal had achieved its own nirvana, the state of being that Heller could not yet emulate despite all the years of meditation and prayer.

There was so much to learn from the unyielding beast before him.

He stood, smiled, and stepped aside. This beast must be recognised as the master it was in this, his domain. Just as he himself must be recognised as the master he was about to become in his own, wider world.

It was relative.

But the same.

The animal and himself.

Masters in their own worlds.

Heller walked on towards the farmhouse and the prey awaiting him there.

Chapter 93

The baby had stopped crying and was sleeping.

It had been a long day. Little Simon had not settled without a struggle. If Faith were here she would have told her all along it was wind, something quite normal for babies that would clear in its own good time and then he would sleep. Julia wished she were here now so she could tell her she was right. But she knew she'd have to settle for the contented look on her baby's face as he lay silently in the crib.

Julia looked around the room before closing the door and heading for the sitting room. She could think about herself for the first time that day.

There was no sound coming from down the hill. The huntsman's dogs were silent though just earlier they'd sounded agitated. That was unusual. Once any immediate intrusion had been dealt with, one or more of them would be expected to be barking or snuffling around. Just as if you live near a stream where the sound of running water is forever present, after awhile you aren't aware of it yet you notice when it stops. It was the same with the huntsman's dogs. Why were they this quiet?

Julia looked at the old mantelpiece clock. Nine PM. Already dark outside.

She hoped for a call from James.

It was about his time if he was going to call. They'd agreed she would not call him unless it was an emergency. She could not call now. What would she say? "Jim, I'm scared. The huntsman's dogs are too quiet."

No, she was being feeble. The huntsman had been here just an hour before and told her everything was fine. She should relax and settle down to making the most of the few hours break she had before baby Simon woke again for his next feed.

Then she saw the shadow of a man pass across the dining room window. Before she could respond, the apparition was gone. She had to convince herself she had seen it, so fleeting had been its appearance.

She was frightening herself. It was all about suggestion, she knew that. The dogs had fallen silent, no doubt for some quite understandable reason, and she was in a heightened state of alert. Scared of a shadow. She needed to set aside these figments of her imagination.

Then came the unmistakable sound of the front door of the farmhouse being forced open, followed by the sound of a man's footsteps approaching along the stone flagged passageway.

Chapter 94

Wolfgang Heller was on Julia before she could defend herself.

Her only thought was for her baby.

Did this man know about the child? Would little Simon stay asleep in the room next door long enough for her to find a way of getting this man to do something, anything that would keep her baby safe?

He had her by the throat. His eyes were fire. His hands massive. His raw power impossible to oppose.

She wanted to shout out but could not speak.

He was mouthing words but she couldn't decipher them. It was as if her fear had placed a veil between herself and this man, as if he were speaking another language. Then she realised, the words she was hearing were German.

He released his grip on her throat for her to be able to speak. "I don't understand."

He tightened his grip again. "You want to hear it in English, Frau Blake? Have you ever thought how arrogant it makes you seem, expecting me to speak your language?"

He relaxed his grip, long enough for her to reply. "Why are you here?"

"To repay you for what you have done. For the damage caused by you and your family."

Through the pain and terror, Julia was beginning to realise who this was. James had told her about the German who had nearly killed him and Miles in East Texas. This was the same man. "Herr Heller, you don't need to do this."

"You know of me? From where do you know of me?"

Julia did not want to turn the attention to James, but she had no choice. "From my husband."

He taunted her. "And where is James now?"

She didn't want to answer but anything that kept him here away from her baby was preferable to what might happen if he was allowed to enter the room next door where Simon was sleeping. "He'll be back any moment."

Heller squeezed more tightly on her throat. "Don't lie to me, Frau Blake. Don't ever lie to me."

The pain was intense. He would not stop unless she told the truth. "He's in Italy."

"At last we begin to understand each other."

He released her, forcing her to sit down in the wingback chair as he loomed over her.

Her throat was burning. He'd come close to killing her. "You won't escape. There are people around here, guarding us."

"Us? Tell me who else is here?"

A sound came from the next room.

The sound of a baby crying.

Heller taunted her again. "So, you have a baby?"

Julia shook her head.

He held Julia's arm in a vice-like grip and twisted. "In that case, I must take a look myself."

Chapter 95

Looking down on the baby asleep in the crib, Wolfgang Heller was aware of the conflict invading his mind and his body.

He was shocked he had not been warned about this by Cleary. He knew the way the man operated – tell them just enough to get the result. Do not tell them how the information was obtained. Do not complicate matters with information like the fact that the target has a three-week old baby.

It was a struggle to hide his annoyance.

His thoughts were back at Town Lake as he prepared to arm the bomb that would blow the compound apart. He was talking to thirteen-year-old Jenny Ravitz who was telling him how excited she was to have met a boy. The turmoil now invading him centred on the realisation that the baby before him would one day become just the kind of boy who would have delighted the young Jenny.

Digging his fingernails deep into his wrist, he drew blood. The pain did not stop the anguish. He thought he was over this. If people were foolish enough to place children in the way of the goals he was destined to achieve, then so be it. It would be their fault if the children suffered. It was none of his business.

Then why did he still feel like this? Why were the days of meditation on this now as nothing when confronted with the simple view of the baby lying before him, helpless?

The Blake woman placed herself between him and the baby. She was pleading. "Go. Please don't harm my child. He has nothing to do with anything you are interested in."

Perhaps, after all, in itself the threat of harm to the child would be enough.

The Blake woman was close to hysteria. "Please don't hurt my baby. I'll do anything you say, but please don't hurt him."

Chapter 96

This was the worst moment of Julia Blake's life.

Worse even than the kidnap and rape she had endured at the hands of Alfieri Lando in Florence. That had been her own pain, her own isolation, her own fear and self-loathing. This was worse.

Heller would kill her; there was no doubt. And when he'd finished with her, he'd kill her child.

No pain, suffering or isolation she had experienced before could prepare her for the prospect of that.

She was desperate to find a weakness, any point of vulnerability she might be able to exploit in this man who had brought such terror into her life.

She had no weapon but she knew that in the kitchen drawer was a set of carving knives. If she could get to the drawer without his seeing she could perhaps be quick enough with the knife to slash him at the throat. But he was not going to let her out of his sight. She would never get to the kitchen without his knowing and even if she were to get the knife and try to use it, the risk that he would harm her child was too great.

She thought about poison. There was rat poison under the kitchen sink. How long did Warfarin take to act? How could she administer it to this man? He would taste it, even if she could contrive a situation in which he would drink anything she set before him. Even if there was a chance of making this work, she did not know how long this man intended to delay the inevitable attack on herself and her baby. There may not be time for the poison to take effect.

She wished now she'd used the mobile phone when she'd been concerned about the silence of the dogs. She should have trusted her intuition. Heller had not thought to ask her about the phone. Perhaps she could find a way to call James. He would alert the police.

Heller must have been reading her thoughts. "I forgot to mention, Frau Blake. Please give me your phone."

He held out his hand.

"I don't have a phone. We only have a landline here."

He took a step towards the baby's crib. "The phone. I will not ask again."

Julia removed it from her bag and handed it to him.

He looked at her long and hard. "I thought you had agreed not to lie to me. You must not lie to me. Do you understand?"

Julia nodded.

"Say it."

"I understand."

Julia was certain she had to stop this man no matter how weak she felt. She made an excuse to go to the kitchen. "The baby needs feeding."

"You are not doing this as in nature?"

She shook her head.

He followed her into the kitchen as she began preparing the baby bottle. If all along he was going to kill her, what kind of perverse pleasure made him want to demonstrate his control and draw her end out like this? Why wouldn't he let his attention slip for just one moment so she could open the kitchen drawer and pull out the carving knife?

Next door, the baby began to cry once more.

Heller turned his head to look.

This was Julia's only chance. She pulled open the drawer behind her and slipped her hand in. Where was the knife? The long one with the serrated edge.

Her fingers gripped the handle. She pulled the knife from the drawer and held it behind her back.

Heller had resumed his attention on her.

She walked towards him. He would notice her arm behind her back but could she get to him and use the knife before he could respond?

It was always going to be futile but what else could she do to save her baby?

He'd seen her coming and had drawn the pistol from his waistband before she could reach him.

It was too late to stop now. Julia raised the blade and rushed at Heller as he prepared to fire. When the bullet hit she would be gone but she would have done all she could.

There was the explosive sound of a weapon going off. Too loud to be Heller's weapon. Then another deafening detonation.

Heller fell backwards. The pistol fell from his hand as he hit the floor and began convulsing.

Julia turned.

Behind her Faith Webster's hands shook as she pointed the emptied double-barrelled shotgun to the floor. "We only ever kept it for scaring rabbits, Julia, you know that. And I never did get on with that cousin of mine."

Chapter 97

Nico Ferrara sought to comfort me as we staggered away from the ruins of San Berado, heading for warmth and light.

"We need to find if there was a word of truth in what Lando told you about Julia. He was trying to hurt you, to use despair to demoralise you."

I couldn't agree. "I wish I could share the same optimism, Nico. I don't believe Lando was lying. There was too much delight in his desire to want to tell me the worst of what was going to happen. I have to tell you, Nico, there's so little left of me to doubt that everything is lost."

"You can't allow yourself to believe that."

We made our way over halfway down San Berado hillside before we came to anywhere that looked as if normal life had resumed after the earthquake. It was a trattoria, one of those small places used by locals. Most were standing outside, looking in awe at the destruction higher up the hillside, discussing how lucky they were their lives and property had been spared.

Inside we found the patron was still attempting to maintain some semblance of normality and he asked if we required drinks or a meal as we came in. Ferrara explained our need for the use of a phone and, when the patron offered use of his and told us it was still working, Ferrara turned to me. "Make the call, James. The time is long gone when you could place Julia in any more danger than she may already be in. If you are so convinced you have nothing left, you have nothing to lose."

Without his insistence I would not have been able to find the will to pick up the receiver and dial.

As the call went through, I could feel the last reserves of strength about to drain from my body. Time stretched out once more. My own heartbeats sounded in my head. There was an eternity between each one.

Then, a voice. "Yes?"

It was Julia. I could not speak. The joy of hearing her voice, of knowing she had survived, was almost too much to bear.

"Is it you, Jim?"

"Yes, my love."

Epilogue

My family was safe but there was much about the events we'd lived through that weren't revealed.

The Italian authorities presented Inspector Manieri as a brave and loyal police officer missing in action, presumed dead. The public media carried extensive details of the after-effects of the earthquake on the lives of the citizens of Florence but nothing emerged about the discovery of an underground complex beneath the San Berado hillside. I was not surprised. I was lucky to count myself amongst the few who'd survived and knew about the secrets entombed there. Knowledge of *I discendenti di Leda* was in the hands of a few. The hope was the earthquake had ended its long history and I felt satisfied with that. Yet what I couldn't shake from my mind was the claim made by Cleary that there were others, elsewhere, ready to continue their madness.

Matteo Lando was reported as having escaped Sollicciano prison only to have been killed in the tragic events of the earthquake, despite the fact that his body had not yet been recovered from the ruins of San Berado churchyard, where he'd last been seen. His luck had run out, the Italian press said, though there were many who supposed he was still alive and living outside Italy. I was not going to second-guess that.

Wolfgang Heller's death was presented to the media in a controlled fashion. The FBI wanted to draw a line under the events surrounding Craven and everything associated with him. The authorities were keen to oblige. The killings in Rook Lane were said to be the work of a loner who'd been traumatised by life as a mercenary in the Far East. He'd been drawn to the UK by the mistaken belief that the woman he'd been with for ten years had escaped there. When he couldn't trace her, he'd chosen victims at random in a psychotic killing spree.

Miles published a series of in-depth features on the drugs war in Tijuana but, in keeping with his agreement with Maynard, revealed nothing about Craven or Town Lake. It was left to Miles to let Luiz Reyas know that while the Lando family had been much weakened by the death of Matteo, Alessa Lando had not been found and his mission was therefore not complete.

Meanwhile I was left with the difficult decision of when to tell Julia about the masterpieces now entombed under San Berado. There was no doubt she would be thrilled to know that such a large number of paintings, presumed to have been destroyed, had been seen there. It was a joy I thought I'd never experience again to be beside her with baby Simon in her arms.

I was not planning to do or say anything to change that. Not for a long time.

Acknowledgements

I would like to express my thanks to Kath Middleton and Jan Warburton for help in getting this book ready for presentation and to many other friends for their kind observations and encouragement.

James Blake Thrillers

Take No More
Regret No More
Forgive No More